Sail Away

ASHLEY FARLEY

ALSO BY ASHLEY FARLEY

Boots and Bedlam

Lowcountry Stranger

Her Sister's Shoes

Magnolia Series

Beyond the Garden

Magnolia Nights

Scottie's Adventures

Breaking the Story

Merry Mary

ONE

E than leads Hannah by the hand, out of the restaurant and down the sidewalk to the horse-drawn carriage waiting on the curb. He bows to her, sweeping his arm at the small white buggy. "Your carriage awaits, mademoiselle."

Hannah rolls her eyes. "Be serious, Ethan. I need to get home to Gus." Grabbing him by the sleeve of his blue blazer, Hannah drags him away from the carriage.

"Wait!" Ethan plants his feet firmly on the uneven brick sidewalk. "I made arrangements for Gus to spend the night with Sally."

Hannah turns on him. "Why would you do that without talking to me first?"

Ethan pulls her to him, wrapping an arm around her waist. "Because we've been together for almost a year, and we've yet to spend one night together."

"I'm a single mother of a three-year-old. You knew what you were getting into when you started dating me."

"And I've been a patient man until now." He brushes his lips lightly against hers. "Gus will be crushed if you ruin his sleepover with Sally."

"True." Hannah's knees go weak at the thought of spending the night in Ethan's arms. "Are you sure Hope doesn't mind?"

"Positive. She was thrilled."

"Maybe I should call her to make sure." Hannah struggles to unzip her clutch.

He snatches the clutch away from her. "That's unnecessary, Hannah. We'll return the favor sometime."

"Hope will like that. She has a new boyfriend." Hannah casts an uncertain glance at the carriage. "What about your car?"

"We Ubered over, remember? Now, quit stalling." He twirls her around and lifts her into the carriage.

The carriage driver turns in his seat to face her. He's approximately the same age, with strong facial features and dark eyes. "Good evening," he says, tipping his straw hat at them.

Ethan climbs into the carriage beside her. "Hannah, meet my friend George. We went to kindergarten together."

"Cool! How did you become a carriage driver?" Hannah's face warms. "Not that there's anything wrong with being a carriage driver. It's just kinda random for someone our age."

George's smile reaches his eyes. "I'm an attorney by day. I give carriage tours on the weekends for fun."

"George is a history buff," Ethan explains. "He aspires to one day be mayor of Charleston."

Hannah's face lights up. "You'll definitely get my vote."

"Awesome. I'll recruit you to work on my campaign."

A breeze brings chill bumps to Hannah's bare arms. "I should've brought a sweater," she says with a shiver.

George tosses her a blanket, "Here. Fresh from the laundry."

Ethan slips out of his jacket. "Put this on." He helps her into his jacket and tucks the blanket around her legs.

George faces forward and lifts the horse's reins. "Where to, mate?"

"Let's cut over to King Street and head toward the seawall," Ethan says.

As the carriage lurches forward, Hannah calls out to George above the sound of hooves clomping on cobblestone. "What's your horse's name?"

"Shadow," George says over his shoulder.

"An appropriate name for a gray horse." Hannah snuggles close to Ethan as they cross over Broad Street and enter the residential section of downtown Charleston. "Was it a coincidence that George was waiting outside the restaurant?"

Ethan shakes his head, a mischievous smirk tugging at his lips.

"First, dinner at our favorite restaurant and now a romantic carriage ride. What're you up to, Ethan?"

He smiles down at her with smoldering brown eyes. "I'm desperate for sex."

"Stop!" She smacks his chest with the back of her hand. "You're not *that* deprived."

The sweet scent of Carolina Jasmine greets them as they pass under a canopy of trees on the narrow house-lined street. When they reach the waterfront, they make a left and ride to the tip of the peninsula at the entrance to Battery Park. George calls out to Shadow to *whoa* as he maneuvers the carriage to the curb.

"Come on. Let's get out." Ethan pulls Hannah to her feet and helps her down from the buggy. She wraps his blazer tight around her as they walk over to the railing and stare out across Charleston Harbor at the full moon.

"Did you arrange for the full moon as well?" Hannah asks.

"Of course. Cost me a fortune." Ethan turns to her, taking her hands in his. "Seriously, Hannah, you ignore me every time I bring up the subject of marriage. I figured if I bought you a ring and formally proposed, you'd have to give me a yes or no answer." He drops to his knees. "Hannah Fuller, will you do me the honor of becoming my wife?"

Hannah's stomach somersaults. This is the moment she's been

dreaming of. She has no reservations about marrying him. But there's no fun in making it easy for him. "What if I say no?"

"I'll keep asking until your answer is yes. We're meant to be together, Hannah. I promise, I'll spend my life making you happy."

"Hmm." She purses her lips as though considering his proposal. "You mentioned a ring?"

Ethan gets to his feet. "Actually, you have it." He slips his hand into the pocket of his blazer and removes a velvet ring box. "Dad helped me pick it out. Mom claims his taste in jewelry is exquisite. I'll let you be the judge. Dad wanted to get something bigger, but I thought this was a more appropriate choice for your petite fingers."

He opens the box, and Hannah gasps at the sight of the sparkling solitary diamond. "Anything bigger and I wouldn't be able to lift my hand. It's exquisite, Ethan. I absolutely love it."

Taking the ring out of the box, he places it on her finger. "Does this mean you'll marry me?"

With glistening eyes, she softly says, "Yes. I can't wait to be your wife."

"I hope you mean it. Because I aim to rush you down the aisle before you change your mind."

"Feel free to rush away. I'm all for short engagements." Hooking an arm around his neck, she draws him close and presses her lips to his.

The sun sets over the horizon, casting Point Pleasant in a golden glow. A sport fishing boat, returning from a day in the ocean, passes through the mouth of the inlet, its waves breaking softly against the shore as it cruises by. Amelia never tires of the landscape, the ocean on one side and the inlet the other, her own private peninsula.

After a pleasant dinner on the porch, when the sun disappears and a chill sets in, Amelia and Jonathan retire to the living room to finish their wine by the fire. Jonathan rests his head against the back of the sofa and closes his eyes. "Your culinary skills are improving by the day."

"Thank you. I'm surprised at how much I enjoy cooking." She places a hand on her belly. "Once the summer's fresh fruits and vegetables come in, I'm hoping to shed these five pounds I've gained."

He cracks an eyelid. "Don't you dare diet. You needed the extra weight. You were gaunt before." His eyes flutter closed again.

"Gee, thanks." Her tone is sarcastic, but she knows it's true. She was too thin when she first came home to Palmetto Island.

Amelia settles back on the sofa, tucking a foot beneath her. "Max's grand opening is tomorrow. The other businesses on the boardwalk are taking part in the celebration. I promised Max I'd help host. If you have time, I'd love for you to stop by. The fun starts at two."

"I have a commitment in the morning, but I should be done by noon." Jonathan rolls his head toward her. "Have you given much thought to your plans for the summer?"

Amelia picks at a loose thread on the sofa. "I've been so busy these past few months. I'm hoping to indulge myself a little. I want to read novels and go for long walks on the beach."

"You deserve to take a break. You've had more than your share of hardship this past year with your husband's horrific murder and your mama's sudden death."

"But come next fall, I have to figure out my purpose in life," she says.

Jonathan lifts his head. "What do you mean by that?"

Amelia shrugs. "I have no career. And no family to take care of. I have to make myself useful."

"What about interior design? You enjoyed helping Max renovate the hotel."

"Decorating is just a hobby. I did a lot of volunteer work in Boston. I could get involved in the community here. Maybe I'll join a turtle conservation program."

"That sounds like a worthy cause. I might be interested as well."

This is not exactly what Amelia has in mind. She's hoping to find an outside interest to keep her occupied while he's at work. "What are *your* plans for the summer? Do you have any projects on the horizon?" She bites down on her lower lip to keep from laughing. She teases him relentlessly about his many home improvement and boat-related projects.

"Ha ha." He bops her with a throw pillow. "Actually, I have a rather enormous project in mind."

Amelia snatches the pillow from him and hugs it to her chest. "Do tell."

"I've always wanted to own a sailboat. And I found one I'm interested in. She's an oldie, but a beauty. She needs a lot of work, though. I'm going to Charleston in the morning to look at it. But I may need your help."

Lines deepen in Amelia's forehead. "How so?"

"Under the best of circumstances, when the moon is full and the tide high, I only have four feet of water off my dock. This boat drafts almost five feet. And you have twenty feet off your dock at low tide. Would you consider letting me tie up here?"

Amelia lowers her gaze. "Oh."

"Oh?" he says, his hazel eyes darkening. "That's not exactly the response I was going for. I thought you'd be excited about the sailboat, as much as you love being out in the ocean."

"I am." Tossing the pillow aside, Amelia leaves the sofa and moves over to the fireplace.

"What is it, Amelia? What're you holding back?"

Staring into the fire, she says, "What happens if we break up? You'll have nowhere to keep your boat."

"Wow. I never considered the possibility of us breaking up." Jonathan comes to stand beside her. "I thought things were solid between us. Are you saying you're unhappy with our relationship?"

Amelia feels his eyes on her, but she can't bring herself to look at him. "Not at all, Jon. I was in an abusive marriage for thirty years. I'm wary of making a commitment. We're both happy with things the way they are. Why rush into something more serious?"

"Something more serious? I didn't ask you to marry me. I asked if I could keep my boat at your dock," he says in a wounded tone.

A pang of guilt tightens her chest. Guilt makes a person vulnerable. Guilt is one emotion she promised herself she'd never again let herself feel. Truth be told, she doesn't mind him keeping his boat at her dock. She loves him. She's never been happier in her life. She senses him waiting for her response. She should tell him how she feels, but the words stick to her tongue.

After an awkward moment, he says, "I take your silence as my cue to leave."

Amelia's conscience screams at her to go after him, but her legs are heavy, her feet glued to the hardwood floor. She remains by the fireplace long after she hears the back door shut and his car start in the driveway. Finally, feeling the weight of the world on her shoulders, she turns off the fire logs, locks up the house, and drags herself up the stairs.

A bay of windows occupies one wall in her bedroom. The moon is full, allowing her to see out across the extensive grounds of Point Pleasant to the waters beyond. The ocean to her left. Creeks and marshes to her right. And the mouth of the inlet straight ahead. She grew up here. This is her home. Her dream of one day moving back to Palmetto Island got her through the tough years with Nelson. And now that dream has come true.

She has everything she's ever wanted, including a wonderful man who treats her the way she deserves to be treated. Why, then, did she shut Jon out when he asked to keep his boat at her dock? Is she terrified of losing her freedom again? Or is it something else? Her love for him isn't in question. She has no doubts about growing old with him. But something is missing, and she can't put her finger on what it is.

She and Jonathan have been together since August of last year. Nine months without so much as a squabble. What made her snap tonight? It's not about the sailboat. She relishes the days spent on his thirty-five-foot center console boat in the ocean, fishing and cruising the shoreline and eating picnic lunches. Jon makes her feel loved and appreciated. She would never have survived those dark months of grieving for her mama without him. But their relationship isn't enough. She needs more. If only she knew what that was.

Moonlight spills through the window onto their blanketed feet as Becca reads the last sentences in the final chapter of *Harry Potter and the Chamber of Secrets* to her nine-year-old daughter. Becca has read to Happy every night since she was a baby. But after Craig left them fourteen months ago, they adopted a new element to their sacred routine. When they finish reading, they turn off the lamp and snuggle together under the covers. The darkness comforts them while they discuss their feelings of sadness and abandonment.

When her daughter was born, Becca named her Harper, using her maiden name to honor her beloved parents who had died the previous year in a car crash. Because the baby was so jolly, always smiling and cooing and blowing raspberries, Becca soon adopted the nickname Happy. Craig never approved of the nickname. Then again, he never approved of any decision Becca made.

Happy appears to be the same even-tempered and happy-go-lucky child she's always been. But Becca senses turmoil brewing beneath the surface. Is it a result of her father's betrayal? Or is Happy exhibiting preadolescent rebellion?

"Can we go to the library tomorrow and get the next in the series?" Happy asks.

Becca closes the book and sets it on the nightstand. "Don't you want to take a break from Potter for a while?"

"Nooo!" Happy cries. "We have to keep reading! Next up is *The Prisoner of Azkaban*. My goal is to finish the whole series by the end of the summer."

"The entire series? That's pretty ambitious." Becca reaches for the lamp. "I'll agree to keep going with Potter as long as we read at least one classic this summer."

"Mo-om. Your classics are so boring."

"Not the one I have in mind. Besides, we'll have plenty of time for reading this summer."

"What do you mean?"

"I have another birthday gift for you," Becca says, mischief tugging at her lip.

"Another one?" Happy's blue-green eyes are bright. "But you already gave me a bike."

"Now you need a place to ride your bike," Becca says, touching her finger to her daughter's pert nose.

"I have a place. Duh. I can ride it in the driveway and around our cul-de-sac."

"True. But you're going to be riding your bike somewhere else this summer." Becca rolls onto her side, facing Happy. "I'll give you a hint. What kind of bike did I give you?"

Happy scrunches up her face. "A beach cruiser." She sits up straight in bed. "Are we going to the beach this summer?"

"Better. I've rented a small cottage on Palmetto Island for the entire summer."

"The whole summer? That's insane, Mama." Happy throws her arms around Becca. "You're the best. When do we go?"

Becca removes a strand of her daughter's golden hair from her mouth. "We have to wait until we both finish school. I'm thinking we'll move down Memorial Day weekend. I'll still have exam papers to grade, but at least we can get settled."

"Can I invite some of my friends down on the weekends?"

"We'll see." The idea of entertaining a pack of nine-year-old girls exhausts Becca. "We've both been under a lot of stress lately, and I want us to enjoy some downtime. We'll read and work jigsaw puzzles. Go swimming in the ocean and explore the little town."

Happy flips onto her back, pulling the cover up to her chin. "That sounds good. Thank you, Mama. This has been the best birthday ever."

Becca understands this is her signal to leave. Slipping out from beneath the covers, she kisses her daughter on the forehead. "Goodnight, angel. Sleep tight."

Happy smooths Becca's hair off her face. "Can we paint my room when we get back from the beach?"

"Maybe," she says, thinking of all the months her daughter has been begging to paint her room. "What color would you like to paint it?"

"I'm not sure. Maybe lavender."

"We'll see." While Becca suspects Happy would quickly grow tired of lavender, she doesn't argue. Happy will change her mind about the color at least a dozen times before she makes her final decision. She kisses her daughter again and walks to the door.

Happy calls after her, "I love you, Mama."

"And I love you, sweetheart. Always and forever."

Always and forever. Their special saying has taken on new meaning for Becca.

Becca goes down the hall to the spare bedroom, which she converted into a home office several years ago when she finally accepted that there would be no more children. Seated at her desk, she accesses the vacation rental website and clicks on the yellow cottage on Palmetto Island. She's been contemplating the rental for weeks. With only two bedrooms, the cottage is ideal for their needs. Becca envisions them spending time on the heavenly screened porch—eating their meals at the picnic table, relaxing with a good book in the daybed swing, having deep discussions in the rocking chairs while staring out into the darkened night. They'd spent last summer moping around the house, picking up the pieces of their lives after Craig moved out. No one knows what future summers will bring. Her doctor's words come back to her. *Live in the here and now.*

Becca enters her credit card information and confirms the booking. The three-month rental will put a large dent in her savings account, but the time she'll be spending with her daughter is priceless.

She accesses the iMovie app on her computer and clicks the arrow to record herself. The green light at the top of her browser comes on and she begins. "Happy, darling, there are so many things I need to say to you. So many things you need to know."

TWO

Ethan is still sleeping when Hannah sneaks out of his condo at the crack of dawn on Saturday morning. She's anxious to retrieve her son, worried he might be missing her. But when she arrives at her downstairs neighbor's apartment, he begs to stay longer.

"I'm sorry, sweetheart. But we have to get ready. We're going to see Birdie today, remember?"

"Yippee! Birdie!" Tossing his hands in the air, Gus gives his fanny a sassy shake.

Hannah and Hope burst into laughter. "Where'd you learn those dance moves?" Hannah asks.

"Sally taught me," he says.

The mothers laugh even harder.

Hope eyes the sparkling diamond on Hannah's left hand. "Ethan mentioned special plans. I didn't know he was going to propose. Congratulations."

Hannah presses a finger to her lips. "We're waiting to tell Gus later today."

Hope gives Hannah a hug. "I'm so happy for you, girlfriend. Ethan is a great guy."

"I think so too," Hannah says, pulling away. "Thanks for keeping Gus last night. I'm happy to return the favor anytime."

Hope grins. "I will definitely take you up on that offer."

Hannah and Gus race each other up the stairs to their second-floor apartment. Tossing her bag onto the sofa, Hannah goes to the kitchen for coffee. "What do you want for breakfast, buddy? A bagel or scrambled eggs?"

"Bagel." Gus says, climbing onto a barstool.

Hannah places a pod in her Keurig and a blueberry bagel in the toaster. "Ethan has a surprise for us today."

Gus furrows his little forehead. "What surprise?"

"If I knew, it wouldn't be a surprise. But he's picking us up at nine. I need to shower and pack."

He rubs his baby blues. "I'm tired, Mommy."

"I bet you are," she says, as she spreads cream cheese on his bagel. "Did you and Sally stay up late?"

He nods. "Sally wouldn't let me go to sleep."

Hannah places his bagel on the counter in front of him. "Girls talk a lot sometimes, don't they?"

"Yeah." Gus sinks his teeth into his bagel, and his eyelids grow heavy as he chews.

Hannah sits down beside her son with her coffee. She, too, is exhausted from a night of lovemaking. As she sips her coffee, her mind drifts back.

After the carriage ride ended, George dropped them at Ethan's condo. Hannah wanted to call her parents to tell them about their engagement, but Ethan was too eager for sex. "They already know about the proposal, anyway," he said, pressing his mouth against hers as he backed her down the hallway to his bedroom.

"My mom too?" she asked, unbuttoning his shirt.

"Mm-hmm. Since your parents are divorced, I felt obligated to ask permission from both of them." He tugged her blouse over her head and unhooked her bra.

"And did they grant it?"

"Yep. Both are eager to get rid of you." He pushed her down on the bed and fell on top of her.

"You're awful," she said, biting his lip until it bled.

Much later, they lay spent in each other's arms. "I meant it when I said I don't want to wait to get married," Ethan said. "Can we make it happen this summer?"

Hannah hesitated, overwhelmed by the logistics of planning a wedding and combining households. "I doubt I can find a venue at this late date, but I can try. The wedding would have to be small."

"That would be my preference anyway," Ethan said.

"Where will we live?"

"I assumed we'd live here." Seeing her disappointment, Ethan added, "I know how much you love your apartment, but you're paying rent and I'm paying a mortgage. We can fix the condo up to your liking. It'll only be for a couple of years. Until we buy a house."

The sound of birds chirping outside her kitchen window brings Hannah back to the present. Gus is now sleeping soundly with his head on the counter. She looks past him into the living room. It will be hard to give up her apartment. She loves her little slice of heaven with its open floor plan and oversized windows. She relishes the thought of buying a house with Ethan and filling it with their children. But everything is happening so fast. Is she ready for marriage? She's been out on her own for less than a year. Maybe they should wait until next spring or summer to get married.

Hannah lifts her limp child from the barstool and carries him to his bed. After luxuriating in a long hot shower, she tiptoes around their bedrooms, gathering articles of clothing and packing them in tote bags.

Gus is grumpy when she wakes him an hour later. But he comes alive when Ethan arrives to pick them up. "Can I ride up front with you, Ethan?" Even at such a young age, he's enamored by Ethan's sports car.

Ethan musses his white-blond hair. "Sorry, buddy. You have to sit in the back."

He stomps the ground in response.

"Gus," Hannah says in a warning tone. "Improve your mood or we're staying home."

"Fine," he huffs.

Hannah buckles Gus into his car seat while Ethan stores their bags in the trunk. "Why so much stuff for one day at the beach?"

Hannah laughs. "Better get used to it. Mothers with young children don't travel light."

"Bring it on," Ethan says as they settle into their respective seats.

During the hour-long drive, Gus pesters Ethan for hints about the surprise, but Ethan refuses to give an inch. Hannah feels the tension leave her body as they drive down Ocean Avenue, the main thoroughfare in her charming hometown. There's no place like Palmetto Island. Southern culture at its finest—Lowcountry hospitality and cuisine in a resort-like atmosphere.

Ethan reaches for her hand, bringing it to his lips and kissing her diamond. "What're you thinking about?"

"How much I love it here. I love Charleston too. But for different reasons."

He gives her a sheepish grin. "You're going to have your very own sliver of paradise."

She stares at him. "What are you talking about?"

"You'll find out soon enough." He kisses her ring again and returns her hand to the console.

They stop in at the Sandwich Shack to pick up their to-go order and continue over the causeway to the ocean side of the island. The sun is bright in a cloudless sky and the ocean is calm, its waves gently lapping against the shore. About a mile down the road, Ethan makes an abrupt left-hand turn into the driveway of a charming gray cottage with dormer windows and pink petunias spilling from containers flanking the yellow front door.

"What're you doing?" Hannah asks. "This isn't a public beach access."

"You're right. It's someone's home." Ethan parks in front of the house and turns off the engine.

Hannah shakes her head in confusion. "But who lives here?"

Digging into the pocket of his shorts, Ethan produces a silver key on a pink spiral bracelet keyring. "You do."

Hannah's mouth falls open. "What're you talking about?"

From the back seat comes Gus's little voice. "Do you mean it, Ethan? Is this really our house?"

Ethan tosses a nod over his shoulder. "All yours, buddy." He looks over at Hannah. "Since we come down so often on the weekends, I figured we might as well have our own place."

Hannah is speechless. No one has ever bought her a house before. "I don't know what to say."

Gus kicks the back of her seat. "Say thank you, Mommy."

Laughter fills the car. Placing her hand on Ethan's face, she says, "Thank you."

He gives her a peck on the lips and opens his car door. "Come on, I'll give you the tour."

Hannah helps Gus out of his car seat, and the threesome approach the house together. Hannah tries to peek inside the paned glass door, but Ethan steps in front of her, blocking her view. "I got a steal on the place. But I should warn you, it needs a lot of work. Mostly cosmetic stuff." Inserting the key in the lock, Ethan opens the front door and steps out of the way.

Hannah enters the house and looks around. The floor plan is simple—one main living room, a breakfast bar separating the adjacent kitchen, with two bedrooms off to the side and a loft area upstairs. Thick wood paneling covers the walls in the living room and the downstairs bedrooms are painted a nauseating gold color. But the kitchen and bathrooms have been recently updated with new appliances, tile, and fixtures. Windows stretch across the back wall and a glass door, identical to the front door, opens onto a screened porch.

"Well? What do you think?" Ethan asks. "The lot is big enough, we can expand the house as our family grows."

Hannah circles the room. "It has good bones. The worn heart pine floors and tabby fireplace hearth add an element of charm. But the wood paneling is dragging it down. If we paint the paneling white, it'll really open up the room." She turns back to Ethan. "I absolutely love it." She throws her arms around his neck, covering his face with kisses. "This is amazing. You're amazing. I don't know how to thank you."

"You already did. By agreeing to marry me," Ethan says in a low voice so Gus, who's standing by the window looking out at the ocean, can't hear him.

Hannah draws away from Ethan. "Now seems like a good time to tell him."

"I agree. I'm not sure I can keep this to myself a minute longer." Ethan crosses the room to Gus. "Hey, buddy, we have something important to tell you. Let's go outside." Scooping Gus up, Ethan carries him out to the sprawling live oak in the back-yard and deposits him on a low-hanging limb.

Swinging his legs, Gus says, "What do you wanna tell me? Is it another surprise?"

Hannah stands behind her son to catch him if he falls. "Ethan and I are getting married. Do you know what that means?"

"It means Ethan's gonna be my daddy."

"Technically, I'll be your stepfather, since you already have a daddy. I'd like for you to think of me as your second daddy."

"Yay!" Gus leaps off the branch onto Ethan, wrapping his arms and legs around him like a baby koala bear. "I love you, Ethan."

"I love you too, buddy," Ethan says, nuzzling his neck. "Let's go look at the ocean."

Whatever reservations Hannah has about getting married this summer vanish as she watches her son and fiancé walk across the thick grass to the sand dunes. Given the opportunity, she'd married Ethan tomorrow. Gus adores him. And Hannah loves him with all her heart. Why wait a year to get married when they can be together now?

THREE

Amelia stands with Max and Birdie at the entrance to the Palmetto Hotel, observing the activity on the boardwalk. Local boutiques have set up booths to display their goods and restaurants offer samples of their menu items. In the adjacent park, a magic show is being sponsored by the mayor. Just beyond the park, on the sidewalk leading to Ocean Avenue, long lines of people wait at the snow cone truck and hot dog stand. On the other side of the park, on the corner opposite the hotel, the staff at Birdie's Nest Cafe is passing out mini crab cakes and Ritz Crackers topped with fried oysters. Next door to Birdie's, the bartenders at Shaggy's offer tasting cups of their specialty drinks—blueberry mojitos and hurricanes.

Max's face beams at the compliments she receives from locals and tourists. *Stunning. Outstanding job with the renovations. The redo will bring a whole new clientele to the area.*

Birdie gives Max a half hug. "Congratulations. You're a success. Your rundown inn is now an upscale boutique hotel. Daniel would be proud."

"I'd like to think so." Tears well in Max's eyes at the mention of her late husband. "I couldn't have done it without the two of you."

"The vision was yours," Amelia says. "I simply helped you execute it."

Birdie adds, "I can only take credit for pouring gallons of coffee down your throat."

Max hip-bumps Birdie. "Never mind all those times you talked me off the ledge when something went wrong, and I threatened to sell the place." Her face becomes serious. "Davis deserves a lot of the credit. He's a brilliant contractor."

Shielding her eyes from the sun, Amelia surveys the crowd meandering about. "Speaking of Davis, where is he? Shouldn't he be here basking in the glory?"

Max shrugs. "I don't know where he is. We're not currently speaking."

Birdie pinches her brow. "What's going on, Maxie?"

Max stares down at the boardwalk. "He's pressuring me to move in with him, and I'm not ready. I haven't yet recovered from my last live-in boyfriend."

"You're not the only one with trouble in paradise," Amelia admits. "Jonathan and I had our first fight last night. He's moving too fast for me, as well."

Birdie chimes in, "I'm glad I'm not the only one having problems with my man. Stan says I work too hard. And I don't deny it. But my work makes me happy. He thinks I should hire someone to manage the cafe, so I can travel around the world with him. I'm only fifty-four. I'm not ready to retire yet. I'm just reaching my stride."

Max says, "Maybe we're too set in our ways."

"Or carrying too much baggage," Amelia adds.

The sea of people in front of them parts to reveal Hannah and Ethan. They're standing at the railing, gazing into each other's eyes. Gus is beside them, licking a snow cone while staring out at the inlet.

"Aren't they the sweetest couple?" Max says with a dreamy expression. "Oh, to be young again and starting out with a clean slate. They don't know how good they've got it."

"Would you do it all over again if you had the choice?" Birdie asks.

Amelia shakes her head. "Not a chance in hell."

Max says, "I would in a heartbeat if it meant being with Daniel again.

"I'm enjoying middle age," Birdie says. "Stan can either take me as I am, or he can leave me. I'll miss him. But I have my business to focus on now. I won't fall to pieces the way I've done in the past."

Max pats her back. "You've come a long way, Birdie, and I'm proud of you."

When Hannah spots the three women, she waves and walks toward them. She holds up her left hand, the enormous diamond on her ring finger sparkling in the sunlight. "Ethan proposed last night."

Amelia's gaze shifts to Birdie. Her eyes glisten with unshed tears as she embraces her daughter. "Congratulations, sweetheart. I'm so happy for you. Ethan is a dear man. The two of you will have a wonderful life together."

"Thank you, Mama. I wanted to call you last night. But Ethan said you already knew."

"Ethan flattered me by asking my permission." Birdie chuckles. "He treated me to lunch. But he only took your father for coffee." She reaches for Hannah's hand. "He showed me the ring. It's beautiful. And a perfect fit. He told me about your other surprise. Oops." Birdie's hand flies to her mouth. "I hope I didn't spill the beans."

Pink spots appear on Hannah's cheeks. She explains to Max and Amelia, "Ethan bought me a beach cottage. It's teeny tiny and needs a lot of work. But we can grow into it. This means we'll be spending a lot more time down here now."

"He bought you a beach house?" Max's blue eyes are wide. "Girlfriend, you have found yourself a keeper."

Hannah hugs herself. "I'm the luckiest girl in the world."

Amelia and Max surround Hannah, offering congratulations and ogling the ring. "You'll make a stunning bride," Amelia says, fingering a lock of Hannah's long mahogany hair. "When's the wedding?"

"Soon, I hope. Neither of us wants to wait. We'd like to get married this summer, if I can find an available venue."

"What about Point Pleasant?" The words leave Amelia's lips before she thinks about them.

Hannah stares down at her ring. "That's a generous offer, Amelia. But I couldn't ask you to do that."

Amelia quickly warms to the idea. "Why not? I would love it. I don't have children of my own. I may never have a chance to host a wedding." She allows her imagination to wander. "I can see it now, you and Ethan exchanging your vows with the ocean in the background."

"That would be amazing." Hannah looks over at her mama. "What do you think?"

"I think it would be lovely." Birdie locks eyes with Amelia. "Are you sure about this?"

Amelia places a hand on her chest. "I'm absolutely positive. Have you chosen a date? Not that it matters. Any date is fine with me. I have absolutely nothing going on this summer."

"I'll have to talk to Ethan, but I'm thinking late July or early August." Hannah is suddenly distracted by the sight of the enormous cake through the window of the hotel lobby. "Whoa. Who made that? It's a replica of the hotel."

"Sydney," Birdie says. "She worked on it for days."

Hannah presses her face against the window. "Do you think she'll make my wedding cake?"

"I'm sure she will," Birdie says. "We've been doing some catering. If you're willing to take a chance on us, we'll cater the whole reception. Although the wedding would have to be on a Sunday, since Saturday night is our busiest night at the cafe."

Hannah turns away from the window. "We should totally get married on a Sunday. It's our special day," she says resting her head on her mother's shoulder.

"How so?" Amelia asks.

"We're closed on Sunday afternoons," Birdie explains. "When Hannah and Gus were living with me, we spent every Sunday afternoon and evening together."

Max says, "If you're planning to have out-of-town guests, which I assume you are since Ethan is from Charleston, a Sunday wedding might be a better choice. I'm booked on Friday and Saturday nights through the summer. If you have a minute, we can go inside and look at the reservations computer."

Hannah glances over at Ethan and Gus, who have moved from the railing and are now watching the magic show. "Sure! I need to get on it, if I'm going to make this wedding happen this summer."

Amelia watches Max and Hannah enter the building before turning back to Birdie. Her expression is now troubled. "What's wrong?"

"I don't see the point in rushing this wedding."

"You've done an excellent job with her, Birdie. She's as lovely on the inside as she is on the outside. And she seems to know her own mind. If she wants to get married this summer, I would be honored to help make that happen."

"Thank you." Birdie presses her cheek against Amelia's. "You're a true friend."

Amelia laughs. "I'm selfish is what I am. I've been trying to figure out how I'll occupy my time this summer. Entertaining is my thing. I've never planned a wedding before, but I've organized every other kind of party imaginable."

"Your expertise is welcomed." Birdie opens the lobby door. "I should provide my input about dates. Do you want to come inside for some cake?"

"Thanks, but I need to head home. Let me know what you all decide about the wedding."

Amelia waves goodbye and walks toward the parking deck. She's been on the lookout for Jonathan all afternoon, even though she didn't really expect him to show up after the way she treated him last night. She and Jonathan were blissfully happy together until she started second-guessing their relationship. He's the one constant in her life. The one thing she's certain of. Why is she pushing him away?

Lowering the roof on her convertible, she cranks the volume on the classic rock station and exits the parking deck, heading in the direction opposite home. The sun warms the top of her head and the wind whips her blonde hair about her face. When she reaches the town limits, she pushes the accelerator, tempting her fate by driving over the speed limit.

She feels a gnawing ache in the pit of her stomach. Whether its fear or loneliness, she can't put her finger on it. And she doesn't know what's causing it. Is she still mourning for her mother? Is she worried about losing Jonathan? Is she afraid of the future? Or is this unsorted pain from the past?

Leaving the main road, she drives down Jonathan's long gravel driveway and parks in front of his Lowcountry farm-house. Getting out of the car, she spots him out on the dock, washing his boat. He doesn't hear her approach, and when he looks up from his work to find her looming over him, he appears startled.

"Can we talk?"

"What's left to say? You made yourself clear last night." He dumps his mop in a bucket of suds and continues scrubbing the floor of the boat.

She climbs onboard, careful not to slip on the wet surface, and takes the mop from him. "I need you to listen to me,

Jonathan. I'm not clear on anything right now. I think I may be suffering from post-traumatic stress disorder."

As her statement sinks in, his expression morphs from anger to concern. "Okay. You have my attention. Let me rinse the soap off, and we'll go up to the house to talk."

She hands him back the mop and gets out of the boat, waiting patiently on the dock while he rinses the soap off with a hose. They walk back to the house in silence and sit down in rocking chairs on his porch.

"So, what makes you think you have PTSD?"

"I've been experiencing a wide range of emotions. Over-whelming sadness and anger, fear and hopelessness. I don't want to feel this way. I've been trying to hide them. But I can't make them go away."

"When did these emotions begin to surface?"

Amelia stares down at her lap. "Weeks. Months. Who knows? Maybe they've been building up for years. But they're becoming increasingly more difficult to ignore."

"You shouldn't ignore them. You need to process them. Your life hasn't been easy, Amelia. At age eight, you witnessed your older sister stab your father to death. You were married to an abusive man for thirty years. Last August, when your mama died suddenly in her sleep and you returned home for her funeral, you found your long-lost sister living in the garage apartment. You discovered said sister killed your mama with sleeping pills, and then, to top it all off, she killed your husband with a knife in front of you."

"Sounds like a soap opera," Amelia says.

His expression is serious when he angles his body toward her. "Have you ever seen a therapist?"

She shakes her head. "I should've. But Nelson wouldn't allow it." Amelia digs in her purse for a tissue and dabs at her wet eyes. "I survived my marriage by keeping busy, organizing benefits and presiding over nonprofit boards. My volunteer work made my life more bearable and prevented me from obsessing about my circumstances."

Jonathan reaches for her hand. "Your coping mechanisms."

"Exactly. And that's what I've been doing since Mama died. Settling estates and helping Max with the hotel. Lately, I've been freaking out about what I'll do with myself this summer."

"What happened to indulging yourself with yoga and romance novels?" he asks in a teasing tone.

"I thought I wanted leisure time, but I'm not sure I can handle it. I just offered to host Birdie's daughter's wedding at Point Pleasant. And I'm thrilled to do it. Hannah's a lovely girl and Birdie is my friend. But I did it as much for me as I'm doing it for her. I need a project. Something else to occupy my mind." Removing her hand from his, Amelia gets up and moves to the edge of the porch, staring out at the marsh. "I've had to be strong for so long. I feel like I'm losing my grip. And I don't know how to handle it."

She hears the creak of his rocker followed by his footfalls on the wooden porch floor behind her. He wraps his arms around her. "You need to stop running, Amelia. Face the pain. Cope with it. You'll be a stronger person at the end of the day."

"I don't know if I can." She relaxes against him.

"Of course, you can. You're not alone. I'll be right here with you."

"You make it sound so easy."

"It'll be anything but easy." He drops his arms and stands beside her. "I hit a bit of a rough patch after Lisa and I split up. While I knew the divorce was the best thing for everyone involved, letting go of the life we built together over twenty-five years was difficult. I learned a lot about myself during my mini breakdown, and you will too. You have to let everything out, let it all fall apart before you can put it back together again. My therapist, Dr. Martie Jackson, is a wonderful woman. She helped me. And she can help you too if you let her."

Amelia sucks in an unsteady breath. The thought of pouring out her secrets to a stranger terrifies her, but she suspects what Jonathan says is true. She'll have to let everything fall apart before she can put it back together. "I'll give her a try."

"I'll send you Martie's contact info. And I'll text her to let her know you'll be calling. I think you'll like her. She's extremely accomplished but very down to earth." Jonathan chuckles. "Be aware. Martie has an uncanny ability to see inside your soul. Don't hide anything from her. You're better off telling her the truth from the beginning, because she'll get it out of you one way or another."

"Sounds like torture." Her lips curl into a smirk. "Is waterboarding one of her techniques?"

Jonathan laughs out loud. "She's refined her methods. You'll never know what hit you."

Turning to him, Amelia gives him a peck on the lips. "I'm sorry about last night. Of course, you can keep your sailboat at my dock. I want to hear about it. Did you make an offer?"

"How about if I tell you over dinner?"

"I'd like that." Amelia's eyes travel across the small lawn to the dock. "Can I help you finish washing the boat?"

"I've got this. I want you to go home, make a glass of sweet tea, and spend the rest of the afternoon reading in your hammock." Jonathan spins her around and walks Amelia to her car. "After I finish here, I'll shower and grab some tuna steaks from the seafood market. I'll be over around six."

"Tuna sounds delicious." She kisses him again. "Thank you, Jon, for being so good to me."

Amelia feels the tension draining from her body on the drive home. She's been on a collision path with a brick wall for too long. She prays Dr. Martie Jackson can save her before she crashes.

FOUR

Tears blur Sydney's vision as she sautés silver-dollar-size crab cakes in a pan. No matter how hard she tries, she can't shake the sadness. The cloud that has been looming over her for years is becoming darker, more ominous. She's all but given up on having a social life. Her career is the only thing keeping her going. She works herself to exhaustion so she can sleep at night.

A voice jerks her out of deep thought. "Sydney! There you are. I've been looking all over for you."

Sydney looks up, startled. "Hannah! I didn't hear you come in."

Hannah crosses the room to her. "Are you crying?"

Swiping at her eyes, Sydney says, "Onions."

Hannah looks around at the spotless stainless-steel counter. "I don't see any onions. Are you okay? Do you need to talk?"

"I'm fine." Sydney returns her attention to the pan of crab cakes. "Can I help you with something?"

"I wanted to compliment you on the cake you made of the Palmetto Hotel. I was wondering if you'd consider making my wedding cake?"

Sydney dumps the crab cakes onto a platter. "Wait, what? Since when are you engaged?"

"Since last night," Hannah says, holding out her hand.

Sydney's eyes pop at the sight of her engagement ring. "Wow! What a gorgeous ring. Congratulations. I know you and Ethan will be very happy."

Eric, the cafe's head server, enters the kitchen with an empty tray. Sydney swaps it out for the full tray of crab cakes, and he's on his way again.

"I would love to make your wedding cake," Sydney says. "When's the big day?"

"We have to clear it with Ethan's parents, but we've tentatively set it for the last Sunday in July."

"Why so soon? Are you . . ." Sydney's gray eyes roam to Hannah's belly.

"No. I'm not pregnant," she says with a laugh. "I've been very careful not to make that mistake again. Not that Gus is a mistake."

Sydney leans back against the counter beside her. "How old were you when Gus was born? I don't mean to pry. But I've often wondered."

"I don't mind talking about it. I was twenty-two when he was born, the summer after my senior year in college. I never would've survived without Mom. She was my rock."

"Did you ever think about not having the baby or giving him up for adoption?"

"I never considered either." Hannah twirls a strand of hair. "I was ready to be a mom, even though I was so young."

"What about Gus's father?"

"He wasn't in the picture," Hannah says in a tone that makes it clear she doesn't want to talk about it.

"So, why the quick engagement?"

"Ethan really wants to get married this summer," Hannah

says. "And I'm fine with it, if I can pull it off. I admit I'm a little overwhelmed."

"Don't think about the big picture. Break it down and focus on one thing at a time."

"That's good advice. You've obviously done this before."

Sydney smiles. "I worked, for a short time, as an event planner before I came to Palmetto Island."

Eric sticks his head through the swinging doors again. "Sydney, we need more sweet potato ham biscuits."

"Coming right up!" she responds.

Hannah steps out of her way so she can get to the oven. "Would you be willing to cater the wedding? Mom mentioned y'all are branching out."

"There's a real need for caterers on the island." Sydney says as she removes a sheet pan from the oven. "Where are you getting married?"

"At Point Pleasant. Amelia's a friend of my mom's."

"Lucky! I've never been on the property, but I've seen it from the ocean. And how many guests will you have?" Sydney asks while transferring the bite-size biscuits from the sheet pan to a serving tray.

"Around a hundred. Although I need to confirm that number with Ethan's parents. The wedding will be late in the afternoon. I'm thinking finger foods."

"That sounds like a manageable size crowd." Sydney takes the tray to the cafe. When she returns, she says, "We'll put our heads together and come up with a menu. But first, we should book your rentals—tents, tables, chairs, and linens. The best party rental companies are in Charleston. I can email you the list."

"I'll call them on Monday morning," Hannah says, looking as if she might cry.

Sydney gives her shoulder a squeeze. "Don't worry, Hannah. I'll walk you through everything. In addition to the rentals, you need to focus on finding your dress and ordering invitations."

Hannah gives her head a determined nod. "One thing at a time."

"Exactly. I've found Pinterest boards really help. Why don't you create one and send me the link? We can go from there."

"That's a great idea. I love Pinterest. Thank you, Sydney. I feel better talking to you." Hannah starts toward the door and Sydney walks with her. "Do you really think this catering thing will fly?"

Sydney hunches her shoulders. "Customers ask us all the time to cater their events. We've done a few small sit-down dinners, but no parties yet. Birdie will ultimately need to hire a separate catering staff and set up another kitchen. If anyone can do it, your mom can. When she gets something in her head, there's no stopping her."

Hannah laughs. "Don't I know it." She tosses her purse over her shoulder. "I'd better go find Ethan and Gus. We promised Gus we'd go to the beach for a while before heading back to Charleston."

"You go. We'll talk soon." Sydney watches Hannah disappear through the swinging doors into the cafe. While she is thrilled for Hannah, she can't help but be a little jealous. She'd love to find an awesome guy like Ethan. If only she could stop comparing every guy she meets to Jake. She's pathetic, a twenty-six-year-old young adult hung up on her high school boyfriend.

Sydney enters the small office she shares with Birdie and closes the door. She avoids the temptation to search for Jake on social media for fear of seeing him with another girl. She's desperate to move on with her life. But she must first face the past. Flipping open her laptop, she searches the most popular social media websites. She has no trouble finding him. He's grown more handsome over the past ten years, but his dimpled smile and eyes haven't changed. Ah, those pale aqua eyes that once melted her heart, sometimes blue and sometimes green depending on his mood and what he's wearing.

His newsfeed shows plenty of pics of football players, but

none of any girls. According to his bio, he's on the coaching staff for the Clemson football team. Good for him. He turned his passion for the sport into a career. When she last saw him, the fall of their senior year in high school, he'd just been awarded a full-ride scholarship to play football at Auburn.

She types a direct message to him. *I hope you're doing well. Would love to catch up sometime.* Taking a deep breath, she clicks Send before she loses her nerve.

She's studying images of wedding cakes on Pinterest five minutes later when his response flashes on her screen. *Great to hear from you. I've been thinking a lot about you lately. Can I call you sometime?*

She responds right away, saying she'd loved to hear from him and giving him her cell number.

She snaps her laptop closed. Tingles of excitement dancing across her chest are quickly replaced by a heavy sense of dread. What has she done? She's opened the can. Is she ready to deal with the worms?

Sydney moves through the rest of her shift with a mixture of emotions. Fear. Hope. Uncertainty. She can always decline his call. But now that she's made the first step, she's eager to talk to him. He could be in a relationship. Maybe even engaged to be married. Even if he isn't, is another chance at a future together possible? The biggest question of all is whether or not to tell him the truth about the past.

Sydney's phone rings with the expected call as she's entering her Ocean Avenue apartment after work. "You kept your old number," she says by way of greeting.

"I'm surprised you didn't." His voice is deeper than she remembers, and his words are slurred as though he's been drinking.

"My parents kicked me off their plan. For work purposes, it made sense for me to get a South Carolina area code." Without turning on any lights, she drops her bag on the sofa and plops down in her favorite chair by the window. Lights twinkling on boats in the nearby marina penetrate the night sky.

"Sorry to be calling so late," Jake says. "I had a team dinner. Senior banquet. I'm a football coach at Clemson."

"I saw that on your profile."

He lets out a grunt. "So, you checked me out. I've been watching your profile for years. You never post about anything but food."

She chuckles. "Because I'm a chef."

"Don't you have any friends?"

That's a bold question, she thinks. "I don't have much time for socializing." Her career is her life. She looks around the room at the bare hardwood floors and white walls. She only has the essential furniture with no art on the walls or decorative accents. She's a cold person with no heart. Hard on the outside. Empty on the inside.

"So, you're a chef," Jake says. "Where do you live?"

"Palmetto Island. Which is on the coast near Charleston. I work at an up-and-coming restaurant called Birdie's Nest Cafe."

"I've heard of it, believe it or not. Several of my players have eaten there. I'm impressed, Syd. That's wonderful. Where did you end up going to college?"

"I didn't." She stares out the window at the still waters of the inlet. "I wasn't feeling the whole college scene, so I attended culinary school in New York."

"Last we talked, you were leaning toward going to Alabama. That was the night before you disappeared. What happened, Syd? Why'd you leave without saying goodbye," he asks, his tone both wounded and accusatory.

A flush creeps up her neck. She wriggles out of her chef's coat and drops it on the floor beside her chair. "Dad was appointed Ambassador to Japan. He had to leave right away."

"According to the rumors, you refused to go with them."

"That's correct. I didn't want to finish my senior year in Japan. My parents agreed to let me live with my sister in Atlanta." She leans her head back and closes her eyes. "You were headed off to Auburn. I was having doubts about college. No strings attached seemed like the best option."

"I'm not buying your story, Syd. We dated for three years. You were my person. We told each other everything. There's more to the story, isn't there?"

Sydney grips the phone. "I knew you'd try to talk me out of going to Atlanta. I was trying to make it easier on both of us."

"Has it been easy for you? Because it certainly hasn't been for me." Silence settles over the line. "I don't need this. I'm not sure why I even called you."

"Then, why did you?"

"Because I can't get you out of my head. Even after ten years."

Sydney hears a loud banging coming from his end of the line, as though he's beating something with his fist. "Jake, are you okay?"

"No, I'm not okay. I need to see you again, Syd. If for no other reason than to put our relationship to bed once and for all."

Whatever she expected from him, this is definitely not it. "You sound angry, Jake. I'm not sure seeing each other is such a good idea."

"There you go again, making decisions for both of us. I *am* angry, Syd. Angry as hell at you. I loved you. I was committed to you. You were my soul mate. But you didn't even have the decency to say goodbye." The sound of leather soles on hardwood floors is followed by the clinking of ice in a glass.

"This conversation isn't going well. Maybe we should talk another time."

"Or maybe we shouldn't," he says, and hangs up on her.

Sydney drops the phone in her lap. His anger is justified. What she did to him was unforgivable. She'd been a fool to hope they might start over. Moving from the chair, she dives onto the sofa and buries her face in the cushion, sobbing until there are no tears left. Plodding on bare feet into the adjacent kitchen, she brews a cup of lavender tea and returns to her chair by the window. She sips her tea as she replays the phone call in her mind. *There's more to the story, isn't there?* He knows she's hiding something. *If for no other reason than to put our relationship to bed once and for all.* What if they meet and there's no chemistry between them? While it's not the ending she wants, at least she'll have closure. From one chapter in her life. But what about the other?

FIVE

On Tuesday morning, Hannah arrives ten minutes late and out of breath for her appointment at the bridal salon. She collapses into the blush-colored leather chair beside Birdie, who is thumbing through a bridal magazine. "Sorry I'm late. I got hung up on a call with a client. I ordered an Uber, because I knew I'd never find a parking place. It took him forever to get to my office."

"Bless your heart." Birdie places the back of her hand against Hannah's forehead. "You're burning up."

"I guess so. The traffic is backed up on King Street. The driver let me out on the corner, and I ran all the way here."

"Sounds like life in the big city is a lot more hectic than Palmetto Island."

Hannah laughs. "I wouldn't exactly call Charleston a big city."

A middle-aged woman emerges from the back room. Birdie says, "Hannah, this is your stylist, Lucy."

Hannah smiles up at the tiny woman. "Sorry I'm late."

"No worries. Let's get a good look at you." Pulling Hannah to her feet, Lucy spins her around as she inspects her from head to toe over the top of her pink rectangular eyeglass frames. "Gorgeous. And what a lovely figure. Nice breasts and a good butt, which is unusual for someone so thin. What sorta dress did you have in mind, hon?"

"I have a picture." Hannah removes her phone from her bag and shows Lucy a photograph of a strapless dress with an overlay of lace.

Lucy takes the phone from her and pinches the image to enlarge it. "We don't carry this designer, but we have some similar gowns. I'll select a few and set them up in a dressing room. Can I offer you a beverage while you wait? Champagne, perhaps, for this special occasion."

"Water is fine," Hannah and Birdie say in unison.

"Water it is," Lucy says and disappears into the back.

Hannah gets up and wanders over to a rack of wedding dresses hanging along an exposed brick wall. She flips through the gowns, finding them too elaborate for her taste. Returning to her chair, she scrolls through her emails and text messages.

"You seem flustered," Birdie says. "Is everything okay? Other than the trouble you had in getting here."

"I'm behind at work. I spent all day yesterday trying to track down tents and tables for the wedding. All the local party rental companies are already booked. I finally located one in Summerville of all places. I hope their tents don't have holes in them."

"I'm sure their tents are fine." Birdie sets down her magazine. "I'm worried about you, sweetheart. I don't know why you're rushing this wedding. Why not wait until the fall?"

"Because of hurricane season. It would be just my luck to have a major storm blow through on my wedding day. We want an outdoor wedding. If we don't get married this summer, we'll have to wait until next spring." Hannah checks the time on her phone. "What's taking this woman so long? Ethan's mom is meeting us for lunch at twelve."

"Lunch?" Birdie pats her blonde hair. "If I'd known I was meeting your future mother-in-law, I would've taken more care with my appearance."

"You always look beautiful, Mom," Hannah says, her eyes glued to her phone.

Lucy returns with two pony bottles of water. "I have your dressing room all set up. Mom," she says to Birdie. "You wait here, and your daughter will provide a fashion show."

Birdie's face registers disappointment, but she doesn't protest.

Hannah follows Lucy to the dressing room and strips down to her bra and panties. Lucy helps her into a strapless dress similar to the picture she showed her. Hannah studies herself in the mirror. "This is awful," she says, and bursts into tears.

"Oh dear," Lucy says, holding a box of tissues out to Hannah. "Is it the dress? Or is it something else?"

Sitting down on the alteration's platform, Hannah buries her face in her hands. "My mom thinks I'm rushing this wedding. I'm afraid to admit she might be right. I don't want to disappoint my fiancé. He has his heart set on getting married this summer."

Lucy sits down beside her, rubbing her bare back. "There, there. Brides often feel pulled in a million different directions. But this is *your* big day. *You're* the star of the show. Do what feels right for *you*, and everything else will fall into place."

Hannah stares at the image of the wedding gown on her phone. "I saw this dress in a magazine years ago. I saved the pic for when my day came. But I look so ugly in it."

Lucy chuckles. "You're far from ugly, sweetheart. But some styles are more flattering than others. I'll be honest, I've never been a fan of strapless. But I have a dress that I think might be perfect for you. Would you like to try it?"

Dabbing at her eyes, Hannah nods. "Please."

Lucy helps Hannah out of the dress. "Now close your eyes while I slip this other dress over your head."

Hannah does as she's instructed, waiting patiently with her

eyes closed while Lucy zips up the back of the dress. "There," Lucy says. "Now you may open your eyes."

Hannah gasps at the sight of her reflection. The front is simple, a satin A-line dress with a boat neck, but the back scoops way down to her waist. "I . . . I don't know what to say. I would never have picked it, but I absolutely love it."

"Not many brides can pull off such a simple dress, but I think it highlights your beauty." Lucy helps her down off the alternation's platform. "Go show your mom."

Tears well in Birdie's eyes when Hannah parades in front of her. "Oh, honey, you're absolutely beautiful," she says, bringing a trembling hand to her lips.

Hannah twirls around. "Do you think so, really? Lucy picked it out. The strapless one was all wrong."

Birdie fingers the dress's fabric. "I think it's stunning. What about a veil?"

"She doesn't need much," Lucy says. "Decide what you want to do with your hair first, and then we'll pick the veil."

"Should you try some other dresses?" Birdie asks. "Or is this the one?"

"I think this is it." Hannah gathers her hair into a loose bun, letting a few tendrils frame her face. "Do you think Ethan will like it?"

Birdie stands beside her in front of the mirror. "He won't be able to take his eyes off you."

After completing the alterations, Hannah rides with Birdie to meet Ethan's mom at the Palmetto Cafe in the Belmont Hotel.

They are making their way up Meeting Street when Birdie asks, "What's Ethan's mother like?"

Hannah taps her chin as she considers the question. "I would describe Clara as elegantly southern. She acts like a snob sometimes, but she doesn't mean half of what she says."

"She can't be all bad. She raised Ethan to be a perfect gentleman." Birdie glances over at Hannah. "Feel better now that you've found a dress?"

"Much better! Now if we could figure out our living situation."

"What's there to figure out?"

Hannah bites down on her lower lip. "The cottage was a generous gift. But I can't furnish it, and the inside needs painting. And how are we supposed to manage three households?"

"Why not move your furniture from your apartment to the cottage? Your lease is up soon. Could you work remotely from the beach for a month or two?"

Hannah's olive eyes go wide. "That's a brilliant idea, Mom. I'm supposed to give my landlord thirty days' notice before terminating my lease, but since we're only a couple of days into May, I'm sure Heidi won't mind. I hope Chris approves." She thumbs off two texts, one to her landlord and the other to her business partner.

Birdie makes a left off of Meeting Street and is turning her ancient Volvo wagon over to the valet attendant when Hannah's landlord responds. *No worries. I already have a prospective tenant. I will miss you, though. Congrats on your engagement.*

Chris's text follows immediately. *We can manage with Zoom. Go for it!*

Hannah skips a step as they enter the hotel lobby. "Yay. Looks like I'm spending the summer at the beach." Then the enormity of the situation hits her. "Now all I have to do is pack up my apartment, hire movers, and figure out childcare for my son." She stops in her tracks. "Gus! I didn't factor him into the equation. Moving away from Sally will devastate him."

Birdie loops her arm through Hannah's, dragging her along. "He'll get over it. He's going to love living at the beach."

"My to-do list keeps growing at an alarming rate. As soon as I cross one thing off, I add another."

Outside of the cafe, Birdie stops walking and turns to her. "I know you have a lot on your plate, and I'm happy to help in any way. Just say the word."

"That means a lot, Mom. And Ethan is a big help. He's on top of his wedding responsibilities."

Birdie tilts her head to the side. "Is he, now?"

"Why the pessimism? Ethan isn't a slacker."

Birdie smiles. "I know that. But most men shy away from wedding planning."

"Maybe in your generation. But not in mine." Hannah walks off, leaving Birdie to follow.

Clara Hayes is waiting for them at an umbrellaed table by the fountain in the lush interior courtyard cafe. She stands to greet them, looking more the bride than Hannah in a white St. John knit ensemble. Birdie's words come back to her. *I would've taken more care with my appearance.* Maybe they both should have dressed a little more appropriately. Birdie is a walking advertisement for Lilly Pulitzer in floral print capris and a pink crewneck, short-sleeve sweater while Hannah feels dowdy in gray pants and a starched white blouse.

Introductions are made, and the three women sit down together. "This is such a special occasion," Clara says. "Shall we order champagne to celebrate?"

Birdie waves her off. "I don't drink, but don't let that stop you."

"I understand. Hannah?" Clara looks at Hannah with anticipation.

She shakes her head. "Sorry, but I'm going back to work after lunch. One glass of champagne and I'll be napping at my desk."

"Well, I'm having a glass. It's not every day a woman's only child gets engaged."

Clara signals the server, who rushes over to the table. The

mothers order the seared salmon and Hannah the shrimp and grits. The server disappears, returning minutes later with two sweet teas and Clara's champagne.

Clara raises her glass. "I'd like to propose a toast to my future daughter-in-law. Hugh and I are crazy about you, dear. We feel so blessed having such a lovely girl enter our family."

Hannah manages a smile. She's a single mother and entrepreneur. She is not a *girl*.

Birdie winks at Hannah from across the table. "Hannah's father and I feel the same about Ethan. He's a wonderful *young man*. The two of them will be very happy."

"We have much to discuss." Clara takes a tiny sip of her champagne and sets down her glass. "Some of my friends have offered to host the welcome party after the rehearsal dinner the night before the wedding. We'll need a block of rooms for both nights at the hotel. I assume you'll be sending out save-the-date cards soon. Although, with so little time before the wedding, you may decide to skip the save-the-dates and send the invitations early. Either way, we'll need at least a hundred and fifty. Maybe even two hundred. We're happy to pay for our invitations if this strains your budget."

"But—" Hannah starts to speak, but Birdie cuts her off. "The budget isn't the issue. Hannah and Ethan want a small wedding. No more than a hundred guests."

Hannah watches for Clara's reaction. Bewilderment, irritation, and anger collide on her face in one unbecoming distorted grimace. "I'm sorry, Clara. I thought Ethan discussed this with you."

"Ethan and I have been playing phone tag." Clara lifts a shaky glass to her lips and guzzles down her champagne. "Okay." She dabs at her lips with her linen napkin. "If this is what you want, I can narrow down my list. But that won't be as easy for Ethan. He has so many friends. He'll have an army of groomsmen."

"Actually, we've agreed to two attendants each."

Clara purses her hot pink lips. "Only two attendants? Why even bother with a ceremony?"

"We're trying to keep things simple," Hannah explains.

"Well." Clara recrosses her legs and smooths out her knit pants. "Will you at least allow me to host a sit-down dinner the night before? We'll only invite the *small* wedding party and our *few* out-of-town guests."

"That would be lovely. Thanks." Hannah's phone vibrates in her lap with a text from Chris letting her know they've won a big account. They've been working on this account for months, their largest to date. She should be overjoyed. Instead, she feels like crying.

When the server arrives with their entrees, Hannah excuses herself to go to the restroom. Outside of the cafe, she heads in the opposite direction of the lobby, exiting the building onto King Street. Collapsing against the brick facade, she inhales deeply to steady her breath.

She clicks on Ethan's number. When he answers on the second ring, she blurts, "We need to postpone the wedding."

"Why would we do that?" Ethan asks.

"So we have more time to plan. So we can invite more people. Your mom is upset because we're having a small wedding. I'm freaking out, Ethan. I have a business to run."

"Hold on a second, Hannah. Where did you see my mom?"

"My mom and I are having lunch with her at the Palmetto Cafe. I told you about it, remember?"

"Right." Hannah hears a creaking noise, which she assumes is Ethan leaning back in his chair. "I'm sorry, Hannah. This is my fault. I didn't realize your lunch was today. I'll stop by my parents' house after work and straighten her out."

"But she has her heart set on a big wedding, and you're her only child."

"This is *our* wedding, Han. We're getting married on our

terms. We agreed to keep it small, so we can get married this summer. Are you having a change of heart about marrying me?"

Hannah hesitates.

"Hannah? Tell me the truth. I promise I won't get mad."

"The truth is, I can't wait to be your wife. I want a small wedding whether we get married this summer or next spring or the following year. I don't really wanna wait. I'm just feeling a little overwhelmed. With all the talk of invitations and rehearsal dinners and moving. By the way, I gave my landlord notice. At the end of the month, I'm moving my furniture from the apartment to the cottage. I'll work remotely from the island until the wedding." Pushing off the brick wall, Hannah looks down at her feet as she paces in small circles. "I hope that's okay with you, Ethan. I made a split-second decision. I should've talked to you about it first."

"That's the perfect solution to your temporary living arrangements. Being on the island will make it easier for you to plan the wedding. I'll miss you during the week, but I'll be down every weekend. You're not alone in this, Han. I'll help you with the move, and I want to do my part in making the wedding arrangements. We'll lean on each other, and we'll get through this together. In three months, we'll be husband and wife."

"Husband and wife. I like the sound of that." The sight of a swimsuit in the window at Tommy Bahama catches her attention. "I need to get back to our moms. I'll call you later." She ends the call and wanders over to the window.

The thought of spending two glorious summer months at Palmetto Island warms her. She'll have coffee on the porch in the mornings, followed by long walks on the beach with Gus. At the end of July, she'll become Mrs. Ethan Hayes, and they'll begin their life together. She's found her dress, hired the caterer, booked the rental company, and notified her landlord she's moving out. The rest will fall into place in time. She needs to relax and enjoy this special time.

SIX

Psychotherapy is messy business. Twice a week, during their hourly appointments, Dr. Martie Jackson chips away at Amelia's armor, the protective outer layer that allowed her to survive the atrocities her husband had imposed upon her. According to the therapist, in order to heal, Amelia must face the past head-on.

"The abuse damaged your psyche," Martie said at their first meeting. "Our job is to repair it."

The all-white decor in Martie's office provides a blank slate for Amelia's crowded brain, enabling her to relax. Seated in leather chairs by the window overlooking the inlet, she works through her feelings. She's angry and humiliated. At times, she experiences actual physical pain, as though Nelson is in the room with them pummeling her with his fists all over again. She grieves for the years she lost, for the carefree young woman she once was.

While the sessions leave her emotionally spent, Amelia typically sleeps well afterward and feels more upbeat the following day. Occasionally, however, she sinks into a depression that stays with her for three or four days. On Thursday during the last week of May, after a particularly grueling session on Wednesday, she falls into the proverbial abyss. She's never known such darkness. She tries meditating and walking on the beach. She drinks gallons of Martie's special homemade chamomile tea. But nothing will chase away the doldrums.

Finally, after vomiting the salad she choked down for dinner, she calls Martie's cell number. "I'm sorry to bother you so late, but I'm really struggling. I feel almost . . ." Her voice trails off. She can't bring herself to say the word. *Suicidal*.

"Hold tight. I'm on my way. Give me your address." Amelia spits out her address, and Martie says, "You're just down the beach from me. I'll be there in less than five minutes. But I want you to stay on the phone with me."

From Martie's end of the line, Amelia hears a car door close and an engine start. "Okay."

"Did something trigger these feelings, Amelia?"

"Sometimes I get down after one of our sessions. This time I can't shake the blues. I feel like I'm tumbling down a stairwell into a dungeon. Something sinister looms at the bottom in the darkness, but I can't tell what it is. What is wrong with me, Martie? I have so much to be grateful for. A beautiful home. A man who loves me. For most women, that would be enough. Why isn't it enough for me?"

"There's nothing wrong with wanting more. In time, we'll figure out what motivates you to get out of bed in the mornings. But for now, we have to deal with the past. You've suppressed these feelings for so long. They can be overwhelming when you finally let them out."

"That's exactly how I feel. Overwhelmed. By everything. I tried all the coping mechanisms. But nothing is working."

"Where's Jonathan?"

"Out of town. He had to go to Spartanburg to take a deposition."

"Does he travel a lot for work?" Martie asks, and for the next

46

few minutes, they talk about Jonathan's hectic work schedule. "I'm pulling into your driveway now. Meet me at the front door."

Ending the call, Amelia crosses the living room to the foyer. She opens the door to find Martie on the front stoop dressed in yoga pants and a tank top with her auburn hair pulled back in a ponytail.

"I'm sorry. I interrupted your workout."

"Actually, I had just finished when you called." Martie enters the house and makes herself at home as she looks around. "This place is stunning, Amelia. Your views are incredible."

"Thank you. As you know, I grew up here. There are so many wonderful memories of my mama here."

Martie stops admiring the living room and turns to Amelia with a serious face. "But some bad stuff happened here as well. During your childhood and not so long ago. These events are the ones we need to address."

Amelia forces a smile. "Are we going to perform an exorcism on my house?"

"Something like that."

Amelia motions her to the sofa. "Can I get you something to drink? Wine? Tea?"

"I have some water. But thanks." Martie removes an oversized bottle of smartwater from her tote bag and sits back on the sofa. "Now, tell me about the events that took place in this room."

For the next half hour, Amelia describes in great detail her sister violently murdering their father in this room in July of 1976. She sits on the edge of the sofa while she talks, wiping her tears and shredding the tissues.

Martie says, "I can only imagine how traumatic it must have been for you, at age eight, to witness your father being stabbed to death. Did your mother ever send you for therapy?"

Amelia shakes her head. "On the contrary. We pretended it never happened. Which led me to suppress those memories."

"That explains a lot. When did the memories begin to resurface?"

"Last summer, when Mama died, and my sister came back to town." Amelia talks on for over an hour about the events leading up to Nelson's death and discovering her sister killed her mother. When she's finished talking, she falls back against the cushions, exhausted.

Martie leaves the sofa and goes to stand in front of the fireplace. "Whether or not you realized it, your eyes remained glued on this spot while you were talking." She runs her foot across the sisal rug. "I can see the faint discoloration from the bloodstain. Have you considered replacing the rug?"

"I'm considering a number of changes. To make the house feel more like mine and less like Mama's. Hannah's wedding provides just the excuse I need for a mini-redo."

"I would get on those changes, sooner rather than later." Martie faces Amelia, placing her back to the fireplace. "Have you thought about returning to your design career? Palmetto Island could use someone with your sophisticated taste."

Amelia shrugs. "Interior design doesn't thrill me the way it once did. But I need to do something productive with my life."

Martie returns to the sofa. "What about opening a home interiors shop?"

"Maybe. Although, I can't really see myself as a shopkeeper."

"Do you like to travel?"

"Not particularly. Nelson traveled all the time, and he insisted I go with him. Now that I've finally come home to Point Pleasant, I don't want to ever leave. Besides, the sunset from my porch offers the best views in the world."

"I can well imagine. You'll have to invite me back sometime for a glass of wine."

Amelia smiles. "I'd like that."

"I admire you a great deal, Amelia. You're much stronger than you think. You're a fighter. You possess inherent survival skills."

This surprises Amelia. "Do you really think so?"

"I never say things I don't mean. Especially to my patients." Martie takes a long drag off her water bottle. "Are you feeling better now? I can stay longer if necessary."

"I'm fine. Unburdening myself of those tragic memories helped. I feel like I hit rock bottom earlier tonight. And now, I'm more hopeful about the future than I've been in a long time."

"Excellent. That's exactly what we're trying to accomplish." Martie stands to go, and Amelia walks her to the door. Martie gives Amelia a quick hug. "Call me anytime."

Amelia remains on the front stoop after Martie disappears around the corner of the house to her car. The familiar sound of waves crashing in the distance sets Amelia at ease. She inhales a deep breath of salty air. This is her happy place. She has no desire to travel to exotic destinations or spend six days a week managing a boutique. Point Pleasant is where she wants to live out her days. Only something is missing. Truth be told, she feels a little lost without Jonathan tonight. But she doesn't hold his absence responsible for her meltdown. There's something missing. Something she can't quite put her finger on. God willing, this *thing,* whatever it is, will reveal itself in time.

SEVEN

Becca lowers herself to the beach chair and digs her toes into the sand. "Stay where I can see you," she calls after her daughter as Happy rides off down the beach on her new bike.

Settling back in the chair, Becca turns her face toward the sun and closes her eyes. When they arrived at the cottage, Becca and Happy unloaded the car, but decided to unpack their bags later. They were both eager to get to the beach. Becca deserves a break, having worked overtime these last few days, grading exams and wrapping things up at school. She'll relax and enjoy the beach for a while.

She's encountered certain challenges these past weeks, developments she anticipated but didn't expect to happen so soon. While leaving the familiarity of her home has disadvantages, the cottage has a simple layout and the town of Palmetto Island is small. The anti-anxiety medication her doctor prescribed is taking the edge off. Still, she has much to worry about. An uncertain future to plan for.

Becca dozes off. When she wakes with a start, she notices Happy's bike abandoned on the beach a short distance away.

Scrambling out of her chair, she shields her eyes from the sun as she searches the landscape for Happy. She spots her talking to a woman and child in the yard next door.

Becca traipses barefoot through the sand to the cottage that is nearly identical to the one she's renting. The only apparent difference is color. Becca's is yellow and this one a subtle gray. She waves as she approaches the yard from the sand dunes. "Hey there! I hope my daughter isn't being a nuisance."

"Not at all." The woman extends her hand as she closes the gap between them. "I'm Hannah Fuller."

Becca is rendered speechless by Hannah's beauty. She's a wholesome green-eyed brunette with a trail of freckles across the bridge of her nose. Remembering herself, Becca accepts Hannah's hand. "Nice to meet you. I'm Becca Godfrey."

"I was just getting acquainted with your daughter," Hannah says to Becca, and to Happy, "What's your name, sweetheart?"

"I'm Harper. But my friends call me Happy."

"Happy?" Hannah says. "What a fun nickname. I love it."

Hannah's towheaded little boy looks up from the ground where he sits with a big yellow dump truck. "And my name is . . ." He looks from Happy to Hannah. "What's my real name again, Mommy?"

"Your full name is Julian Augustus Fuller."

"Right. Augustus. But my friends call me Gus." He scrambles to his feet and takes off, spewing rumbling noises as he pushes his truck through the grass.

Becca laughs. "He's adorable."

"He's a mess," Hannah says. "Happy tells me you're here for the summer. So are we. Well, most of it, anyway. I'm getting married at the end of July. My fiancé and I live in Charleston. Where are you from?"

"Mount Pleasant," Becca says. "We arrived this morning. We dumped our bags at the door and headed straight to the beach."

"I don't blame you. This weather is incredible." Hannah

gestures at her house. "We haven't actually moved in yet. We just bought the cottage as a weekend home. My fiancé is bringing a load of furniture down on Monday. I've invited some friends over for a painting party tomorrow. I'd love for you and Happy to come. Not to paint, of course. I wouldn't ask you to do that since we just met. But you might enjoy meeting some locals."

Happy bounces on her toes. "Can we, Mom? Please!"

"Sure! I don't see why not."

Happy furrows her brow as she looks up at Hannah. "Where are you sleeping, if you don't have any furniture?"

Becca nudges her daughter. "Don't be nosy, sweetheart."

Hannah smiles at Happy. "That's a legitimate question. Gus and I are staying with my mom. She owns a cafe over on the boardwalk. She lives in the apartment above the cafe."

Gus returns with his truck, parking it at his mother's feet. "Birdie makes the best donuts ever. She's bringing my favorite, peanut butter brownie, to the party tomorrow."

Becca thinks the donut flavor sounds disgusting, but she keeps her opinion to herself. "I gather your mom is Birdie. As in Birdie's Nest Cafe?"

"That's the one," Hannah says. "Have you heard of it?"

"Who hasn't?" Becca says. "Birdie's Nest is the newest hot spot in the Lowcountry."

Happy asks, "Can we go there for dinner tonight?"

Becca shakes her head. "I don't think so, sweetheart. The cafe's cuisine is more for grownups. At least that's my impression. Miss Hannah would know better."

Hannah winks at Happy. "My mom keeps a bag of frozen chicken nuggets in the freezer for Gus, if that tells you anything about the menu. Shaggy's, on the other hand, is right next door, and they are very kid friendly. You'll love eating on the porch."

"Shaggy's sounds perfect." Becca takes Happy by the hand. "Come on, sweetheart. We need to make a run to the grocery before lunch."

Happy pries her hand free of Becca's. "What time should we come for the painting party tomorrow, Miss Hannah?"

"Around two," Hannah says.

"What should we bring?" Becca asks.

"Just yourselves. And your appetites. Mom is providing refreshments." Hannah picks Gus up. "Come on, buddy. We need to think about lunch as well."

Gus wriggles free and takes off again with his dump truck.

Hannah rolls her eyes. "I'll never get him out of here. He loves having a big yard to play in."

"We're gonna have the best summer ever," Happy says, and heads off down the sand dune path toward the beach.

"She's a cutie." Hannah watches Happy go and turns back to Becca. "Well then, have a great afternoon. Enjoy Shaggy's, if you decide to go."

Becca furrows her brow. "Shaggy's?"

"The restaurant on the boardwalk with the porch," Hannah says with a curious stare.

Becca's face heats. "Oh, right. Sorry. It's been a long week."

Hannah laughs. "Tell me about it."

Becca traipses through the dunes, retrieves her beach chair, and follows Happy's tire tracks to the cottage. She considers the pros and cons of being friendly with her next-door neighbor. What if Hannah gets too close? What if she discovers Becca's secret? Then again, if things continue to progress as rapidly as they have this past month, she'll be grateful to have someone her daughter can turn to in case of an emergency.

***

Becca feels her daughter watching her as she studies the menu at Shaggy's.

"Why are you wearing sunglasses when the sun isn't even out?" Happy asks.

Becca continues to stare down at the menu. "Because my eyes are sensitive after being on the beach all day."

"What about the hat? Did you forget to wash your hair?"

"You don't like my straw hat?" Becca tugs the hat lower over her face. "It's part of my ensemble."

"Your ensemble?" Happy laughs. "Strapless dress, sandals, sunhat. Are you going for resort casual?"

Becca pulls the sunglasses down her nose. "Since when did you become a fashionista?"

"Since I'm going into the fourth grade." Happy sits back in her chair and crosses her arms. "My friends get to pick out their own clothes. Why won't you let me?"

"Because you never asked. I'm thrilled for you to pick out your clothes."

Happy smiles. "Okay. Sweet."

Readjusting her sunglasses, Becca returns her attention to the menu.

"Maybe something is wrong with your eyes," Happy says. "We weren't on the beach *all* day. Only for a short time this morning. And you slept most of the afternoon."

Becca's head shoots up again. "That is not true. I unpacked my suitcases and read for a while. I'm tired, sweetheart. I worked overtime to finish up my work at school, so I could have the weekend free to spend with you." She looks back down at the menu. "Now, I'm starving. Should we order some fried calamari?"

Happy glares at her. "Seriously, Mom? I'm allergic to seafood."

Fear grips Becca's chest, but she manages to appear calm. "Silly me. I wasn't thinking about calamari being seafood. What about some nachos?"

"Whatever. Nachos are fine."

Becca signals the server and places their order. Settling back in her chair, she surveys their surroundings. They're seated at a table along the edge of the porch with a direct view of the boats in the marina. The mood at Shaggy's is lively with patrons of all ages celebrating Memorial Day weekend, the official kickoff to summer. She couldn't ask for a more perfect venue to celebrate their first night at the beach. If only things could be different.

After dinner, they walk up to Ocean Avenue and order mint chocolate chip ice cream cones from Scoops. They take their cones back down to the park and sit on a bench by the fountain. Happy chatters about which friends she wants to invite down for which weekends while Becca observes the young woman making her way from table to table in the outdoor seating area at Birdie's Nest Cafe.

Happy startles her when she elbows her in the ribs. "Who are you staring at, Mom?"

Becca straightens, smoothing her dress over her crossed legs. "What do you mean? I'm not staring at anyone."

"Yes, you are, Mom. I've been watching you watching her."

Becca feigns confusion. "Her, who?"

"The lady over there in the white coat. Is she the cook or something?"

Becca's eyes follow her daughter's finger. "I assume she is. She's dressed like a chef. That's Birdie's Nest Cafe. Miss Hannah's mother's restaurant. I wasn't staring at the woman. I was just checking the place out."

Happy squints, glaring at Becca with her piercing blue-green eyes. "You're acting strange, Mom. Is something wrong?"

Becca finishes her cone and tosses her napkin into a nearby trash can. "What could possibly be wrong? This is our first night on Palmetto Island. We have the whole summer ahead of us. How should we spend our day tomorrow?"

"We're going to Miss Hannah's painting party, remember?"

"I remember," Becca lies. "What time is the party again?"

"At two o'clock. And we're not supposed to bring anything, because Birdie is providing treats from her cafe."

"That's right." As they walk back to the car, Becca removes

her phone from her straw clutch and creates an event in her calendar app with an alert for tomorrow morning, reminding her of the party. From now on, she'll have to be more diligent about keeping track of her commitments.

EIGHT

Sydney works the lunch shift on Sunday, filling in for Sadie, who is out of town for the holiday weekend. She's leaving the cafe around two, scrolling through text messages instead of watching where she's going, when she collides with a giant of a man. Her phone flies out of her hand and crashes to the boardwalk. She bends down to pick it up. When she straightens, she comes face to face with Jake. Her breath hitches. The handsome teenager she once knew has morphed into a drop-dead gorgeous man with chiseled features. Even his aqua eyes are more electric.

"Is it broken?" Jake asks, eyeing her phone.

Sydney looks down at her phone and back up at him. "It's fine. What're you doing here?"

He stuffs his hands in the pockets of his linen shorts. "I couldn't stop thinking about you. I probably should've called first. But I worried you wouldn't agree to see me."

She casts a nervous glance toward Ocean Avenue. "When we talked . . . our phone conversation . . ."

"Didn't go well. You're obviously in a hurry. Are you going somewhere?"

"I've been invited to a friend's painting party." She shifts her weight from one foot to the other. "Did you happen to be in the neighborhood? Or did you drive all the way down here specifically to see me?"

"I came to see you." He rakes his fingers through his wavy brown hair. "In hindsight, it was a risky move on a holiday weekend when you might have been out of town."

"Nope. I'm here." She rarely leaves the island. Her parents still live in Japan, and her sister invites her to visit only on major holidays.

"How long will your party last? Maybe we can meet up later. Take a walk on the beach or something."

"The party's not a big deal. A walk on the beach sounds nice." She looks down at her chef's attire. "But I need to change first. I only live a block away." She sweeps her arm in the direction of the park. "Why don't you wait for me here? I'll be right back."

"Sounds good. Take your time."

Hurrying up the sidewalk, Sydney shoots off a text to Hannah, explaining an old friend has come to town unexpectedly and she wouldn't be able to make the party. When she reaches the avenue, she pockets her phone and increases her pace. Jake's sudden appearance has taken her by surprise. He will press her for answers. If she tells him the real reason she left San Antonio all those years ago, she'll risk losing him forever. Where's the harm in waiting? Why not find out if any chemistry still exists between them?

At her apartment, she quickly freshens up and changes into denim shorts and a cropped pink T-shirt that reveals a sliver of tanned midriff. When she arrives back at the park, she finds Jake sitting on a bench eating a snow cone. "That was fast. Do you want a snow cone?"

Her lip curls in distaste. "No thanks."

He laughs. "You always were a food snob. No wonder you

became a chef." He studies his cone. "This isn't nearly as good as I remember."

"I guess not. It's nothing but sugar and water."

"True." Jake takes one more bite of the snow cone and tosses the rest in a nearby trash can. "Let's hit the beach. I'll drive." He leads her to a gray Ford truck parked parallel on Ocean Avenue.

"I see you're still driving a pickup."

Aiming his key at the truck, he clicks the doors unlocked. "You can take the boy outta Texas—"

"But you can't take the Texan out of the boy," she finishes. "Why didn't you go back to Texas after college?"

"I interviewed with all the major football programs. Clemson gave me a better offer."

The interior of his truck smells like Old Spice, and when he starts the engine, country music blasts from the radio. "Sorry" he says, turning down the volume. "Which way?"

"Straight. The beach is just over the causeway." Sitting beside Jake in the passenger seat is surreal, as though the years have fallen away and they are back in high school again, headed off to spend the day at Canyon Lake. She yearns to stroke his arm, to reach over and hold his hand. The spark is definitely still there.

She directs him to one of the more popular beach accesses. They leave their flip-flops at the end of the boardwalk and run across the hot sand to the edge of the surf. The beach is crowded with children and adults of all ages, enjoying the glorious early summer weather. When the wind whips strands of her blonde hair about her face, she ties it back into a ponytail with the elastic she wears around her wrist. They stroll for a while without talking, the silence reassuringly familiar.

They've gone about a quarter of a mile when Jake says, "I owe you an apology. I'd been drinking the night I called you. I'm not much of a drinker, but I was nervous about talking to you. I was rude to you, Syd. And I'm sorry for that. After I hung up, I realized how angry I've been at you all these years. We had something special. Why did you throw it all away?"

Sydney kicks at the water. "I already told you. My parents were moving to Japan."

"You could have lived with us. You were already like part of the family."

"Several of my friends offered for me to finish out the year with them. But my parents insisted I stay with my sister."

"We could've convinced them, if only you'd confided in me." He picks up a shell and skims it into the ocean. "That's the part that hurts the worst, Syd. You didn't trust me enough to even talk to me."

She didn't trust him? Or she didn't trust herself?

Jake takes her by the arm and turns her toward him. "I can't shake the feeling there's something more. Something you aren't telling me?"

A trickle of sweat runs down her back. What difference will it make now? Telling him won't change the past. But not telling him could change the future. She stares beyond him at the ocean, grateful her eyes are hidden behind dark sunglasses. He once knew her so well. He could always tell when she was lying. Then again, she's become an expert at hiding her emotions.

"I was terrified of losing you," she says. "Not only were you a football star, you were also good-looking and intelligent with a bright future. I saw how other girls looked at you. I knew they would be throwing themselves at you when you went to Auburn —big SEC school with gorgeous cheerleaders and sorority girls. I was leaning toward not going to college, and I didn't want to be the obsessive psycho girlfriend. I thought it was easier to make a clean break."

"I was committed to you, Sydney. I would never have cheated on you."

"You don't know that for sure." She tugs her arm free of his grip. "I made the decision that was right for me at the time. If I had to do it over again, knowing what I know now about life, I might do things differently."

She continues on down the beach, and he jogs to catch up with her. "What does that mean exactly?"

Her shoulder brushes his, sending tingles down her arm. "I had no idea how hard it would be to get over you. Ten years later, and I can't stop thinking about you, can't stop wondering what things might have been like if I'd made a different choice."

"I came here looking for closure, so that I can finally move on with my life. But being with you again . . . There's still something between us. Is it me, or do you feel it too?"

A single tear spills over her eyelid and slides down her cheek. "I feel *something*, Jake. It may be real, or it might be misguided hope."

"Are you willing to explore our feelings further to find out?" He smiles and dimples appear at the corners of his mouth. She never could resist those darn dimples.

"And how do you suggest we do that when we live at opposite ends of the state?"

"We take it one step at a time. I booked a room at the Palmetto Hotel for tonight, hoping you'd have dinner with me. Unless you have to work."

Sydney stops walking and faces him. If she accepts his invitation, there will be no turning back. How can she possibly say no? This is the chance she's been waiting for. "I don't typically work on Sundays and Mondays. And I would love to have dinner with you tonight."

Jake steps closer to her, closing the distance between them. "That leaves the rest of the afternoon free. I noticed the marina on the boardwalk rents wave runners."

She laughs out loud. "You haven't changed one bit."

"Nope. I'm still the same old thrill seeker. What do you say, Syd? Are you up for an adventure?"

The heat of his body sends a wave of pleasure to her sensual organs. She imagines herself riding on the back of a wave runner with her arms wrapped tight around his body. "I'm totally game."

A second chance with Jake is within her reach. This time she won't screw it up.

NINE

Amelia is among the first to arrive for the party. "Who else is coming?" she asks Hannah as they spread out drip cloths and sort painting supplies.

"The usual crowd," Hannah says. "Mom and Max and their significant others. Plus, my next-door neighbor, Becca, and her daughter, Happy."

Amelia smiles. "Happy? What a quirky nickname. I love it. I wonder what it's short for."

"Harper," Hannah says, opening a can of white paint for the living room. "Wait till you meet her. The name suits her. She's a precious little nine-year-old. Gus is absolutely smitten. He's forgotten all about Sally, his best friend in Charleston."

As Hannah suggested, Amelia is immediately taken with Happy when she arrives with her mother a few minutes later. She's as talkative and inquisitive as her mother is reserved.

Hannah has created a diagram assigning her helpers to various rooms. But when Happy claims the white paint in the living room boring, Hannah sends the little girl to the master bedroom to help Amelia.

"You don't mind, do you?" Hannah whispers to Amelia.

Amelia watches Happy slip her arms into a paint smock. "Not at all. She's adorable."

"Please keep an eye on her. I don't want paint all over the floor."

"Understood," Amelia says. "I will give her a demonstration."

Happy appears at Amelia's side. "I'm ready if you are. I should warn you. I've never done this before."

Amelia holds her hand out to Happy. "Well, I've painted more rooms than I care to admit. I'll teach you everything you need to know." She leads the child to Hannah's bedroom, where sunlight filters through a set of french doors that lead onto the screen porch.

Happy carefully removes the loose lid from the bucket of powder blue paint. "Ooh. This is much prettier than boring old white."

Amelia nods. "I agree. A lot of people prefer white walls. But I need color in my life."

"Me too!" Happy dips the tip of her finger in the paint and runs her finger across the wall. "What's your favorite color, Miss Amelia?"

"Gosh, I have so many. But I have a tendency to pick shades of blue. What about you?"

"I like blue and green and yellow. And pink, although it depends on the shade. Mama's gonna let me paint my bedroom when we get home after the summer. I can't decide what color. I was thinking of lavender. But now I'm not so sure."

Amelia hands Happy a rag to wipe her finger. "If you're having trouble deciding, you can buy sample-size containers at the paint store and try them on the walls in your room."

"That's a great idea," Happy says.

Amelia and Happy each select a brush. "Hannah has done most of the hard work," Amelia says. "She's primed the walls and taped off the woodwork. We get to do the fun part. First, we're going to cut in around the edges." She pours paint into two plastic cup-size containers and shows Happy how to dip the brush into the paint.

Happy hovers over her. "Can I try?" she asks, her expression eager.

"Of course. But let me guide you." Amelia wraps her hand around Happy's as she runs her brush around the doorjamb. Once Happy's gotten the hang of it, Amelia releases her hand and moves across the room to the opposite wall.

Happy is quiet at first, focused intently on her work. But after a few minutes, she begins telling Amelia about her friends and school and all the books in the Harry Potter series she's planning to read with her mom this summer.

"Do you rent the house next door every summer?" Amelia asks.

"No," she says, her tone suddenly serious. "My dad used to take us to Wild Dunes for a week every summer. But then he found a new family and moved to Colorado. We didn't go on a vacation last year. My mom pretty much cried the whole summer. She wanted to do something special this summer to make up for it."

"I'm sorry about your dad," Amelia says. "That must be hard for you. My dad died when I was about your age."

Happy takes her eyes off her painting to look at Amelia. "I'm sorry. Sometimes I wish my dad had died. I know I'm not supposed to say things like that. But I'd rather feel sad than angry."

"That's understandable. You'll feel better in time. You're lucky to have a mama who obviously loves you very much. I was close to my mama too."

"My mom's the best. Except . . ." Happy's voice trails off.

"Except what, sweetheart? Is there something you need to talk about?"

"She . . . um . . ."

Gus appears in the doorway with his nanny who could be his

65

sister with white hair and baby blue eyes. "Happy, do you wanna come swimming with me at Mia's pool?"

"Yes!" The excitement on Happy's face is quickly replaced by uncertainty. "I doubt my mom will let me, though."

"She will," Mia says. "I already asked permission. I'm a certified lifeguard, and my parents only live a few houses down the beach."

Happy looks down at her paint-splattered smock. "I have to go put on my bathing suit."

"Come on." Gus waves her on. "We'll go with you."

Happy looks over at Amelia. "Do you mind, Miss Amelia?"

Amelia smiles at her. "Not at all, sweetheart. We're almost finished with our first coat."

"Awesome! Thanks." Happy gently sets the paint roller in the tray and runs out of the room after them.

The child's departure is like a vacuum sucking the positive energy out of the room. Amelia is suddenly overcome with inexplicable sorrow. Feeling short of breath, she throws open the french doors and steps onto the porch. At the opposite end, Becca is seated in a rocker, staring blankly out at the ocean. Amelia moves to the refreshment table and pours herself a glass of sweet tea. "Can I get you something?" she calls out to Becca.

Becca shakes her head. "I'm fine, thank you."

Amelia goes to stand beside her. "Are you taking a break from painting?"

Becca aims her thumb over her shoulder. "It's really crowded in there. Too much confusion for me."

Amelia looks through the window into the living room where Birdie and Stan are cutting up with Max and Davis as they work. "They're a rowdy crowd for sure." She gestures at the empty rocker next to Becca. "Do you mind if I join you?"

Becca spreads her lips thin, as though intending to smile, but it comes across as a grimace.

Amelia sits down in the chair next to her. "The ocean is gorgeous today."

"Yes, it is. I've been watching that sailboat." She points at a catamaran, its sails billowing in the wind as it glides across the water. "I've always wanted to go out on the ocean in a sailboat."

"I grew up on Palmetto Island and, believe it or not, I've never been sailing either. But my boyfriend just bought an old schooner. We went out on our maiden voyage yesterday."

"Your boyfriend?" Becca cranes her neck to see inside the window behind her. "Which one is he?"

"Jonathan's not here. He's actually working on his boat today. Say . . ." Amelia shifts in her seat. "Would you and Happy like to go sailing in the ocean sometime?"

"That would be nice."

Amelia finds Becca's reluctant tone odd when just moments ago she admitted she'd always wanted to go sailing. Something about this woman tugs at Amelia's heartstrings. She seems lonely, as though she could use a friend. "Are you free next Saturday?"

"As of now, I'm free the whole summer."

"Then it's a date. Why don't you come around eleven. I live at Point Pleasant. It's the very last house on Ocean Avenue. Head south, and you can't miss it."

Becca pulls out her phone. "I'll create a calendar reminder."

Amelia wonders why Becca needs a reminder if her whole summer is free. She studies the woman as she taps on her phone's screen. She's striking with warm brown hair and a shapely figure. But there's a sullenness about her, a vacancy in her hazel eyes.

Becca returns her phone to the arm of the chair. "What can I bring?"

"Just yourselves and some sunscreen," Amelia says. "I'll pack a picnic lunch for us."

"Happy will be thrilled. Thank you."

A cool salt-infused breeze rustles Amelia's hair. "What do you do for a living? Do you work outside the home?"

"I'm a high school English teacher."

"Teaching is a noble profession. I'm an avid reader. I like all genres. Happy told me about some of the books on your summer reading list. She has a thing for the Harry Potter books."

Becca nods. "She's totally hooked. I'm encouraging her to branch out. I've convinced her to read at least one classic this summer. She's letting me pick. I think she would identify with Scout in *To Kill a Mockingbird.*"

"One of my all-time favorites. *The Swiss Family Robinson* might be another good choice," Amelia suggests.

Becca doesn't respond. She's too distracted by the sailboat that has come back into sight. "I'm excited about going sailing. Where did you say you live, again?"

"At Point Pleasant. The very last house on the beach south of here." Amelia points at Becca's phone. "You put a reminder in your phone."

Pink dots appear on Becca's cheeks. "Oh, right."

Amelia drains the rest of her tea. "I should get back to painting."

Becca rises out of her chair. "I should help since my daughter abandoned you."

"That would be great."

The two women return to Hannah's bedroom and resume painting. They settle into a comfortable silence while they roll a second coat of blue paint on the walls. Amelia thinks back to her earlier conversation with Happy. *Mom's the best. Except . . .* What was the little girl about to say before Gus and Mia interrupted her? Becca rented an oceanfront beach cottage for three months. She obviously doesn't have financial problems. Perhaps she's emotionally unstable, which would be understandable considering her husband left them for another family. But how does that impact her nine-year-old daughter? Is Happy in any kind of danger? Becca doesn't seem like the abusive type. But Amelia knows all too well how people often act out of character when under pressure.

Amelia wishes she could rescind the sailing invitation. She has enough problems of her own without taking on those of a total stranger. She's wracking her brain for an excuse to cancel sailing when she's overcome by a strong premonition. Her relationship with Happy and Becca is only beginning. Somehow, in some way, Amelia is meant to play an important role in their lives.

Becca and Amelia are finishing up with the final coat of paint when Becca hears the crunch of gravel in the driveway, followed by the slamming of the front door. A deep voice comes from the living room. "This place looks amazing."

Becca crosses the bedroom and peeks around the door frame at the tall man with sandy hair and a smile that warms the room. Through the paned front door, she spies a moving truck in the driveway.

Amelia joins her in the doorway. "Is that Hannah's fiancé?" Becca asks.

"Yes. Ethan. Isn't he adorable?"

Hannah emerges from Gus's bedroom with paintbrush in hand. "Ethan! What're you doing here? I wasn't expecting you until tomorrow."

"I missed you too much. I couldn't wait another twenty-four hours to see you." He bends down and plants a kiss on her lips. He walks about the room, admiring the fresh white paint. "Your crew does excellent work. Are they for hire?"

The weary painters let out a chorus of groans in response.

"I know you all are tired. But your efforts are greatly appreciated." Ethan greets everyone in turn, pausing briefly to introduce himself to Becca and kiss Amelia's cheek.

He returns to Hannah's side. "Looks like you're almost done painting. Which means we can start moving furniture in tonight."

"That would be awesome," Hannah says. "Gus will be thrilled."

"Speaking of the little devil, where is Gus? I have a surprise for him."

"Here I am," Gus says, appearing in the porch doorway. He sprints across the room and leaps into Ethan's arms. "What'd you bring me?"

"I can't tell you. It's a secret."

Gus's chubby hands pat Ethan's cheeks. "Give me a hint."

"I'd rather show you," Ethan says, rubbing noses with Gus.

Becca experiences a surge of anger as she watches the little boy and his soon-to-be stepfather. Craig never showed Happy affection, never brought her surprises. She deserves a devoted father like Ethan. And Becca is determined to get her one.

Ethan sets Gus down on the floor. "Wait for me by the oak tree in the backyard. I'll be there in a minute."

The group, their curiosity piqued, migrates toward the porch. When they reach the yard, Becca distances herself, standing off to the side, feeling awkward and out of place amongst these lifelong friends and family members. Minutes later, Ethan comes around the side of the house carrying a large round swing with a netted webbed seat.

"What is it?" Gus asks, looking from the swing to Ethan.

"It's a giant swing. We're going to hang it from this tree."

"Really? Cool!" Gus says, dancing around him as he inspects the swing.

"You're gonna need a ladder for that," Stan calls out. "I just happen to have one in my truck."

The group laughs.

Birdie plants her hands on her hips. "You didn't just *happen* to have a ladder in your truck. You were in on this surprise and didn't tell me."

Stan winks at her. "I'm a good secret keeper."

When Stan goes out to the truck for the ladder, the others gather around to investigate the swing.

Mia comes to stand beside Becca. "I had a blast with Happy. She's a trip. A few of my friends and I are having a backyard camp for some girls her age week after next. We have a few spaces left, and we'd love for her to sign up. The hours are from nine until one, and the price includes lunch," she says and tells Becca the amount.

"That's reasonable, I guess." When Becca decided to rent the cottage for the summer, she assumed the beach itself would provide plenty of entertainment. But they've been here only one day, and she can already see her daughter needs more socialization than Becca can provide.

Happy sees them talking and rushes over to Mia, throwing her arms around her waist. "Did you tell her about the camp?"

Mia smooths back Happy's golden hair. "I did. She's going to think about it and let me know."

"Please, Mama." Happy presses her palms together under her chin as though praying. "Think of all the new friends I'll make."

This idea appeals to Becca. If Happy makes new friends here, she won't have to invite her friends from home to come down on the weekends. "All right. I don't see why not."

"Thank you, Mama." Happy gives her a quick hug before running off to find Gus.

Mia pulls out her phone. "I'll add her to the list. If you'll give me your number, I'll send you the details."

Becca recites her cell number as Mia's fingers fly across the screen. Seconds later, her phone pings.

Mia pockets her cell. "Call me if you need a sitter. I'm nannying for Gus during the afternoons. I can easily keep both kids if you have errands to run or need some time to yourself."

A thought occurs to Becca. "There is one important thing I need to take care of. It involves a day trip to Charleston. Could you keep Happy after camp one day until I get home? My schedule is flexible."

"Of course," Mia says. "Any day is fine. Just let me know."

Becca had planned to schedule the appointment later in the summer, but with things happening faster than anticipated, she should do it sooner.

TEN

On Tuesday morning, Hannah and Becca address wedding invitations at the table on the porch while the children fly back and forth through the air on Gus's new swing.

"How thoughtful of Ethan to surprise Gus with the swing," Becca says. "You're a lucky woman to have found such a kind-hearted man."

"He's a good guy," Hannah says with a soft smile. "You'll find the right man too. Just give it some time."

Becca mumbles something Hannah doesn't understand.

"I'm sorry. I—"

Becca pushes abruptly back from the table. "I'm gonna get some more coffee. Want some?"

"Sure," Hannah says, handing over her empty mug.

Becca is gone much longer than it takes to pour two cups of coffee. When she returns, she appears flustered, and Hannah's coffee is cold.

"I took a look around," Becca says. "I hope you don't mind. The cottage really came together. Did you have all this furniture in your apartment in Charleston?"

"Most of it. Except for the rockers and this table." Hannah runs her hand across the glass-topped table. "They were in Mom's storage unit. They came from our old house, the house I grew up in on the inlet." A faraway look settles on her face. "My parents and I ate dinner at this table most nights when the weather was nice. Growing up on the water is a blessing. Being surrounded by nature helps keep kids grounded. I hope Happy and Gus realize how fortunate they are."

Becca pauses before responding, "I agree. Having the ocean and wildlife in your backyard offers a sense of calm."

Hannah's phone vibrates with an incoming call. Looking at the screen, she says, "This is the party rental company. I need to take this." She leaves the table and walks to the edge of the porch, looking out at the ocean.

"This is Agnes at Summerville Rentals. We have an issue with your tent order. According to our inventory, we don't have the size tent you need available for your date."

Hannah white-knuckles the phone. "What do you mean? I made a deposit. Will you double-check the contract?"

After a moment of silence, Agnes says, "Are you getting married on Saturday or Sunday?"

Hannah says, "Sunday. The last weekend in July."

"I apologize for the confusion," Agnes says. "I was mistaken. We have a big event the night before, but we *should* be able to accommodate your wedding."

"*Should* is not good enough, Agnes. Please reconfirm that you *will* accommodate my wedding and get back to me."

Hannah ends the call and returns to the table, plopping down in her chair. "Who knew there were so many details involved in planning a wedding?" she says to Becca, who is looking back and forth between her phone and an invitation.

Becca looks up at Hannah. "Didn't you say your wedding was on a Sunday?"

"That's correct. Why?"

"I hate to tell you this, but I think the printer made a mistake with your date."

Hannah snatches an invitation from the pile and reads through the wording. "Ugh. You're right. How did this happen? I proofed them myself." Opening her laptop, she accesses her inbox and searches for the email from the printer. "The date is wrong on the proof. This is my fault." She falls back in her chair. "This is bad. Really bad."

"Maybe you should call the printer, to see if they have more invitations in stock."

Hannah's mind races. "Actually, my business partner designed them. Which is good news, I guess. I'll only have to pay the printing fees plus the cost of the cardstock. And we won't need to reprint the envelopes." She sits up in her chair. "Okay, maybe this isn't so bad after all. I'll call them."

Becca taps on her phone's screen. "Looking at my calendar, you still have almost nine weeks until your wedding. That should be plenty of time."

Hannah calls the printer and remains on hold for a representative for five minutes. She explains the situation, taking full blame for the error, and begs for a rush order.

"Don't worry, hon," the representative tells her. "Happens all the time." Hannah hears typing on the other end of the line. "We can have a replacement order to you in ten days."

"Thank you. And please expedite the shipping no matter the cost." Hannah ends the call and drops her phone on the table. "At least we can finish addressing and stamping the envelopes. That way, we'll only have to stuff and seal them when the invitations get here."

Still holding the invitation, Becca says, "Point Pleasant? Why does that name ring a bell?"

"That's where Amelia lives. Wait until you see it. The property is gorgeous."

"That's right. Happy and I are going sailing with Amelia on Saturday."

An hour later, when Hannah and Becca are addressing the last of the envelopes, Sydney calls. "Hannah, can you come over to the cafe? Sadie and I are experimenting with cake flavors. This would be a good time for you to decide what kind of batter and filling you want."

Hannah's looks over at Gus and Happy, who have abandoned the swing and are now playing with Matchbox cars in the edge of the sand dunes. "I'll have to bring Gus with me."

Sydney laughs. "Is that a problem? I can't imagine he'll mind being forced to taste cakes."

Hannah smiles at the thought of her son stuffing his chubby face with cake. "No, I don't guess he will. We'll be there in a bit."

"More wedding drama?" Becca asks when she ends the call.

"Not drama, thank goodness. Sydney—she's my mom's head chef and event planner—has summoned me to the cafe to choose the flavor for my cake."

Becca begins organizing the addressed envelopes into piles. "What's Sydney like? I read an art . . ." She pauses, as though searching for the right word. "A piece about her in a local magazine. She's so young to be so accomplished."

"She's driven and talented. But there's something mysterious about her as well. I get the impression she had a troubled past."

The lines in Becca's forehead deepen. "What kind of trouble?"

"I'm not sure. She doesn't talk about herself much." Hannah glances at her watch. "I need to get going.

"I'll watch Gus for you. The kids are having so much fun. I'd hate to interrupt them."

"I hate to ask you to do that." Hannah's gaze travels back to the kids. "Although they are having fun. I don't know many nine-year-old girls who are willing to play Matchbox cars with a little boy."

"That's her nature. She's as content being with younger children and adults as she is with her own peers." Becca stands. "Go. I'll hold down the fort here."

"If you're sure. I'll be back well before lunch, but if the kids get hungry, there's plenty to eat in the refrigerator."

Becca moves over to the rockers. "Take your time. We'll be fine."

Hannah gathers the stacks of envelopes in her arms. "I'll run these up to my office, where they'll be safe from little sticky fingers, and be on my way."

Sydney is waiting for Hannah in the kitchen with five thick slices of cake arranged on plates on the counter in front of her. She comes from behind the counter and gives Hannah a hug. "I hope you brought your appetite."

"I'm starving." Hannah inspects the cake slices. "They all look yummy. But where's the icing? That's the best part."

Sydney laughs. "We start with the cake flavor first. Then we'll work on the filling."

"Makes sense." Hannah points to the brown cake. "Obviously that one is chocolate. What are the other flavors?"

"Vanilla, coconut, lemon, and almond," Sydney says, pointing at each one in turn. "In my experience, people prefer the more traditional cake flavors. You can go crazy with the filling and frosting or keep it simple. Whichever you prefer."

Hannah picks up a fork and takes a small bite of vanilla cake. "This is delicious. So light and airy. What frostings and fillings go best with each of these cakes?"

"The options are limitless. For the vanilla, you could do buttercream frosting with lemon curd or raspberry filling. Coffee caramel with the chocolate makes for a rich cake. I like a mango filling or cherry with almond for the coconut cake. Strawberry shortcake has become popular in recent years." Sydney throws her hands up. "Really, it's whatever you want."

"You're making my head spin." Hannah sets down the cake plate. "You decide."

Sydney shakes her head. "No way. This is your wedding. But I can help you narrow it down. Have you given any thought to flowers?"

"Actually, that was one of the easier choices. I'm using citrus-colored flowers. Roses, ranunculus, and peonies in shades of hot pink, coral, and yellow."

"Perfect! Bright and cheerful like you." Sydney hands Hannah the slice of lemon cake. "Try this. If you like it, we could do lemon on lemon with buttercream frosting decorated with a spray of the same fresh flowers you're using on the tables."

Hannah forks off a chunk of cake and slides it in her mouth. "That's incredible," she says, digging in for another bite.

"We can definitely get more creative if you prefer. But sometimes simple is more elegant."

"I agree. Let's go for simply elegant." Hannah studies Sydney more closely. "You seem chipper today. And your complexion has a rosy glow. Have you met someone?"

A flush creeps up Sydney's cheeks. "In a manner of speaking."

Hannah digs her fingers into Sydney's arm. "Ooh. Do tell."

Sydney hesitates. "I could use some coffee. Care to join me?"

Hannah glances at the wall clock. "I can spare a few minutes to hear more about your *manner of speaking.*"

"Let's go out front," Sydney says.

Exiting the kitchen through swinging doors, Hannah and Sydney help themselves to fresh brew from the carafe on the coffee bar and sit down opposite one another at a table on the banquette in the cafe.

Hannah blows on her coffee before taking a sip. "Start talking."

Coffee in hand, Sydney sits back on the bench and folds her

arms over her chest. "So, the old friend who showed up in town on Sunday, the reason I wasn't able to attend your painting party, was actually my high school boyfriend."

Hannah's eyes pop. "And you had no idea he was coming?"

"None," Sydney says. "I'd reached out to him on social media about a month ago. He called me, but the conversation was awkward, and ended abruptly. I honestly never expected to hear from him again."

When Sydney grows silent, Hannah prompts her to continue. "And?"

She hunches a shoulder. "Turns out there's still chemistry between us. I'm driving up to see him on Sunday for a couple of days."

"You go, girl. I hope it works out for you." Hannah's expression grows pensive. "I was in a similar situation once. With Gus's father, actually. I hadn't seen Ryan in years. I desperately wanted our relationship to work, so that we could be a family."

"What happened?" Sydney leans into the table.

"It didn't work out. We were on two different planets. I was a single mother and Ryan was in law school. I'd grown up and he hadn't."

"Were you disappointed?"

Hannah thinks before answering. "Not really. I gave it an honest try. I'd recently met Ethan, and closing the Ryan chapter of my life allowed me to consider a relationship with Ethan."

"Closure is what I'm hoping for in my situation as well. We have some logistical issues to work out. But we once had something special. If those feelings are still there, if we're meant to be together, we'll find a way to make it work."

Hannah smiles. "Yes, you will. And if not, you'll move on with your life." She stands to go. "I hate to run out on you, but I need to get back to Gus. I think we're on the right path with the wedding cake."

Sydney walks with her through the kitchen to the back door. "I'd like to set up a time next week to go over the menu."

"That works for me. I'm flexible. Let's check with Mom to see when she's available."

On the drive home, Hannah reflects on her conversation with Sydney. Having her boyfriend back in her life has drastically improved her demeanor.

Hannah is surprised to find her father waiting for her in the driveway at the cottage. She gets out of her Jeep to greet him. "Dad, this is a pleasant surprise."

Cary plants a peck on Hannah's cheek. "What's up with your babysitter?"

Hannah narrows her green eyes. "What'd you mean?"

"She wouldn't let me in the cottage. She claims she doesn't know anyone named Hannah."

Hannah looks through the glass door. She can see through the house to where Becca is standing on the porch. She's holding up her phone, and Hannah assumes she's videotaping the children in the swing. "That's Becca. She's not my sitter. She's my next-door neighbor. She knows who I am. She was watching Gus while I ran an errand. I'm sure she misunderstood you." She looks back at her father. "Did you need to talk to me about something?"

"In private. Can you get rid of that woman?"

Hannah studies her father. Something's different about him. His hair is darker. Is he coloring it now? In recent months, she's noticed subtle changes in him—more muscular biceps and less wrinkles in his forehead as though he's getting Botox treatments. Hannah attributes these changes to his new girlfriend, Violet, a woman only a few years older than Hannah. "I need to feed Gus his lunch. If it's that important, we should set aside time another day to talk."

Her father's chest deflates as he lets out a deep breath. "This can't wait. I have a conflict with your wedding date. Violet won a

Mediterranean cruise through work. The only available dates happen to fall over the weekend of your wedding. I'm torn, sweetheart. I wanna walk you down the aisle, but this is a once in a lifetime trip."

Hannah's blood boils. "Are you kidding me, Dad? If choosing between a cruise and my wedding is that difficult, I don't want you to walk me down the aisle. Go on your Mediterranean cruise. And have a nice life."

Spinning on her heels, Hannah storms off and around to the side yard. She leans against the house as she fights back tears. Emotions crash over her. Disappointment. Anger. Hurt. She can't let anyone see her upset. She doesn't want Becca to know her father has chosen a Mediterranean cruise over her. She forces her mind to go blank, letting the feelings roll off her back as she composes herself. She continues to the back porch where she finds Becca still videotaping the kids. "What're you doing?"

Becca taps on her phone, stopping the video. "I wanted to capture this moment. They grow up so quickly." She pockets her phone. "Was your errand successful? Where did you go again?"

Hannah's jaw goes slack. How did Becca forget? "To the cafe, to taste cake flavors for my wedding." Her father's words rush back to her. *She claims she doesn't know anyone named Hannah.* "Is everything okay, Becca? You seem distracted."

"Everything's fine. I've just got a lot on my mind." Becca collects her handbag from the table. "I'd better go. Happy will get hangry if I don't feed her some lunch soon. Enjoy your afternoon."

A chill travels Hannah's spine. Is this woman some kind of weirdo? Did Hannah just trust her child's care to a pedophile? Hannah shakes off the negative vibe. She considers herself a good judge of character. Becca seems like a genuine person. And Happy is certainly a well-adjusted child. There must be a logical explanation. Everyone has bad days.

Hannah's mind travels back to her childhood as she watches

Becca and Happy cross the yard hand in hand. Hannah is a child again, and the hand she's holding belongs to her father. They were inseparable back then. Her father is responsible for her love of nature. He taught her to fish and crab. How to track tidal cycles and moon phases. She can't pinpoint when he changed. Was it during her teenager years? Or was it after she went away to college and her parents became empty nesters? The father she worshiped back then would never have abandoned her, never would've let her think he was dead. She forgave him for running off with another woman. She thought she'd moved past the pain. Such wounds don't heal so easily. And now he's choosing to miss her wedding. This time she won't forgive him. He just drove the final nail in the coffin of their relationship.

Hannah comes crashing back to the present when Gus jumps into her arms. She hugs him tight. She loves her son with her whole heart. On Gus's wedding day, she'll be seated on the front row beaming with pride.

ELEVEN

All week long, Happy peppers Becca with questions about going sailing on Saturday. *What time did Miss Amelia say to be there? How big is the boat? Are we going out in the ocean?* While Becca doesn't admit it to her daughter, she's dreading the outing. Her apprehension confuses her. Going sailing in the ocean is a dream come true. Then again, there's much she finds confusing about herself these days.

Happy and Becca—dressed in bathing suits and cover-ups with Becca carrying a tote bag packed with towels and sunscreen —arrive at Point Pleasant a few minutes before eleven. When Amelia greets them at the front door, Becca presents her with a gift-wrapped bottle of beach-scented hand wash.

"We're a few minutes early," Becca says.

"No worries. I was just packing our picnic." Amelia motions them inside.

They pass through the foyer to the living room, which offers a widespread view of the inlet.

"Whoa!" Happy says with mouth open and eyes wide. "Your house is amazing. Do you live here alone?"

"That's none of your business, Happy," Becca says in a scolding tone.

"I don't mind." Amelia smiles down at Happy. "I live alone now. But I grew up in this house with my mama."

Happy says, "That's so cool! Can I see your bedroom?"

Amelia laughs out loud. "Maybe when we get back from sailing. Jonathan's waiting for us on the boat." She sweeps her arm at the living room. "Please make yourselves at home while I finish up in the kitchen. I won't be long."

"Can we help?" Happy asks.

Amelia plants a hand on her hip. "Now, what kind of hostess would I be if I put my guests to work? I won't be long." She starts off toward the kitchen, calling, "Have a look around. There's a nice breeze out on the porch this morning."

Becca follows Happy as she investigates the living room, admiring the furnishings and collection of Lowcountry-inspired art. Happy opens the right side of a pair of french doors, and they step out onto a wraparound porch. Standing at the edge, they look out over the property. Water is visible in three directions across the expansive lawn.

"Imagine waking to this view every morning," Becca says, unable to contain her awe.

"When I grow up, I wanna get married here too," Happy says.

Becca looks over at her daughter. "Too? Do you know someone who got married here?"

"Duh, Mom. This is where Hannah's getting married."

"Right." Did she know this? Becca can't remember.

"Do you think we'll be invited to the wedding?"

"I wouldn't count on it," Becca says. "We've only just met Hannah and Gus."

Amelia emerges from the house carrying two soft Yeti coolers. "Ready?"

"Yes! Here, let me help," Happy says, and takes a cooler from Amelia.

Becca trails behind Amelia and Happy across the yard to the dock on the back side of the property. A handsome gentleman with a scruffy beard and salt-and-pepper hair waves at them as they approach. "Welcome to the Miss Amelia."

Amelia peers at him over the top of her sunglasses. "Stop it already. You're not naming your boat after me."

Happy smacks her chest. "I'm Happy. You can name your boat after me."

He grins at her. "The Miss Happy has a nice ring to it. I'll give it some thought. I'm Jonathan. Welcome aboard." He takes their belongings from them and helps them onto the boat. "Are we ready to get this voyage underway?"

Amelia lifts the coolers. "Give us a minute to get settled first. Come with me, ladies. I'll give you the tour."

Becca and Happy follow Amelia inside to the small cabin, one main room that serves as kitchen and lounge. Amelia opens a door leading off the cabin. "Here's the head, aka restroom. Toilet paper only please." She closes the door and opens another that leads to a small bedroom with two twin beds. "Here's the stateroom, if you need to change. But I see you're wearing your bathing suits under your cover-ups. Which is good, because the wind is up and you're likely to get wet."

They return to the deck and a few minutes later, Jonathan steers the sailboat away from the dock. Much commotion is involved in putting up the sails. Becca and Happy stay out of the way as Jonathan barks orders at Amelia. As they clear the mouth of the inlet, the wind picks up and they soar through the breaking waves.

Amelia sits down next to Becca in the cockpit. "As you've probably surmised, I'm a novice sailor."

"I think you did a fine job," Becca says.

"Do you wanna help me steer the boat?" Jonathan asks Happy.

Her face lights up. "Can I really?"

"Sure!" He steps aside, letting her take the wheel.

Happy grins over at Becca. "Take my picture, Mom."

Pulling out her phone, Becca snaps several images before switching to video. Happy begins bombarding Jonathan with questions, which he answers patiently.

"Is it okay if I go up to the front of the boat?" Becca asks Amelia.

"Of course. Just be careful and hold on to the railing."

Becca makes her way up to the bow and sits down on the deck with her knees drawn up under her chin. With the salt air whipping her brown hair, she lifts her face to the warm sunshine. She feels close to heaven out here on the wide-open water. If only she could spread her wings and fly off over the horizon. But she's stuck on earth, forced to face her new reality. Even though she's surrounded by people, she's never felt so alone. These are Happy's new friends. And Becca is grateful to them for taking her daughter into the fold. But she can't help feeling out of place in their company. Her once bubbly personality is gone. She's now a walking, talking zombie. Distancing herself is the only way. The less she says to her new friends, the better.

Becca is staring off into space when a shadow crosses her plane. "Mind if I join you?" Without waiting for an answer, Amelia drops down beside Becca. "You were a million miles away just now. What were you thinking?"

"I was wondering if, when a person dies, they just sail away to heaven. A morbid thought, I know. I'm sure you're sorry you asked."

"Not at all. I wonder about death sometimes too. Wouldn't it be lovely if a person's death experience is based on a dream they never fulfilled or an adventure they particularly enjoyed? For example, you might sail off into the sunset, and I might hang glide off the cliffs of the California coast."

"That's an interesting concept. I hope you're right."

"Is there a reason you're thinking about death, Becca? You're not considering hurting yourself, are you?"

Becca jerks her head toward Amelia. "No! What makes you ask such a thing?"

Amelia places a hand on Becca's shoulder. "Happy told me about her father. If you want to talk about it, I'm a good listener. Divorce is traumatic. Especially when you're not the one who wants out of a marriage."

"I'm managing just fine," Becca snaps.

Amelia removes her hand from her shoulder. "I didn't mean to offend you. But I understand hard times. I was married to an abusive man for thirty years. I'm finally seeing a therapist, and I'm feeling more like myself every day. If you're interested, I can provide an introduction."

"I'll think about it." The idea of unburdening herself to an unbiased person appeals to Becca. Unfortunately, money doesn't grow on Becca's trees the way it obviously does on Amelia's. She's sorry for Amelia's past troubles, but the woman clearly has everything going for her now. Incredible home. Perfect boyfriend. Rosy future.

After seeing Becca and Happy off, Amelia showers, dresses in loungewear, and retires to the porch hammock with her romance novel. She reads three paragraphs before dozing off. Jonathan wakes her hours later, when the sun is beginning its descent over the horizon.

Amelia struggles to keep her eyes open. "I don't ever remember napping so long."

Jonathan smiles down at her. "The hard work you're doing

with Martie is paying off. You're defeating your inner demons, and your sense of calm is being restored. Now that you're able to relax your mind, your body is telling you it's exhausted."

Amelia considers this. "That's very perceptive of you. I've finally accepted that Nelson is gone, that he can never again hurt me, and I've stopped looking over my shoulder. The sense of security is incredibly reassuring."

"You've been through so much. Hopefully soon, you'll be able to put the past behind you for good." Jonathan kisses the tips of his fingers and touches them to her lips.

"I picked up steaks on the way back from my house. Do you wanna eat now or wait a bit?"

Amelia rubs her tired eyes. "Give me a few minutes to wake up first."

"Fine by me." Nudging her to move over, he climbs into the hammock beside her.

As they snuggle, Amelia reflects on the day. "I offered to pass along Martie's contact information to Becca today. She just went through a difficult divorce, and I get the feeling the poor woman is struggling with depression."

"Her daughter certainly isn't. I admire Happy's spirit."

"Isn't she the most precious child you've ever met?" Amelia says. "She's really gotten under my skin. I mean that in a good way."

Jonathan puts his arm around her. "You never talk about your infertility. Did you go through many procedures in your attempt to have children?"

"We exhausted every avenue. Except adoption. Nelson refused to consider raising another man's child."

Jonathan hugs her close. "You would've been a great mother. After we get married, and when my girls have children, you'll have grandchildren."

"Anna and Kayla just graduated from college and neither is in a serious relationship." Amelia snickers. "Maybe, by the time they get around to having children, I will have given in and married you."

"Maybe," he says with a chuckle. "Since we're on the subject of commitment, I need to talk to you about something. But I need a glass of wine for courage." Jonathan rolls out of the hammock, taking her with him.

Amelia allows him to drag her through the living room. She knows what's coming, and she's dreading the conversation. In the kitchen, he opens a bottle of her favorite pinot noir and pours two glasses, handing one to her.

Jonathan leans back against the counter, crossing his legs. "I promised I wouldn't pressure you into making a commitment. But I feel very unsettled in our current situation. Why not try living together this summer on a trial basis? We're already together every night, anyway."

Anger pulses through her. She's not ready for a permanent situation. "First of all, we're not together every night."

He looks at her from under a furrowed brow. "We're together more often than we're not. You probably don't realize it, because you're not the one constantly driving back and forth between our houses."

Amelia looks away. She admits Jonathan is doing most of the heavy lifting in their relationship. When he leaves work in the evenings, he drives twenty minutes in the opposite direction to his house to change out of his work clothes and get more clothes for the following day before coming to Point Pleasant. "There are times when I need to be alone, Jonathan. Like on the evenings following my sessions with Dr. Martie."

"Those are the times when you shouldn't be alone."

She can't argue with this either. Sometimes, she wants to crawl in bed and cry herself to sleep. Other times, she feels euphoric after unburdening herself. Either way, she's on edge and shouldn't be alone after her sessions.

Jonathan continues, "My work schedule for the summer is

chaotic. I'll be traveling a lot, which will give you plenty of time to yourself. And if you're having a bad day and don't want me around, I can easily spend the night at my house." He folds his arms over his chest, his wine glass dangling from his fingers. "This is more about logistics than commitment, Amelia. Living together would make my life a whole lot easier."

Why is she being so difficult about this? She trusts him to respect her privacy. If she needs time alone, he'll accommodate her. "When would you want to move in?"

"My girls are coming for Father's Day weekend. After they leave, I'd like to close up my house and move my clothes over."

"You didn't tell me Anna and Kayla are coming for a visit," Amelia says, opening the refrigerator and removing a bag of chopped salad.

"I just found out today. Kayla left a message for me while we were out on the boat, and I called her back on my way over here. They are moving to New York soon. I don't know when I'll see them again. They're excited to meet you."

A smirk plays on her lips as she dumps the salad greens into a wooden bowl. "Will you tell them we're moving in together?"

Crossing the room to her, he spins her away from the counter to face him. "Are you saying what I think you're saying? Are you agreeing to us living together?"

She bobs her head. "Let's give it a shot. On a trial basis."

"Right. For the summer." Leaning down, he brushes his lips against hers. "I love you."

"And I love you." Hooking an arm around his neck, she pulls his face to hers. When they kiss again, their tongues meet, and hands begin to roam. She pushes him away. "There's time for this later. For now, we need to eat."

"You're killing me, Amelia."

"Get used to it, if you're going to be my roommate," she says, and returns her attention to making the salad.

Taking the steaks out of the refrigerator, he unwraps the

white butcher's paper and places the meat on a plate. Standing next to her at the counter, he begins sprinkling the steaks with seasonings. Amelia finds working side by side with him comforting. She and Nelson never did anything as mundane as cooking together. They always had a chef, and Nelson insisted they eat every night in the formal dining room. She thinks it's wonderful that Jonathan likes to cook. And she relishes their time together in the kitchen. "You didn't answer my question earlier," she says. "Will you tell the girls we're living together?"

"Of course. I don't keep secrets from my children. They're adults. They'll understand."

Amelia adds crunchies to the salad and squeezes the dressing out of the plastic sleeve. "Father's Day is two weeks away. Why wait until after they leave to move in? I have plenty of room for them to stay here. Unless you want to spend time alone with them, which I totally understand."

"Are you sure? They would love being here at Point Pleasant. Anna and Kayla have always been fascinated by this house."

"Great! We'll cook on the grill and take them for a picnic lunch on the ocean like we did today with Becca and Happy."

"I'll call them tomorrow and break the news," Jonathan says, and takes his plate of steaks outside to the grill.

Following him with placemats and flatware, Amelia sets the table on the porch while he cooks. Over a candlelit dinner, Jonathan and Amelia discuss all the things they want to do together this summer. As the evening wears on, she warms to the idea of them living together. She knows this man. She trusts him. He treats her like a queen. He's not going to suddenly become abusive. Who knows? Maybe at the end of the summer she'll decide to marry him.

TWELVE

Late on Sunday morning, Sydney is speeding up I-26 toward Columbia when Jake calls. "I booked a room in Greenville. I hear the town has great vibes, and I've been wanting to check it out. It's only thirty minutes from here and right off I-26. It'll cut down on your driving time."

"Okay," she says with hesitancy in her tone.

Jake rattles on, "Greenville is a foodie town. I thought you, being a chef, might enjoy some of the restaurants. Soby's comes highly recommended. They're usually booked, but because today is Sunday, I was able to get a reservation."

"Don't they have good restaurants in Clemson?"

"Of course." He pauses a beat. "I can cancel the reservations, if you'd rather come here."

His wounded tone makes her feel guilty. "Don't do that. I'm fine with meeting you in Greenville. Text me the address for the hotel."

As she ends the call, annoyance crawls across Sydney's skin. She was already wary of staying with him. She's never seen his apartment, but presumably, he has multiple rooms if she feels confined and needs some privacy. She can sleep on his sofa if things aren't going well between them. But a hotel room offers no escape. Despite the chemistry between them, she's terrified of being intimate with Jake. They were once best friends, soul mates, and first-time lovers, but they are virtual strangers now. Over the years, her sex life has been limited to drunken hookups that have left her unsatisfied and wrecked her self-esteem. She can't remember when she last kissed a guy. Lately, she's been too absorbed in her work to even go out for drinks with friends.

As she nears Greenville, excitement over seeing Jake replaces her concerns. Besides, she has a credit card. If things go south, she'll simply book her own room.

Jake is waiting for her in the lobby of the Westin Poinsett when she arrives in Greenville.

"Our room isn't ready," Jake says. "Let's explore the town while we wait."

Some of the tension subsides as he takes her bag and gives it to the desk clerk.

They exit the lobby onto Main Street. Jake reaches for her hand, and they stroll in companionable silence toward the river. The weather is warm with only a few puffy white clouds dotting the brilliant blue sky. They cut over to Falls Park and walk out onto the footbridge, pausing in the middle to look over the waterfalls.

Jake brings her hand to his lips. "I'm glad you came, Syd."

She smiles at him. "Me too."

For over an hour, they meander the winding paths of the park's garden. When they come across a bistro with an outdoor sitting area, they stop in for a glass of champagne. He lifts his glass. "To us."

"To us," she repeats, and takes a sip of the golden liquid, the bubbles tickling her nose.

He sets down his glass. "I owe you an apology. It was presumptuous of me to book a hotel room without talking to you first."

"This is all very confusing for me, Jake. Being with you feels so familiar in some ways, yet awkward in others."

"I know what you mean. I have to remind myself we're not the same people we were in high school. I'll book a separate room if it makes you feel more comfortable. I already checked with the desk clerk. They have availability."

"That's not necessary. Just because we're sleeping in the same room doesn't mean we have to . . . you know . . ." Sydney's face warms at the thought of being physical with him.

He places his large hand over hers. "You're in the driver's seat, Sydney. You determine how slow or fast we go."

She looks down at her bubbly. "That takes some of the pressure off. Thank you."

Finishing their champagne, they walk the long way back to the hotel, pausing to look in some of the boutique windows. They retrieve their packet of key cards from the desk clerk and take the elevator to the third floor. Jake unlocks the door, and they step inside the room. Their eyes bounce around, looking everywhere but at the king-size bed.

"Our dinner reservations are in an hour," Jake says. "I don't need to shower. Why don't I change clothes and wait for you in the lobby."

"That would be great."

He takes his duffel bag into the bathroom and emerges ten minutes later in khaki-colored jeans and an aqua gingham shirt that brings out the green in his eyes. The sight of him nearly takes her breath, and she refrains herself from seducing him.

As soon as he leaves the room, she peels off her clothes and steps into the shower, letting the tepid water return her body temperature to normal. There's no denying her attraction to him. She's in the driver's seat, and she knows exactly what road they'll travel tonight.

After drying her long golden hair, she carefully applies her makeup and slips on a simple A-line black dress with high halter neck and cut-in shoulders. She steps into strappy black sandals and grabs her metallic clutch. Jake whistles when she emerges from the elevator. He crosses the lobby to her and kisses her cheek. "You look amazing. I'm taking back control of the car."

In her most seductive voice, she says, "You may chauffeur, *after* you buy me dinner."

"Then let's get this show on the road," he says, offering her an arm.

A block away, Soby's, a trendy restaurant for people of all ages, is hopping despite being a Sunday night. Jake flashes the pretty young hostess a smile and is rewarded with a table by the open doors.

"I wish Birdie would install sliding doors," Sydney says after they're seated. "You can bring the outdoors inside without ever having to worry about the weather."

"You're wasting your talent at Birdie's," Jake says as he studies the menu. "You would have more opportunities in a town like Greenville. I can see us living here one day. I could handle the thirty-minute commute."

"You're getting way ahead of yourself, Jake. This is only our first weekend together." She leans across the table and whispers, "We haven't even done the dirty yet."

He blushes. "We will soon enough. I'm warning you, Sydney, I'm going to ask you to marry me, sooner rather than later. You got away from me once. I won't let that happen again."

The server appears at their table, saving her from having to respond. Running his finger down the menu, Jake orders for both of them, appetizers and main courses followed by dessert.

When the server leaves, she says, "We can't possibly eat all that food."

"We taste, Sydney. We don't gorge. I read the reviews. I want you to sample the most popular dishes."

"That's very considerate of you." Given the choice, she would've picked different items from the menu, but when the plates arrive, she savors every bite. Fried green tomatoes and tuna crudo for appetizers. And for the main course, smoked short ribs for Jake and shrimp and grits for Sydney. She doesn't admit it to Jake, but she thinks the shrimp and grits are better than her own, and she pays particular attention to the combination of flavors. They share a slice of white chocolate banana cream pie for dessert, which Sydney thinks is nothing short of heaven.

They polish off two bottles of pinot noir with dinner, and by the time Jake pays the bill, they are more than a little tipsy. Clouds have built in during dinner, and the first sprinkles from an approaching system fall as they race-walk back to their hotel.

They have the elevator to themselves on the way to the third floor. As soon as the doors close, Sydney is all over Jake, laying a kiss on him that surprises herself. They run down the hall to their room, and once inside, they tug off their clothes and come together, their naked bodies pressed tight.

They make love with all the tender passion she remembers from high school. But there's another element mixed in as well—an urgency created by the years they've spent apart.

Sydney and Jake wake on Monday to torrential downpours. "I guess we'll have to spend the day in bed," he says, running a hand over her bare breast.

"You shouldn't have changed our plans. If I'd gone to Clemson, you could've saved money on this room."

"Ah . . . But this is more fun, more adventurous."

They order room service for breakfast and lunch, and when the rain slows to a drizzle, they take an Uber to Hall's Chop House for dinner. They share a salad, a porterhouse steak, and a bottle of red wine. In ninety minutes, they're back in bed together.

"Can I come see you next weekend?" Jake asks as Sydney is packing her things on Tuesday morning.

"I have to work. Birdie is launching her catering company, and she has a large cocktail party booked for Sunday night. Considering the long distance, I think it's more realistic for us to try for every other weekend."

While he seems disappointed, he doesn't argue. "I understand."

She zips her suitcase and kisses him goodbye. Cupping his face, she says, "This was lovely. Let's enjoy whatever time we can manage together without putting pressure on ourselves."

"My schedule will get considerably more hectic beginning in late July. I was offering to make the trip while I have spare time. But I understand this is your busy season." Swinging his feet over the side of the bed, Jake brings the blanket with him when he walks her to the door. "We'll take it as it comes. I'm just grateful to have you back in my life."

"Me too, you." She stands on her tiptoes and pecks him on the lips.

On the drive south, she has plenty of time to ponder their relationship. Jake's appearance may have changed. His perspective on life has matured. But deep down he's the same headstrong boy she dated in high school. He was a success on the football field and in the classroom because of his drive to succeed and determination to never give up. He's on the coaching staff with one of the top college football programs. He can't leave Clemson without taking a step back in his career. He admitted he wants to marry her, and he won't be satisfied until she moves to Clemson or Greenville. But she doesn't want to leave Palmetto Island for reasons he knows nothing about.

On her way through Charleston, she makes a detour through Mount Pleasant. She used to come here once a week, but she hasn't been here since the end of April. She's trying to break the bond. Some days are easier than others. She parks on the cul-de-sac, watching for activity at the yellow one-story house across the street. But it appears no one is home. She waits for nearly an hour, but when there's still no sign of life, she drives away.

Maybe it's time for her to make a clean break, to leave the Lowcountry once and for all. But a nagging voice warns her this chapter in her life isn't over.

THIRTEEN

Becca pulls into the circular drive of Mia's family's sprawling oceanfront home, where counselors are greeting campers at the front entrance. Happy jumps out of the minivan and runs over to Mia. Becca is impressed by the teenager. For someone so young, Mia seems grounded and wise beyond her years. Life will get confusing for Happy in the coming weeks. And Becca's grateful her daughter has someone she looks up to, who's nearer her age, to confide in.

Leaving the engine running, Becca gets out of the minivan and approaches Mia. "Are you still able to keep Happy after camp today? She packed an extra bathing suit."

"Yes, ma'am. I'm counting on it." Mia places a hand on Happy's head. "After the other campers leave, we'll chill out here and watch a movie or something."

"She'll love that. My appointment is on the other side of Charleston, and I need to stop by my home in Mount Pleasant to check on things. Unless I get stuck in traffic, I'll pick her up around four."

Mia's smile reaches her sparkling green eyes. "Take as long as you need."

Becca returns to her minivan and heads toward Charleston. An hour later, she pulls into her driveway in Mount Pleasant. After pausing to water a row of drooping hydrangeas at her back door, she walks through the house, spending a few minutes in each room to make certain everything is in order. She brews a cup of tea and sits down at the breakfast table. Being here brings back the heartache of Craig's betrayal. While renting the beach cottage has brought about a host of complications she didn't anticipate, she's at least been able to let go of some of the sadness that has plagued her this past year.

She picks up her phone and places the dreaded phone call to the principle at the high school where she works. The conversation is brief. Randal expresses his concern and offers his support. They speak for a minute about health insurance before hanging up.

Becca remains at the table after she finishes her tea. Closing her eyes, she has a strange premonition she won't be coming back to this house to live. Her world has been thrown off-kilter. She's alone at an amusement park, spinning around and around on the tilt-a-whirl. The ride stops, but she's too dizzy to find the exit. She looks around for someone to guide her. Happy takes her by the hand and leads her out of the park. Their roles have reversed. Happy is now the parent and Becca the child.

Placing her mug in the dishwasher, she locks the door and continues on to her appointment. The director of the facility is waiting for Becca in the reception area. Gloria Rowe is a woman about Becca's age with warm brown eyes and a sympathetic smile. "I'll give you a brief tour, and then we can talk more in my office."

"That works for me," Becca says.

The tour offers no surprises. The facility is exactly what she expected, nothing more or less. When they retreat to Gloria's office, Becca explains the uncertainty of her situation.

"You have come to the right place, Becca. I know this is a

difficult time for you. But rest assured, we will take excellent care of your needs." The director gives Becca a packet of information. "This is a pamphlet highlighting our facility and the programs we offer. There are a couple of forms you can fill out and return at your leisure. We're here for you whenever you're ready."

Gloria walks with Becca to the front entrance. "Thank you for your time," Becca says, shaking her hand in parting.

Desolation sets in as she exits the parking lot. She takes a right-hand turn and speeds off down the highway. Becca has made plans for her future. Now she must see to Happy's.

Becca's eyes are on the road, but her mind is on her problems. She has no concept of how far she's driven until she passes a mileage sign alerting her that Beaufort is ten miles ahead. Beaufort is nowhere near Palmetto Island. She must have taken a wrong turn somewhere. Panic grips her chest, and she careens her minivan off the road, onto the shoulder. Blue lights reflect in her rearview mirror, and seconds later, a uniformed officer appears at her window.

She rolls down the window and looks up at the large man. "Can I help you, officer?"

"Are you okay, ma'am? You're driving erratically. You nearly caused me to wreck."

"I'm sorry, officer. I just realized I'm lost."

"Perhaps I can help. Where are you headed?"

"I . . .um . . . I missed my turn a while back. I'll figure it out. Sorry if I caused any trouble."

Removing his aviator sunglasses, he studies her more closely. "Are you sure you're okay? You seem flustered."

She fans her face with her hand. "It's hot as blazes out. I don't do well in the heat." She forces a smile. "Once I get where I'm going, I'll have myself a large glass of sweet tea."

Taking a step backward, the officer tips his hat at her. "All right, then. But be careful." He returns to his patrol car and peels out onto the highway.

Becca squeezes her eyes shut, clenching and unclenching her fists. *What to do? Who to call? Where is she going? Why is she on the way to Beaufort?* Her brain is firing off signals, but none of them are connecting. Her breathing is shallow, and she worries she might hyperventilate. *Happy. Where is Happy?*

Spotting her phone in the console, she scrolls through texts until she finds one from Mia. *The babysitter.* Becca's head falls back against the headrest as a wave of relief washes over her. Happy is at Palmetto Island with Mia. Accessing her maps app, she scrolls down to recents, clicking on the address of her beach rental. The app calculates the route. Two hours. She'll have to drive halfway back to Charleston before she can get on the road to Palmetto Island. Putting the car in gear, she carefully pulls out onto the two-lane highway, heading in the opposite direction.

She grips the steering wheel. Her circumstances are not only serious, they are dangerous, as evidenced by what just happened. What if her daughter had been with her? Things worked out for Becca this time. Next time she might not be so lucky. And one thing's for certain. There will undoubtedly be a next time.

Her heart aches. She has a plan, but once she instigates it, there will be no turning back. Everything will change. Life as she knows it will be over. She needs a little more time with her daughter. The Fourth of July is in a few weeks. If she's careful, if she keeps to herself and doesn't venture far from the cottage, she can wait until after the holiday weekend to set things in motion.

Hannah is ending a Zoom call when Birdie arrives with Gus. "Thanks for picking him up, Mom. That was a new client. I couldn't reschedule."

Mia offered to bring Gus home, but Hannah needed an excuse to see her mother alone. There are always people around at the cafe, and Birdie spends most evenings with Stan.

"I hope your call was productive," Birdie says, hanging Gus's backpack over a barstool.

"Very much so. The client was receptive to our ideas. Not only will his website be fun to build, his brand will be a nice addition to our portfolio."

Gus tugs on the hem of her blouse. "Can I watch TV, Mommy?"

"Of course." Hannah looks down at her son's upturned face. "You look exhausted. Did you have fun at Mia's?"

He gives her a vigorous nod. "Happy was there. We went swimming and played Capture the Flag."

"That does sound like fun." Hannah looks back at her mom. "Can you hang around? I need to talk to you about something."

Birdie checks her watch. "I can spare a few minutes. But I'm parched. You get him settled while I fix us a cold drink."

"There's a pitcher of lemonade in the fridge," she says to Birdie as she scoops Gus up and deposits him on the sofa. She powers on the television, tuning in to an episode of *SpongeBob*, and returns to the breakfast counter.

Birdie places a glass of lemonade in front of her and sits down beside her. "What's up, sweetheart? More wedding drama?"

"You could say that. Have you talked to Dad lately?"

"Not in weeks." Birdie gulps down lemonade. "Why do you ask?"

"Because he's decided to go on a Mediterranean cruise with Violet instead of coming to my wedding."

Birdie blinks hard and then opens her blue eyes wide. "You've gotta be kidding me?"

"Nope." Hannah buries her face in her hands. "Why did I let you convince me to give him another chance? He's not worth it."

Birdie rubs her back. "I'm so sorry, sweetheart. I don't know what to say. I honestly thought he'd changed."

"He's changed, all right. He's not the same man who raised me. He'll always put his current girlfriend ahead of me. I only have myself to blame. He fooled me once. It's my own fault for letting him fool me a second time."

"Listen to me, sweetheart." Birdie tilts Hannah's chin toward her. "This is *his* loss. Not yours. Don't you dare let this ruin your wedding."

"What am I supposed to tell Ethan and his parents?"

"The truth. What else can you do? This is on him, not you."

Hannah's eyes fill and tears stream down her cheeks. "Really? Because it doesn't feel like that to me. This feels like before. He's abandoning me all over again."

Birdie thumbs away a tear. "Let me talk to him."

"No, Mom! Please don't. He chose Violet over me. I don't want him to feel obligated to be here. I guess I'll walk myself down the aisle. Unless . . ." Hannah swivels the stool toward Birdie. "You'd be willing to walk me down the aisle. I know it's unconventional, but . . ."

Birdie smiles at her. "I would be honored, sweetheart. And there's nothing conventional about the Fuller women. Besides, our friends know how close we are."

Hannah hugs Birdie. "Thank you, Mom. You've always been here for me."

Birdie shakes. "Not always. I remember a time, when you were pregnant with Gus."

"That doesn't count. You and I were both struggling to move on after Dad disappeared. But you haven't let me down since."

"And I won't in the future. Not if I can help it." Birdie stands up. "But I'm still going to tell your father he's a fool."

"I hope he has a nice life with Violet. Because he's not getting another chance with me. He's dead to me."

Birdie kisses the top of her head. "I'm sorry you feel that way, but I don't blame you."

Hannah grabs hold of her wrist. "Why did you marry him, Mom?"

"Because I loved him. And sometimes love is blind."

"I love Ethan with all my heart. Is there something about him I can't see?"

Birdie pries Hannah's fingers from her wrist and brings them to her lips. "No, sweetheart. Ethan is nothing like your father. He's honest and trustworthy and considerate. And he loves you every bit as much as you love him."

Not trusting herself to speak, Hannah nods.

Birdie digs her keys out of her pocket. "I hate to leave you so upset."

Hannah waves her on. "I'm fine. I'll call you later."

She takes their lemonade glasses to the sink, and through the kitchen window, she watches her mom drive away in her ancient Volvo wagon. Her father was a rotten husband. Hannah blames him for her mother's drinking problem. Birdie has worked hard to overcome her addiction, and she's built a life for herself with her cafe. If things don't work out with Stan, Birdie will have her career to fall back on. Just as Hannah has her web design business if, god forbid, her marriage to Ethan doesn't work out.

Needing to take her mind off her father, Hannah busies herself with making dinner. Thirty minutes later, she slides the ziti casserole into the oven and takes her laptop into the living room. She's sitting on the sofa beside Gus, typing notes from the meeting with her new client, when Mia and Happy come walking up from the beach. She closes her laptop and stands to greet them. "Hey there! What're you girls up to?"

Happy plops down on the sofa beside Gus. "My mom's not back from Charleston yet. Is it okay if we wait here for her?"

"Of course." Hannah notices Mia's troubled expression. "I need to pay you for earlier. Let me get my wallet." Mia follows her to the dining table where she left her bag. "Is something wrong?" Hannah asks the babysitter as she's digging her wallet out of her bag.

"I'm not sure. Miss Becca said she'd be home no later than

four. I haven't heard from her, and it's past six o'clock. I tried her cell, but she didn't pick up. Should I call the police?"

"Not yet. Let's give her a while longer. I'm sure there's a logical explanation." Hannah removes several bills from her wallet and hands them to Mia. "Happy can stay with us if you need to get home. I know you're tired after taking care of kids all day."

Mia hesitates a beat. "I'll wait a little longer. I wanna make certain Miss Becca gets home okay."

"Do your parents know where you are in case Becca shows up at your house?"

"Yes, ma'am." Mia flashes her phone. "I just texted them."

"Good." Hannah looks closely at the babysitter. "Is something else wrong, Mia?"

With a quick glance at the kids, Mia pulls Hannah into the kitchen. "To be honest, I'm kinda worried about Miss Becca. I hardly know her, but I get the impression something is wrong."

The lines in Hannah's brow crease. "What do you mean?"

"Don't get me wrong. She seems like a nice person." Mia gnaws on a hangnail. "It's just that . . . well, sometimes Miss Becca seems confused. And I'm worried she's having some kind of mental problems."

Hannah doesn't admit she has her own doubts about Becca. "She just went through a bad divorce. She's finding herself again, and we need to support her."

This seems to pacify Mia. "I guess that makes sense."

Seconds later, the front door bangs open and Becca rushes in. "Happy! There you are."

Happy jumps to her feet and scurries across the room. "Mama! You're home!"

Becca looks at Mia over the top of her daughter's head. "I'm so sorry I'm late. My phone was on silent, and I missed your calls. My meeting ran over, and I made a wrong turn on the way home."

"It's fine. I'm just glad you made it back safely." Mia moves toward the living room. "I'd better get going. My mom will be having dinner soon."

"Do you want me to drive you?" Hannah offers.

"No, thanks. I enjoy the beach this time of night. See you kiddos tomorrow." Mia kisses Happy's hair and pats Gus on the head on her way out.

Hannah turns her attention to Becca, who appears disheveled and confused. "Why don't you stay for dinner? We're having baked ziti. The recipe makes enough to feed an army."

"Sorrow. I mean, sorry. I wish we could. But it's been a long day. I'm ready to get home."

"Then take some ziti with you." Returning to the kitchen, Hannah removes the ziti from the oven and spoons half of it into another casserole dish, covering it with foil. She takes the casserole to Becca. "Here ya go."

"Bless you," Becca says, her eyes moist with tears.

"Any time." She walks Happy and Becca to the door. As Becca is getting in her van, Hannah calls out, "We're around all weekend. Let's have coffee one morning."

Becca waves at her in return.

As Hannah watches the minivan retreat down the driveway, she wonders about Becca's appointment in Charleston today. And how she could've possibly gotten lost on a two-lane highway on the way back. Hannah feels for Becca. Something is seriously wrong. Is it her health? She has no family and, apparently, no close friends. Hannah vows to be a better friend to Becca during the weeks they have left together.

FOURTEEN

Amelia and her family's longtime housekeeper, Bebe, spend a week getting ready for Jonathan's daughters' visit. Bebe deep cleans the house, putting a shine on every surface, while Amelia cooks. She makes sweet potato ham biscuits and roasts two chickens for salads and sandwiches. And she bakes cookies and lemon bars and a coffee cake for breakfast. She's a nervous wreck. She wants so much for Anna and Kayla to approve of her. She daydreams about being their father's hip live-in girlfriend. She'll buy them expensive trinkets and entertain their friends at Point Pleasant on long weekends. Jonathan and Amelia will visit them often in New York. They'll take the girls out to dinner, to Broadway Shows, and on lavish shopping trips.

On Friday afternoon of Father's Day weekend, Amelia stands in front of her bathroom mirror for an hour, trying out different greetings. But when the girls arrive with Jonathan around six o'clock, she's rendered speechless. Not just at their beauty—although they are stunning creatures with creamy complexions, silky black hair, and their father's hazel eyes—but at how much they look alike. The girls are identical in every way.

"Don't worry," the twin on Amelia's right says. "We often have this effect on people."

"You'll be able to tell us apart once you get to know us," the other twin says. "I'm Anna. I wear a lot of blue. My sister, Kayla, has a pink fetish."

Amelia takes in their attire. The twin on her right is wearing a pink sundress while the one on her left has on a pale blue top with white jeans. She points at them, one at a time. "Kayla. Anna."

"Right," Kayla says. "My sister always wears her Apple Watch, and I usually have on this ring." She holds out her right hand, revealing a silver band on her middle finger.

Taking hold of her hand, Amelia fingers the engraving on the ring. "I can't read it without my glasses. What does it say?"

"*Carpe Diem.* Seize the day." Kayla leans into her sister. "We're all about living in the moment."

Jonathan moves toward them. "Don't let these two fool you. I'm their father and I can't tell them apart. And a word of warning, they love to play tricks. The whole Apple Watch/pink fetish thing is a farce. They switch clothing and jewelry all the time."

Amelia lets out a laugh. "In that case, I'll call both of you Kayanna. That way, I have a fifty percent chance of being right."

Anna jabs her finger at Amelia. "I like your way of thinking."

Amelia spreads her arms wide. "Welcome to Point Pleasant. Would you girls like to take a swim before dinner?"

"I'd like to have a drink before dinner," Kayla says.

Amelia hides her surprise. These twins are not bashful. "I'm certain we can accommodate you. Why don't I show you to your rooms first, so you can freshen up after your trip."

The twins, with duffel bags dangling from shoulders, comment on Amelia's lovely home as they follow her through the living room to the foyer and up the stairs. "You're welcome to stay in any of the rooms. But, if you don't mind sleeping together, this guest room has a king-size bed with en suite bath and the best view of the ocean." When she opens the first door on her right, the twins gasp in unison.

"OMG." Kayla enters the room, and tossing her bag onto the bed, goes straight to the window.

Anna joins her sister at the window. "This is dope."

"We may never leave," the girls say in unison.

Amelia beams. "You're welcome to stay as long as you like." She backs out of the room. "I'll leave you to get settled. Let me know if you need anything."

Amelia goes down the hall to her room to touch up her makeup. On the way back down the stairs, she overhears one of the twins say her name. "Amelia's pretty, don't you think?"

"Ooh. Gross. No. She's way too thin," the other twin says.

"I guess she is kinda thin. But I like her outfit."

"I think it's tacky. She should dress her age instead of trying to be young like us."

Tears sting Amelia's eyes as she hurries down the stairs to the kitchen. She pours herself a splash of rosé and gulps it down. In her case, being too thin is about genetics. She has a high metabolism like her mama. She eats whatever she wants and never gains weight.

She stares down at her outfit. What's tacky about her yellow maxi skirt and cream-colored, off-the-shoulder top? Do they disapprove of her showing a hint of tanned midriff? Their daddy sure likes her wardrobe. *Why not, Amelia? If you've got it flaunt it.*"

Amelia pours more wine and takes her glass out to the porch. She's thumbing through a home interiors magazine when Jonathan and the girls emerge through the french doors an hour later. Her anger and humiliation have diminished, but the memory of their insults still hurts.

Jonathan takes Amelia's empty glass. "I'll get you a refill. Girls, what would you like?"

"Tequila, please," the twins say in unison. Both girls are dressed head to toe in white and neither is wearing any jewelry.

"Tequila it is," Jonathan says. "I just bought a new brand. You can be my guinea pigs."

The girls watch their father leave the porch before sitting down in rockers opposite Amelia. To allow for more engaged conversation, she'd arranged the chairs in a circle around the coffee table and is sitting with her back to the ocean. But instead of enjoying the view, the girls stare down at their phones and giggle as they share social media posts. Amelia thinks they're being rude, and when Jonathan returns, he takes their phones away from them.

They whine like toddlers, and Jonathan appeases them by agreeing to give the phones back after dinner.

Amelia sets down her magazine. "Tell me about New York. I'm dying to hear about your jobs."

"Anna got a job as an event planner," the twin on her right says, and Amelia makes a mental note that she's Kayla. "I'm going into publishing. I haven't found a job yet, but interviewing will be easier once I'm living in New York."

"I imagine it will," Amelia says. "Are you girls living together?"

"We are! In Gramercy Park," Anna says and describes the tiny apartment they've rented.

"Which of your friends are living in New York?" Jonathan asks, which prompts a lengthy conversation about the goings-on of their high school and college classmates. Since Amelia doesn't know any of these kids, she takes the opportunity to sneak away and prepare dinner.

With Jonathan's help, Amelia brings out a platter of shrimp and grits, a basket with squares of moist corn bread, and a bowl of arugula and goat cheese salad. The foursome gathers around the iron table, which Amelia has set with pale blue linens, her mother's favorite Herend china, creamy fat candles in hurricane globes, and a large arrangement of blue hydrangeas from her garden. After saying the blessing, Jonathan opens a bottle of Pinot Grigio and fills their glasses.

"What time are we going sailing tomorrow?" Kayla asks.

"I figure we'll leave the dock around eleven," Jonathan says. "Amelia and I plan to pack a picnic lunch."

Kayla is unable to hide her disappointment at the mention of Amelia's name.

"I'm taking orders now," Amelia says. "We have tuna salad, pimento cheese, and roasted chicken. Unfortunately, I won't be able to go sailing with you."

Jonathan looks at her over a forkful of grits. "Why don't you wanna go?"

Amelia sets down her fork and dabs her lips with her napkin. "Birdie called this afternoon, asking if they could meet here tomorrow to discuss the wedding. I feel obligated to be here, since I know the property better than anyone."

"I'm not sure I can handle the boat without you," Jonathan says with eyebrows pinched.

A broad grin spreads across Kayla's face. "We'll help, Dad. We know how to sail."

Anna adds, "You insisted we take all those sailing lessons when we were little, remember?"

Amelia smiles at Jonathan. "You'll be fine. You need to spend this time alone with the girls."

Anna says, "This would be a fab place for a wedding. Who's getting married?

"Hannah Fuller. Her mother, Birdie, is an old childhood friend of mine."

"We know Hannah," Kayla says. "Although she's a few years older than us. Is she marrying the guy who knocked her up in college?"

Jonathan casts her a warning look. "Don't be crude, Kayla."

"It's true," Kayla says, stabbing a shrimp.

"Maybe so, but you can think of a more sensitive way to say it."

"I'm sorry. Is Hannah marrying her baby daddy?" Kayla says, and Anna bursts out laughing.

In a curt tone, Amelia says, "Hannah is not marrying the father of her child. Her fiancé is from Charleston. His name is Ethan Hayes."

Kayla brings her fist crashing down on the table. "Bullshit! Hannah Fuller snagged Ethan Hayes? You've gotta be kidding me."

The twins have been gulping down first tequila and now wine, and they're both well on their way to being sloppy drunk. Amelia looks over at Jonathan, who shrugs as if to say there's nothing he can do about his wayward daughters.

"I take it you know Ethan," Amelia says.

"Duh," Anna says. "Ethan's the biggest catch in the Lowcountry. He's good-looking as sin, and his family has more money than God."

Amelia pushes back from the table. "Hannah has been through a lot. She's compassionate and hardworking, and she deserves someone who loves her as much as Ethan does. Now, if you'll excuse me, I'll get dessert." She gathers the empty plates and takes them to the kitchen.

She's cutting slices of strawberry shortcake when Jonathan joins her a few minutes later. "I sent them to bed. I apologize for their behavior. I don't know what got into them tonight. Other than the obvious—they had way too much to drink. I haven't spent any quality time with them since last summer. Maybe it *is* best for me to take them sailing alone tomorrow. They need a good old-fashioned tongue lashing. Otherwise, they're going to make fools of themselves in New York."

Amelia remains silent. She's not a parent, which makes her unqualified to comment.

He peers over her shoulder at the strawberry shortcake. "That looks delicious. Did you make it?"

"Mm-hmm. I spent hours on it." She forks off a bite and feeds it to him. "What do you think?"

"Delicious. Like you." When his lips meet hers, he tastes like strawberries and angel food cake.

"Yum. That is good." She feeds herself a bite and then another one for him.

"I don't think your daughters like me very much."

"Anna and Kayla are complex creatures. Give them some time." His mouth travels to her ear. "I'm sure they're passed out by now. Why don't we forget the dishes and go to bed?"

"Sorry." She shoves him away. "No sex while your daughters are in the house."

"Why not? They know we're sharing the same bedroom."

"Still. I wouldn't feel right."

A mischievous glint appears in his eyes. "Have you ever made love on the beach?"

Her body tingles in anticipation. "Can't say that I have. What're you thinking?"

He takes her by the hand "Come with me and find out."

Amelia made the right decision in choosing the wedding meeting over sailing. The representative from the tent company has a long list of logistical questions no one else could've answered. And she enjoys being part of the planning. Based on her vast experience entertaining crowds of all sizes, Amelia voices her opinion on floral arrangements and table placements. She suggests where to place the chairs and arbor for the ceremony and offers input on the schematic for the stage, dance floor, and tables. But she has little to add to Sydney's proposed menu. The young chef has created a well-balanced smorgasbord of food items to be passed by servers as well as arranged on one long banquet table.

When the others leave, Amelia invites Birdie to stay. "I haven't seen you in weeks. If you have time, I'd love to catch up."

"I'd like that as well." Birdie fans her face. "But it's a scorcher. I wouldn't say no to a glass of something cold."

Amelia motions Birdie to the house. "Sweet tea or lemonade?"

"Tea, please," Birdie says, following her through the front door to the kitchen.

Amelia pours tea into two glasses and transfers a handful of shortbread biscuits onto a plate. "I'd suggest we go outside to the porch, but I think we're better off in here where it's cool."

"I agree," Birdie says. "There's not even a hint of a breeze today."

"Which doesn't make for good sailing conditions for Jonathan and the girls," Amelia says, and takes the tray with the tea and biscuits to the breakfast room table.

Birdie runs her hand over the worn pine. "This table brings back memories of late-night gossip sessions."

"Here's something to gossip about," Amelia says with mischief tugging at her smile. "Jonathan and I are living together now."

Birdie grabs Amelia's arm. "Get out of town! How's it going?"

"Better than I expected. Jonathan convinced me to try it on a trial basis. Turns out, I really like having him around."

"That's encouraging. Stan has asked me to move in with him, but I'm not ready. He also keeps pressuring me to work less." Birdie laughs. "But I'm working more, not less. Our catering business is taking off faster than I anticipated. I'm meeting with Sydney in the morning to discuss restructuring the business. Do you have any interest in working for me as head party planner? With your experience, I'd hire you in a second."

"Me? Gosh, Birdie, I don't know." Amelia sits back in her

chair, twirling her mother's Tahitian pearls while she considers Birdie's offer. If she were twenty years younger, she'd jump at the chance. And while she's hoping to find purpose in her life, the catering business involves long hours she'd have to spend away from Jonathan. "I'm flattered. And I'm happy to consult with you on big events. But I'm still sorting out my past, and I'm not ready to commit to a full-time career just yet."

"I understand. If you don't mind, I may need to consult with you from time to time."

"I would love that," Amelia says.

Birdie takes a bite of a shortbread biscuit. "This is seriously delicious. Did you make these?"

Amelia grins. "Yes, I'm learning to cook, if you can believe that, at my age."

"We're never too old to learn something new, Amelia. I've experienced that time and again these past four years."

"Why don't you try living with Stan on a trial basis? His house is only a few miles from the waterfront. The commute would take you five minutes, tops. Maybe then he'd stop pestering you to work less."

"Maybe. I could use my apartment as office space, which we desperately need. Especially if I'm going to expand my business." Birdie pops the rest of her biscuit into her mouth and swallows it down with tea. "How's it going with Jonathan's girls?"

Amelia lowers her head. "Not great. I set my expectations too high."

"What were your expectations?"

"I was hoping we'd share a magical bond. I desperately wanted to be their father's cool live-in girlfriend. But these girls are catty and self-centered. They aren't kindhearted and considerate like Hannah."

"How old are the twins now? They're younger than Hannah, but I vaguely remember them."

"They just graduated from college in May."

"That explains a lot," Birdie says. "Kids that age are full of themselves. Hannah was too, although in a different way. She was pregnant with Gus. She was ready to be on her own, while at the same time, she was terrified of raising a child alone. Once they get their first taste of the real world, they'll grow up."

"That's a good point. They're moving to New York next week. By the time we see them again, they will have gotten a reality check."

"Kids go through stages. One minute, you're their best friend, and the next, they can't stand the sight of you. I made a lot of mistakes in raising Hannah. No parent is perfect. You have to give them space to find their own way. Be there to help pick up the pieces when they fall. And to celebrate the victories when they succeed."

"That's excellent advice, Birdie. Thank you." Amelia looks away, watching the mast of Jonathan's sailboat approach the dock behind Birdie. "Speaking of the divas. There they come now. Maybe it's a good thing I never had children. I'm not sure I would've had the patience."

"You would've been fine. Every mother enters into parenthood blindly. We do the best we can and hope everything turns out. Sometimes it does. Sometimes it doesn't." Birdie stands to go. "I'd better get back to the cafe."

"I'll walk you out." They exit the house through the mudroom door and stroll to Birdie's car at the end of the gravel driveway.

"Lordy be, it's hot out here," Birdie says. "My poor guests will wilt outside tonight."

Amelia looks up at the cloudless sky. "We could use a thunderstorm to cool things off."

Birdie opens her car door and tosses her bag onto the passenger seat. Turning back to face Amelia, she says, "I hope we have nice weather for Hannah's wedding. The thought of an early-season tropical storm keeps me awake at night."

"We have tents and porches," Amelia says. "We can even clear out the furniture in the living room if necessary."

"No, honey. We are not having all those people in your beautiful home. Worst case scenario, Hannah and Ethan can get married in the cafe."

"Let's pray it doesn't come to that."

Birdie fingers Amelia's cheek. "You look lovely. I want a piece of your rosy glow. Perhaps I'll take your advice and move in with Stan."

"You should. What do you have to lose?"

Birdie drops her hand. "My apartment, if I convert it into offices. I'll have nowhere to live."

"Then you'll buy a house of your own. You've been talking about it for a while now, anyway." Amelia shrugs. "If you get in a bind, you can always live in my garage apartment until you figure something else out. Don't let logistics stop you from spreading your wings and trying something new."

A wicked smile spreads across Birdie's lips. "How scandalous of us, living with our boyfriends at our age."

Amelia laughs out loud. "Our mamas are rolling over in their graves."

Birdie kisses the air beside Amelia's cheek. "I enjoyed our talk. Let's do it again soon." She slides behind the steering wheel, wiggling her fingers at Amelia as she drives off.

The *Carpe Diem* inscription on Kayla's ring pops into Amelia's head. Seize the day for what? This nagging feeling tells her she's meant to be doing something. But she can't, for the life of her, figure out what that something is.

FIFTEEN

Birdie is waiting for Sydney in the kitchen when she arrives late morning on Sunday. "Here," Birdie says, handing her a coffee. "The cafe is hopping this morning. I thought we'd talk upstairs in my apartment where it's quiet."

Sydney follows Birdie up the narrow stairs to the large room that serves as living room, dining room, and kitchen. "I've never been up here before. I love it." She moves over to the floor-to-ceiling windows. "The natural light is glorious, as is your view of the inlet."

Birdie joins her at the window. "I'm considering moving in with Stan. If I do, we can use this space for our catering company. The bedrooms will provide the office space we so desperately need."

Sydney turns her back to the window. "We can meet with clients and host tastings out here."

"Exactly. As you know, the catering business is taking off much faster than we anticipated. You are the key to my success, Sydney. And not just on the catering side. You are the reason Birdie's Nest Cafe has become the most popular new dining spot in the Lowcountry."

Sydney's face warms and she looks down at her coffee. "You give me too much credit, Birdie. But I appreciate your vote of confidence."

"I want to make certain you're happy. I can see our expansion happening in one of three ways." Birdie ticks the options off on her fingers as she speaks. "You stay on as head chef, and I hire an event planner. You become the event planner, and I hire another head chef. Or I hire an event planner *and* a chef, and you oversee both. The third option gets my vote."

"Wow." She's intrigued by the idea of being involved with both sides of Birdie's business, but what would that mean for her future career as a chef? "That's a lot to think about."

"I realize that. And you don't have to give me an answer today. But I will need to know soon."

"Can I let you know on Tuesday?"

"Tuesday would be great."

Sydney walks around the apartment. "Having the catering offices up here solves one problem. But you're eventually going to need more kitchen space."

Birdie gets to her feet. "I've thought about that. Do you have any ideas?"

"I do, actually. Come with me." She waves at Birdie to follow and heads for the stairs. "I wanna show you something."

At the bottom of the stairs, they pass through the kitchen and the double doors into the cafe. As they're skirting the long line of customers waiting to order breakfast, Birdie says, "We need to address this bottleneck problem."

Sydney holds up a finger. "And I have the solution."

They continue outside. Standing in front of the building, she gestures at the storefront wedged between the cafe and Shaggy's. "There's your solution."

Confusion crosses Birdie's face. "What does an office that sells tickets for wave runner rentals and offshore fishing adventures have to do with my cafe?"

"The space is for sale."

Birdie's mouth falls open. "No kidding. How do you know that?"

"I'm friends with the girl who manages the office. They're building a ticket hut closer to the dock."

Birdie hesitates while she considers this. "That makes sense for them."

"My friend asked me if you'd be interested in buying the storefront. I told her I'd talk to you."

Birdie walks over to the ticket office and peers in the window. "It doesn't look very big. Have you been inside?"

"Once. It's big enough to house the coffee and pastry bars and still have enough room for a few tables. The storefront extends the depth of your building. You could use the back for the catering kitchen."

Birdie, her face still pressed to the glass, says, "I'd have to talk to an architect, to see if we could blow out the brick wall."

"I wouldn't necessarily go to all that trouble. If you connect the two separate spaces with double glass doors, you could close off the coffee shop when you rent out the cafe for private events."

Birdie spins on her heels to face Sydney. "I love your way of thinking."

"And while you're remodeling . . ." She guides Birdie back to the front of the cafe. "You could install sliding floor-to-ceiling glass doors. Outdoor dining with climate control. If you install awnings off the building on both sides of the front door, you will have an even larger outdoor seating area. Which would make it much easier for our waitstaff to serve our guests."

Birdie draws her in for a half hug. "You're brilliant. What would I do without you?"

Sydney laughs. "I'm full of great ideas when I'm spending someone else's money."

"I prefer to think of it as an investment. In the long run, we'll be able to operate more efficiently and effectively. I'm going to talk to your friend at the ticket office now. What's her name?"

"Laurie. Tell her I sent you." When Birdie marches off toward the ticket office, Sydney calls after her, "I've gotta run. I'll see you on Tuesday."

Sydney heads in the opposite direction, around the corner of the cafe. She's nearing Ocean Avenue when her phone vibrates with a text from Jake. *I'm here. Where are you?*

Increasing her pace, she thumbs off a response. *Coming. Be there in a sec.*

Jake is waiting with his overnight bag at her apartment. Unlocking the door, she grabs a fistful of his shirt and presses her lips to his as she drags him through her living room to her bedroom. Stripping off his clothes, she makes love to him with reckless abandon.

Afterward, they lay with their naked bodies entwined atop her comforter. "Someone missed me," Jake says. "You couldn't even wait to turn down the covers."

She cuts her eyes at him. "Next time, I'll have my way with you on the kitchen floor."

"Ooh. I look forward to it. When will that be? When *will* I see you again?"

"Seriously?" She smacks his bare chest. "Do we have to talk about that now? You just got here."

"True, but our time together always flies by. Can you come to Clemson for the Fourth of July? Our head coach is throwing a massive party at his lake house."

Sydney doesn't relish the idea of spending the holiday with football coaches and their wives, but she's not in a position to protest since it will be her turn to travel. "That could work, since the Fourth conveniently falls on my day off."

Jake sits up against the headboard, taking Sydney with him. "What're we doing today?"

"Having a lazy day on the beach. I brought home some left-overs from the cafe for a picnic."

He kisses her forehead. "And then we can come back and do this again?"

"All night long, if you want," she says, snuggling closer.

They make love again before changing into their swimsuits and packing up their belongings. They drive her car to the beach and set up their chairs at the edge of the surf. A pleasant breeze is blowing, and while Jake wades into the ocean, Sydney turns her face to the sun and closes her eyes.

She replays her conversation with Birdie over in her mind. She's torn between the positions Birdie offered. While she's currently enjoying both aspects of her job, being chef and event planner, she agrees they need more staff. If she takes the head job, she'll be managing the new people Birdie hires. Her primary responsibility will be signing off on *their* creations, not hers. She'll have creative control, but she'll no longer be the artist. After Jake leaves on Tuesday, she'll call her mentor from culinary school for advice.

She watches her incredibly sexy boyfriend emerge from the ocean. She should ask his opinion about her dilemma. But she knows what he'll say. He'll tell her to accept the head job, to train her underlings to take over for her when she marries him and moves to Greenville or Clemson. But she doesn't want to leave the Lowcountry. After two years of living here, Palmetto Island finally feels like home. And Birdie and Hannah and Max are becoming her family. She and Jake have only been back together a few weeks. She needs to make the decision that's right for her, not for him. Her love for him isn't in question. But there future together is. She can't fully commit to Jake until she's honest with him about her past. And she's not ready to do that. Not this weekend, anyway.

SIXTEEN

Amelia spends much of her designated fifty minutes telling Dr. Martie about her weekend with Jonathan's daughters. "Jon claims he gave the girls a firm talking-to while they were sailing. If anything, they were more ill-behaved at dinner on Saturday. They talked about their mother all night long. Don't get me wrong. I expect them to talk about her. She's their mama. But this wasn't normal. They were trying to get under my skin."

Martie uncrosses her legs and leans toward Amelia. "And? Did you let them?"

Amelia stares down at her lap. "I tried not to. But I couldn't help myself. They didn't ask one single question about me the whole time they were staying in my house."

Martie recrosses her legs and sits back in her chair. "That's not unusual for kids their age. They haven't yet developed conversation skills. How did you feel when you overheard the twins say you're too thin and made fun of your clothes?"

"I was angry and hurt at first. But I got over it. I can't help that I have a genetic predisposition to high metabolism." She smooths her navy cropped linen pants. "As for my wardrobe, after being married to a man who insisted on picking out my clothes, I now dress for myself and no one else."

"Good for you, Amelia." Martie clasps her hands together. "I'm thrilled with your progress. You're getting stronger every day. But I sense something else about this visit with the twins is bothering you. Can you pinpoint what it is?"

"I really wanted to connect with the girls. I was hoping we'd be a family. That Jon and I would visit them often in New York. That we'd exchange texts, and they'd ask for my advice about women issues." Amelia lets out a sigh. "I guess it was unrealistic of me considering they already have a mother."

"Wanting a relationship with Jonathan's daughters is not unrealistic at all. This is about the girls. Not you. They just graduated from college. They're going through some big changes right now."

Amelia nods. "That's what Birdie said. Let them get a taste of the real world."

"And let them get used to the idea of their father having a live-in girlfriend."

Amelia gets up and goes to the window. Over the course of her treatment, she's discovered it easier to share her deepest secrets with her back to the therapist. "There's something else I need to talk to you about."

"Go ahead. Whenever you're ready."

"It's about Happy, the nine-year-old little girl I told you about. I can't stop thinking about her. Why do you think I'm obsessing about her?"

"*Obsessing* is an interesting choice of words. Is that what you think you're doing?"

"Sort of. But not in a perverted way. I just think about her a lot. About the kinds of things she likes to eat, and the types of clothes she likes to wear. I wonder how she's spending her day, if she's riding her bike on the beach or hanging out at a friend's house."

"Different people impact our lives in different ways, Amelia. We've talked at length about your infertility, but maybe we need to revisit the issue. Maybe a child is the *thing*"—Martie uses air quotes—"that's missing in your life. You were so close to your mother. Perhaps not being a mother yourself has been a greater loss than you realize."

"I'm acutely aware of the void inside of me created by not having children. I try not to dwell on it, because there's nothing I can do about it."

"Says who?"

Amelia watches a young mother pushing a baby carriage along the boardwalk. "No adoption agency would give a baby to a woman my age."

"Why does it have to be a baby? You could foster an older child. Oftentimes fostering leads to adoption."

Amelia turns to face Martie. "Jon has raised his children. He'd never agree to being a foster parent."

"He might, when he realizes how important it is to you."

"I'll think about it." Amelia glances at the old-fashioned alarm clock Martie keeps on her desk. "You let me go over my allotted time."

"No worries. My noon appointment canceled on me." Martie gets to her feet. "I'm getting hungry, though. Can I interest you in lunch at Shaggy's?"

Amelia retrieves her purse from the sofa. "Only if you let me pay."

"Deal!" Martie says, switching off the overhead lights as they exit her office. Leaving the building, they stroll around the corner to the boardwalk and get in the short line at Shaggy's. When their turn comes, the hostess shows them to a table for two on the railing. Their server appears right away, and both women order sweet tea and Caesar salads topped with fried shrimp.

Martie waits for the server to leave before saying, "I work

with a number of foster families in the area. If you decide to try fostering, I can connect you with the right people."

"I promise to give it some thought, Martie. But can we please change the subject. I'm tired of talking about me." Amelia plants her elbows on the table. "Tell me about you. Is there a special someone in your life?"

Martie offers her a sheepish grin. "There is someone. I'm still deciding how special he is," she says, and tells Amelia about the orthopedic surgeon she's been seeing for the past month.

Amelia is so engrossed in Martie's comical tales of her new relationship, she doesn't notice Happy and Becca approach until they are standing beside her.

Happy flaps her hand at Amelia. "Hi!"

"Hey there, Happy. What a pleasant surprise. I'd like you to meet my friend Martie." She gestures at her therapist. "Martie, this is Happy and her mother, Becca."

"Very nice to meet you, Happy and Becca," Martie says, smiling at daughter and mother in turn.

Amelia shifts in her seat toward the child. "How's your summer going so far?"

"Awesome! I've made a bunch of new friends. They're so lucky. They all live on the beach and have pools in their yards. Why don't you have a pool, Miss Amelia?"

"Happy," Becca says in a warning tone. "That's none of your business."

"I don't mind," Amelia says. "I've actually been thinking of putting in a pool. If I do, you'll have to come back next summer for a visit."

"I'd like that," Happy says. "I had so much fun sailing with you and Mister Jonathan. Do you think he'd take us again soon?"

"I'm sure he would," Amelia says. "I'll talk to him and figure out a time."

"Awesome!" Happy says bouncing a little on her toes.

Becca places a hand on her daughter's back. "Come on, Happy. You're gonna be late for your playdate."

"Mo-om." Happy swats at Becca's hand. "We don't have play-dates anymore. We hang out. Besides, I'm not supposed to go to Miranda's until four."

Becca's face remains expressionless. "Regardless, we need to let these ladies enjoy their lunch."

"See you soon, sweetheart." Amelia puckers her lips and blows Happy a kiss.

"Bye." Happy waves again and they leave the table.

Amelia turns back toward Martie whose smile has faded. "What's wrong?"

"How much do you know about Happy's mother?"

"Not that much. She's a high school English teacher from Mount Pleasant. Why?"

"She's hiding something," Martie says, her eyes still on Happy and Becca as they exit the porch and stroll down the boardwalk.

"I don't think that's it. She's unhappy. She recently went through an ugly divorce."

"There's more to it than that." When Becca and Happy are out of sight, Martie's gaze shifts back to Amelia. "It's nothing she said or did. There's something in her eyes. I have a sixth sense about people. Which is why I became a psychiatrist. Something about her is off."

"Off how?" Amelia says, the lines in her forehead creased.

"I'm not sure. But something is definitely not right in that woman's world."

Amelia moves through the afternoon in a daze, preparing dinner and paying a few bills. But she can't stop thinking about Becca. She agrees with Martie. *Something is definitely not right in that woman's world.* Amelia recognized it the first time they met. And

Becca made that strange comment about death the day they went sailing. Which Amelia interpreted as Becca's intention to harm herself, even though Becca denied it. There's an undeniable aura around her, whether it's sorrow or dejection or fear. Is Becca in trouble? Maybe she's hiding from someone. Her ex-husband, perhaps? What if her *troubles* impact Happy? Is Happy in danger?

Becca and Happy continue to preoccupy Amelia's thoughts during dinner with Jonathan on the porch. She barely touches her food while Jonathan devours every bite of his mushroom ravioli. Pushing his empty plate away, he reaches across the table for her hand. "You're awfully quiet tonight. What's on your mind?"

This is ridiculous, she thinks. She has to do something to take her mind off of Becca and Happy. "I was thinking we should have a Fourth of July cookout."

Jonathan's eyes light up. "Yes! Let's! Can I be in charge of the fireworks?"

"Men and their toys," Amelia says with a chuckle. "By all means. Have at it."

"Who were you thinking of inviting?"

"The usual crowd. Stan and Birdie. Max and Davis. Hannah, Ethan, and Gus. I guess we should invite Becca and Happy." The words slip out before she can stop them. So much for taking her mind off them. "Is there anyone else you'd like to include?"

"That sounds like a good crew. If I invite one of my law partners, I'd have to invite them all."

"Maybe we can have them over for dinner one night later in the summer." Jonathan is usually so worn out by week's end, he's content to stay close to home. Which suits Amelia fine. Since moving back to Palmetto Island, she's made no effort to branch out beyond her friendships with Birdie and Max. For Jonathan's sake, they should entertain his friends more.

"We'll do that. I think you'd enjoy their wives."

Amelia and Jonathan gather their plates and take them to the kitchen. While they're doing the dishes and storing the leftovers, Jonathan asks, "Tell me more about our Fourth of July party."

"I haven't given it much thought. We should keep it simple since we're having children. We'll have the typical Fourth of July menu with hamburgers and deviled eggs and blueberry cobbler. I'll invite them to come late afternoon and stay through fireworks."

"That sounds perfect. This will be our first party together."

The idea came to her in a flash, but now that she's had a chance to wrap her mind around it, Amelia is excited to have an event to plan. Maybe she should reconsider Birdie's job offer after all.

SEVENTEEN

As June wears on, Becca and Hannah establish a habit of walking every morning on the beach. Hannah pays Happy a nominal sum to keep an eye on Gus. The arrangement suits everyone. Happy feels like a big kid with her first babysitting job, and Gus is thrilled to have her dote on him.

Becca is content to let Hannah do most of the talking. She has much to say about the wedding, and Becca enjoys hearing about the pending festivities. Everything is coming together ahead of the big day. The invitations have gone out. The menus are set. The bluegrass band is booked.

An easy friendship develops between them. Becca can tell Hannah suspects something amiss, but she never pries into Becca's life. The close proximity of Hannah living next door gives Becca peace of mind.

Happy, too, makes new friends with some of the local girls. They travel in a pack, roaming back and forth between their houses. Whenever they're at the cottage, Becca observes them closely. Celeste is their unspoken leader. Her sassy, sometimes rude, behavior rubs Becca the wrong way. The other three girls—Becca can never remember their names—have nice manners with more pleasant demeanors. Happy is not in their league. These girls come from wealthy families. Their parents give them more freedom than Becca allows her daughter, and before long, Happy begins pushing back on the rules. While the friction exhausts Becca, she doesn't give in to her daughter. She will parent Happy as long as she can. Happy begins spending less time at the cottage and more time at her friends' houses. Happy claims it's because they all have pools. But Becca was young once. She knows her daughter is trying to escape her mother.

Happy's absence leaves Becca with too much time on her hands. Her video diary is nearly complete. Which is a good thing since the storage on her laptop is reaching capacity. Whereas Becca once spent hours at a time reading novels, she can no longer focus on more than a few pages at a time. Mostly she sits on her porch, staring out at the ocean. She senses her time is running out. After the Fourth of July, she'll proceed with her plan.

On Monday during the last week of June, Becca and Hannah return from their walk on the beach to find Amelia nestled between the children on the sofa, watching cartoons and eating Fruit Loops out of the box.

Amelia jumps up to give them a hug. "This is an unexpected surprise," Hannah says.

"I probably should've called first. But I wanted to give you these." Amelia hands envelopes to Becca and Hannah. "Jonathan and I are having a Fourth of July party. I hope y'all can come."

"Are Gus and I invited?" Happy asks.

Amelia says, "Of course."

"Are you having fireworks?" Happy asks.

Amelia says, "Yes! And hamburgers for dinner."

Hannah smiles at Amelia. "The party sounds like fun. Count us in."

"What about us, Mommy? Can we go?" Happy asks.

Becca has no interest in attending a party. But she can't think of a legitimate reason to decline the invitation. And this might very well be her last Fourth of July with Happy. "Of course. Thank you for including us."

Happy bounces on the sofa. "Awesome! I'm so excited! You have the coolest house on the beach."

"No doubt about that," Hannah says, offering Happy a high five.

At least Happy will be spending the holiday with Becca instead of Celeste and the gang. Becca senses trouble on the horizon where those girls are concerned. And she gets her first dose of adolescent drama three days later.

She's napping in the rocker on the porch when Happy comes up from the beach. Her daughter's footfalls on the boardwalk startle her awake, and Becca jolts upright in her chair.

"Celeste invited me for a sleepover. Can I go, Mama? Puh-lease."

Sinking back down, Becca rests her head against the back of the chair and closes her eyes, letting the fog clear from her brain. "I don't think so, honey."

Happy stomps her foot on the porch. "Why not?"

"Because I said so."

"But, Mo-om. That's not a legit reason."

Legit? Since when does her daughter use slang. Becca rolls her head to the side and opens her eyes again.

"Please, please, please, Mama! Everyone else is going."

She can see how much this sleepover means to Happy. Becca remembers how important friends are at her age. And she knows all too well what it's like to be left out.

"All right, honey. You can go. Get your things together, and I'll drive you to Celeste's house. I want to speak to her mother, to make sure it's okay."

"But—"

"That's the only way, Happy. If you argue with me, you can stay home."

"Okay. Fine," Happy says and sulks off to her room to pack an overnight bag.

Fifteen minutes later, Becca pulls into the driveway of Celeste's family's multi-million-dollar estate. Celeste is waiting out front with the other girls. Becca and Happy get out of the minivan and approach them. "Is your mama home?" Becca asks.

"She went to the grocery store. My older sister is here," Celeste says, but doesn't offer to get her sister.

"Are you sure your mom is okay with everyone spending the night?"

"It's fine," Celeste says, dismissing Becca's concern with a flippant wave of her hand.

"I need to make sure it's *fine*. Please ask your mom to call me when she gets home."

"Yes, ma'am," Celeste says, faking a sweet voice.

Becca is headed back to the van when she hears the girls snickering. She knows they are laughing at her. She has a bad feeling about leaving her daughter here. She's tempted to make Happy go home with her. But that would embarrass her daughter, and Becca would have to endure her foul mood for the rest of the evening. In a moment of weakness, against her better judgment, she gets in her car and drives away.

Becca waits for hours for Celeste's mom to call. Finally, around ten o'clock, she convinces herself she's being overprotective and goes to bed.

When her cell phone rings in the middle of the night, she springs out of bed to her feet. Becca is confused at first. It takes a moment for her to grasp that the angry woman on the phone is Celeste's mom. But then she remembers Happy is spending the night out.

"Please come pick your daughter up immediately."

Becca grips the phone. "Wait a minute. Why?"

"I just told you. The girls have gotten into trouble."

"What kinda trouble? Is Happy okay?"

"No one was hurt, fortunately. But they easily could've been. They snuck out of the house without permission, and we found them down on the beach. They weren't doing anything wrong. They just scared us to death."

"I'm sure they did." The thought of Happy being out on the beach unsupervised at two o'clock in the morning scares the heck out of Becca too. This isn't like Happy. She barely recognizes her daughter anymore. "I'm on my way. I'll be there in a few minutes."

Becca throws on her robe and drives to Celeste's house in her pajamas. Hazel, Celeste's mom, comes to the door dressed for a night on the town in white jeans and a tunic.

Becca wraps her robe tighter around her. "If you don't mind me asking, where were you when the girls snuck out?"

Hazel squares her shoulders. "At a friend's house. We left our older daughter, Eliza, in charge."

Becca stares at the woman in disbelief. She doesn't know any middle-aged people who stay out until two o'clock in the morning. "I would not have let Happy spend the night if I'd known you wouldn't be here. I asked Celeste to have you call me. Did she not give you the message?"

"Sorry. No. She must have forgotten to tell me."

When Happy appears in the doorway, Becca takes her by the arm and marches her to the minivan. On the way home, she says, "You're grounded for two weeks."

"Grounded? Are you kidding me? We didn't do anything wrong. We were just hanging out on the beach in front of their house."

"I shouldn't have to tell you that sneaking out of the house at night is dangerous. I thought you had better judgment than this."

Happy folds her arms over her chest. "None of my friends' parents are making a big deal about it."

Becca takes her eyes off the road to look at her daughter. "I don't care what the other parents do. I'm grounding you. End of story."

But Happy isn't the only one being punished. For the rest of the weekend, Happy makes Becca's life miserable. She mopes around, complaining about being bored, and when Becca tries to have a normal conversation with her, Happy talks back to her in a sassy tone. Becca threatens to cancel their plans to go to Amelia's Fourth of July party, but Happy convinces her that would be rude.

She wanted to spend these precious last few months with her daughter. But now, all mother and daughter ever seem to do is fight.

EIGHTEEN

Hannah is buckling Gus into his car seat on the way to the Fourth of July party when she notices Happy in front of their cottage next door. The little girl is leaning against the hood of their minivan with arms hugging her midriff and face set in a scowl. Hannah's never seen Happy angry before. Did mother and daughter have a fight? Becca exits the cottage and stands on the front porch with a bewildered expression, as though she's forgotten something.

"Come on, Mom!" Happy yells at Becca. "We're gonna be late."

Becca locks the door and plods across the gravel driveway to the van. Hannah feels guilty. She's been too busy doing weekend chores with Ethan to walk with Becca these past few days.

She calls out to Becca. "Why don't you and Happy ride with us to the party?"

From inside the car, Ethan says, "Is that really necessary?"

"Be nice," Hannah warns. She's expressed her concern about Becca to Ethan. With every passing day, she grows more convinced Becca has a mental health disorder.

"You're right. I'm sorry."

Without waiting for her mom's approval, Happy dashes across the yard and jumps in the back seat beside Gus. Becca, a tote bag slung over her shoulder, follows with eyes glued to the ground. "Are you sure you don't mind?" she asks.

"Not at all," Hannah says. "Get in."

Becca climbs in beside her daughter in the back seat, and Ethan peels out of the driveway toward Amelia's. Hannah turns around in her seat to face Happy. "Did you bring your bathing suit?"

Happy nods. "Are we going swimming?"

"We have something better than swimming planned. Stan is bringing his wave runners over."

Happy cuts her eyes at her Mom. "I doubt Mom will let me. She doesn't believe in kids having fun."

"Give it a rest, Happy," Becca snaps.

Hannah is taken aback. She's never heard Becca use a harsh tone with Happy.

"But, Mo-om," Happy whines. "I've never ridden a wave runner before."

"You may go on the wave runner, if an adult is willing to ride with you."

"Why can't you?" Happy asks.

"Because I didn't bring my swimsuit."

"I'll ride with you on the wave runner," Hannah says with a sympathetic smile. "Ethan can take Gus."

"Yes!" Happy says, punching the air. "We'll have a race, boys against girls."

"You may regret that," Ethan says to Happy in the rearview mirror.

She sticks her tongue out at him in a playful manner. "We'll see."

The other guests are on the porch sipping blueberry mojitos when they arrive. Hannah greets everyone and gives her mom a kiss on the cheek. "Happy Fourth of July."

Birdie smiles at her. "The same to you, darling."

Happy and Gus make a beeline to Stan. "Can we ride your wave runners?" Happy asks.

Stan gestures at the dock. "Help yourself. But don't forget to wear your life jackets."

When Hannah notices Becca standing awkwardly by herself, she whispers to Birdie, "Maybe I should stay here."

Birdie follows her gaze. "That's not necessary. You go ahead. Have some fun. I'll take care of Becca."

Hannah shoulder-bumps Birdie. "Thanks, Mom. You're the best."

Birdie wanders over to Becca. "You need a drink. Sweet tea or mojito?"

Becca appears grateful. "Sweet tea, please."

Hannah and Ethan take the kids down to the boathouse where they fit them for life jackets. Ethan nestles Gus in front of him on one wave runner. On the smaller of the two wave runners, Happy climbs onto the seat behind Hannah, wrapping her arms around her waist. They start the engines and take off. The ocean is slick as glass, and they ride north for thirty minutes before turning around. When they return to the inlet, they pull up to a deserted beach. "Wanna go for a swim?" Hannah asks Happy who bobs her head.

Ethan watches Gus dig sandcastles while Hannah and Happy float on their backs in the water. "Things seemed tense between you and your mom in the car on the way over," Hannah says. "Is there anything you wanna talk about?"

"I'm mad at Mom for grounding me."

"Uh-oh. What'd you do to get grounded?"

"Well, you see, three of my friends and I spent the night with Celeste on Thursday night. We went out on the beach to hang out. It was late, and we probably should've asked her sister's permission, but we weren't doing anything wrong, and we didn't think it was a big deal. Celeste's parents came home from their party and freaked out. Her mom called our moms to come pick us up in the middle of the night."

"Was the sister supposed to be babysitting for y'all?"

"Hannah! Please! We don't need babysitters anymore."

Hannah laughs. "Sorry. Let me rephrase. The sister was responsible for you while the parents were out?"

"I mean, I guess. We were all just hanging out." She smacks the water with her hand. "I have the meanest mom ever. None of the other girls got in trouble." Happy rolls onto her belly and swims over to the sand, sitting down with her knees tucked under her chin.

Hannah joins her on the sand. "I was in your shoes once, not so long ago. I know all too well what it's like to have a strict mom."

Happy gathers her long hair and squeezes the water out of it. "You do?"

"Yep. But I see things differently now that I'm a parent myself. Trust me, it is much easier to tell your child yes than no. The hardest thing about being a parent is depriving your kids of the things they desperately want. But we don't do it out of meanness. We do it to protect you, to keep you safe."

Happy considers this before responding. "I haven't thought of it like that."

"Your mom is doing the best she can. Maybe you should cut her some slack."

Happy hangs her head. "I guess you're right. Now I feel guilty for being mean to her."

"You can make it up to her. Your mom adores you. She'll forgive you." Hannah touches her finger to her temple. "Just remember to think next time about how your actions might affect your mom."

"Okay." Happy gets to her feet and holds her hand out to Hannah. "Can we go back now?"

"You bet!" She places her hand in Happy's, letting the little girl pull her off the sand.

On the ride to the dock, Hannah thinks back on all the difficult times she'd put Birdie through. Yet Birdie never held it against her. Hannah hopes she'll be as good a mom to Gus when he enters the difficult years.

Amelia sets up a banquet table on the porch from which she serves the usual Fourth of July fare—hamburgers and hot dogs and an assortment of different salads. After fixing their plates, her guests gather at the long picnic table on the lawn. Conversation at dinner is lively, centering around the fireworks show Jonathan has planned for later. Even Becca is more talkative than usual.

Amelia is slicing blueberry cobbler and passing dessert plates around the table when she notices dark clouds moving across the inlet. "Looks like we might get some rain."

"But what about the fireworks?" Happy says.

Jonathan pulls out his phone and consults his radar app. "It's just a passing storm. Shouldn't last too long."

They are finishing cleaning up after dessert when the rain begins to fall.

Jonathan says, "I could use some help in the garage organizing the fireworks while we wait out the storm." And the other men eagerly volunteer to go with him.

Amelia starts a movie for the children in her study before joining the other women in the living room for an after-dinner glass of wine. She thinks nothing of it when Becca sneaks off, and when she doesn't return, she assumes Becca is watching the movie with the children. Max is entertaining them with a funny story about her hotel guests when they hear a woman scream in a distant part of the upstairs. The four women jump to their feet and dash up the stairs to the second floor. They follow the sounds of loud sobbing down the hall to Amelia's room where they find Becca standing at the window, her face wet with tears.

Amelia hurries to her side. "What is it, honey?"

"I got lost," Becca cries. "I was looking for a bathroom, and suddenly, I didn't know where I was."

"You're fine, now." Amelia walks the hysterical woman over to the bed, pulling Becca down beside her. "You're shivering." She looks up at Birdie. "Will you grab the mohair throw off the chaise lounge?"

Birdie retrieves the blanket and drapes it around Becca's shoulders.

"Has this ever happened before?" Amelia asks.

Becca buries her face in her hands. "I can't do this anymore."

Hannah sits down on the other side of the distraught woman. "Do what, Becca? We're your friends. You can trust us. Whatever you say won't leave this room."

"I have early onset Alzheimer's Disease," Becca blurts.

Hannah pulls her close. "I'm so sorry. I suspected something was wrong. I wish you'd told me sooner."

Everything suddenly makes sense to Amelia. Becca's strange comment when they were out sailing. *I was wondering if, when a person dies, they just sail away to heaven.* Tears prick her eyes at the thought of what this poor woman must be going through. And what about Happy? What will happen to that sweet child?

Becca says, "I booked the cottage for the summer, hoping to spend some quality time with Happy. But the disease is progressing much faster than the doctors anticipated. Now I'm praying I make it through August without something bad happening. There's no way I can go back to teaching in the fall."

"Do you have any family?" Amelia asks.

Becca shakes her head. "I'm an only child, and my parents are both dead."

"Does your ex-husband know?" Hannah asks.

Becca stares down at her lap. "He wants nothing to do with us. He made that clear."

"But he's Happy's father," Amelia says. "He has a right to know."

"The situation is complicated," Becca says.

Birdie crouches down in front of Becca. "You have us, Becca. We'll see you through this."

"I don't wanna be a burden," Becca says, bringing her balled fist to her mouth.

"You're not a burden," Hannah says, stroking Becca's leg. "You're a friend. We want to help you. Does Happy know about this?"

"I'm not ready to tell her yet. But I need to go check on her." Shrugging off the blanket, Becca slowly rises and plods across the room. She stops when she reaches the doorway. "Will one of you take me to her?"

"Of course. Come with me," Hannah says, taking her by the hand.

Amelia, with Max and Birdie on her heels, follows them down the stairs to the study. Gus is sound asleep, but Happy is nowhere in sight.

"Where'd she go?" Becca says, her brow furrowed.

"She probably went to the bathroom," Birdie says.

But a quick search of the downstairs yields no results.

"Let's not panic yet. Hannah, you and Becca wait in the living room. Birdie, you and Max check the second floor. I'm going out to the garage to see if the guys have seen her." Amelia waves her phone at them. "I have my cell. Call me if you find her."

She exits the back door. The rain has slowed to a drizzle, but her sandaled feet are soon soaked from the wet lawn as she hurries over to the detached garage. The fireworks are organized by type in the bed of the Gator, and the guys are standing around talking.

"Have y'all seen Happy? She's disappeared."

"What do you mean she's disappeared?" Jonathan asks.

"She was watching a movie with Gus in my study. But now we can't find her."

"Is Gus okay?" Ethan asks with narrowed eyes.

"Yes. He's sound asleep." Amelia's phone rings with a call from Birdie. "Did you find her?"

"Not yet," Birdie says. "She's not upstairs. We even looked in the attic. Max and I are thinking Happy may have heard her mama scream. What if she went looking for her and overheard us talking about Becca's disease?"

Panic rises in Amelia's chest. "Oh, dear. You might be right. Let me tell Jon. He'll know what to do."

She ends the call and explains to the men about Becca's revelation.

"And you're certain she's not in the house?" Jonathan says.

"I'm positive. We checked everywhere."

"Maybe she wandered down to the beach to see if we were starting the fireworks," Stan suggests.

Jonathan walks over to the work bench where Amelia keeps a surplus of flashlights. He hands out flashlights as he issues orders. "Ethan, you and Davis search the property on foot. Stan and I will take the Gator to the beach. Amelia, get in your car and drive down the road a ways. Everyone keep your cell phones with you and let us know if you find her."

Amelia is heading for the door when Jonathan calls after her. "Better tell Max to call Toby."

A chill travels her spine. "Do you think we need to get the police involved already?"

He nods. "I do. Considering the circumstances. A young girl is missing. She's likely to be upset and confused. It's pitch black out tonight, and we're surrounded by water."

"Say no more." Amelia runs to the house where she finds Max and Birdie in the kitchen with their heads close together.

"The guys are searching the property and the beach. Max, Jonathan says you should call your nephew."

Max nods. "I'm on it."

Amelia removes her keys from the hook beside the back door. "I'm going to look for her in the car. Y'all hold down the fort here."

Amelia drives slowly out of the driveway, flicking her head-lights to high beam. The road is desolate, but off in the distance, fireworks light up the dark sky. The farther down the road she goes, the more certain she is that Happy overheard them. She must be so devastated, to lose her father and now her mother's future is uncertain. Amelia's heart breaks thinking about what's in store for Becca and Happy in the days, weeks, and months ahead.

Hannah moves a sleeping Gus to the living room, and he snores softly with his head in her lap. On the other side of her, Becca is understandably fraught with worry. Hannah can't imagine how terrified she would be if Gus had run away into a stormy night. She tries to reassure Becca, but her words sound empty and appear to offer little comfort.

For the third time in five minutes, Becca asks, "Do you think Happy went in the water?"

Repeating herself is nothing new for Becca. But now Hannah understands why. She rubs circles on Becca's back. "Happy is a smart girl. She knows better than to go in the ocean alone at night."

Becca wrings her hands. "This is not how I wanted her to find out about my disease."

"There is no easy way, Becca. When were you diagnosed?"

"In early May. The doctor thought I'd have a year or two of quality time." Becca sighs. "Sometimes, as in my case, the disease is more progressive."

"I know so little about Alzheimer's. Are you in any kind of pain?"

"I wouldn't necessarily call it pain. But it's frustrating. I lose stuff all the time and forget how to do the simplest things. I used to cook elaborate meals, but now, depending on the night, I struggle to heat up a can of soup. What if Happy went in the ocean?"

Hannah patiently answers, "She knows better than to go swimming alone, especially at night."

Becca chews on a fingernail. "What if she ran into a stranger? What if someone tries to hurt her?"

"Point Pleasant is private property. People don't typically wander this far up the beach." Hannah is grasping at straws. She has no idea whether this is true. "Maybe she went to a friend's house."

"Maybe." Becca stares blankly at the phone in her lap. "I don't know if I have any of their numbers."

"Why don't I call Mia?"

"That's a great deal. Ideal." Becca draws in a breath. "Idea."

Gently removing Gus's head from her lap, Hannah goes outside to the porch to make the call. When Mia answers on the third ring, Hannah tries to sound calm despite the tightness in her voice. "Hey, Mia. Have you, by any chance, seen Happy?"

"Not tonight," Mia says. "Why? Is something wrong?"

Hannah considers how much to tell Mia. While the news of Becca's illness isn't hers to share, in order for Mia to understand the urgency of the situation, Hannah quickly walks her through the events of the night.

"That's awful," Mia says. "Poor Miss Becca. I had a feeling something was wrong. Have you called the police?"

"Yes, Max's nephew is the police chief. He's on the way with several units. Do you know how to get in touch with any of Happy's friends?"

"Yes. Most of them live near me. I'll reach out to them. Also,

I'm having some people over. I'll recruit them to help look for Happy."

Hannah lets out a deep breath she didn't know she'd been holding. "That'd be awesome, Mia. Let's stay in touch."

Hannah is pocketing her phone when she notices Ethan standing near the sand dunes. Cupping her hands around her mouth, she calls out to him, "Hey, Ethan! Any sign of Happy?"

He shakes his head. "But the police are here." He points north, and she follows his finger to where a long line of patrol cars with blue flashing lights are making their way up the driveway.

Police swarm the house and grounds. When their search yields no results, they call in the coast guard. Within minutes, Helicopters are hovering overhead, and boats are cruising the shore with beams of light directed at the inky waters.

Hannah returns to the living room. Gus sleeps through the commotion, but Becca, completely beside herself, paces the floors and cries a torrent of tears.

Mia calls around ten o'clock. "None of Happy's friends have seen her. But they're all helping in the search. We're combing the beach and surrounding houses. So far, we haven't had any luck."

"Neither have we. Keep looking." Hannah's heart sinks. Seemingly everyone on the island is looking for Happy. Why can't they find her? Happy wouldn't go into the ocean at night, would she?

Hannah remains at Becca's side throughout the long night. Amelia answers questions and fields phone calls from the neighbors while Birdie and Max hand out coffee to the rescue workers.

Finally, a few minutes before midnight, Mia calls Hannah. "We found her! She was hiding in our outdoor shower. I checked the shower earlier, when you first called. She must have snuck in sometime after that. She's terribly upset. She feels bad for causing so much trouble. Do you want me to take her home?"

All eyes in the room are on Hannah. She gives them a

thumbs-up to let them know Happy has been found. Becca drops to a nearby chair, her face buried in her hands.

"No need for you to go out, Mia. We'll pick her up on our way home in a few minutes. Tell her not to worry. No one is mad or upset with her. We love her. You've outdone yourself, Mia. I don't know how to thank you."

"I'm just glad we found her."

Ethan carries a limp Gus to the car while Hannah helps Becca out of the chair. "I don't know what to say," Becca says to the room. "I'm so grateful for your help."

"We are your family." Amelia gives Becca's arm a squeeze. "Get some sleep. If you need anything during the night, you call me."

Nodding, Becca inhales an unsteady breath.

Placing an arm around Becca, Hannah walks her out to the car. On the ride over to Mia's, Becca says, "What do I say to Happy?"

Hannah shifts in her seat to face Becca. "Say what's in your heart. She may not be up for talking tonight. In which case, you hold her in your arms and let her know you love her. She'll probably have a lot of questions. If you don't feel like answering them, I'd be glad to talk to her." Hannah reaches through the seat and gives Becca's knee a squeeze. "Anything you need, Becca. Like Amelia said, we're your family now."

NINETEEN

Jake's boss knows how to throw a party. Coach Massey's lakefront residence, a sprawling multistoried home with porches and shingles, sits on acres of manicured lawn. Servers meander about, passing out drinks and bite-size nibbles. Chefs roast pigs and cook burgers, chicken, and hotdogs on commercial grills. Boats in all shapes and sizes come and go from the pier, some towing water skiers while others take guests on tours of the lake.

Sydney and Jake sip margaritas while lounging on the second-floor deck, watching the activity below. "I could get used to this lifestyle," she says. "When do *you* get to be head coach?"

Jake rolls his head to the side to look at her. "Does this mean you're considering a future with me?"

"Maybe," she says in a teasing tone. Truth be told, she's thought of little else since she accepted the job overseeing both Birdie's Nest Cafe and the catering business.

For the remainder of the afternoon, they mingle with the rest of the coaching staff and their significant others, some of them already married while others are living together. She spends most of her time talking to three young women who live in Greenville.

One is an elementary school teacher, another a landscape architect, and the third a Realtor. Sydney picks Erin's brain about the average price per square footage in the most desirable neighborhoods in Greenville.

Sydney and Jake stay at the party until the professional fireworks show ends. On the drive back to Clemson, Jake says, "Admit it. You had a good time today."

She smiles at him. "I admit it. I had a good time. I met some nice people. I think I could be friends with some of the girls."

Jake's lips part in a mischievous grin. "Does this mean—"

"It means I like your friends." She turns away, staring out the window into the darkness. "I'm not moving up here without a commitment, Jake."

He lowers his voice. "I understand. And I wouldn't ask you to."

Neither speaks during the remainder of the drive. But when they arrive at Jake's townhome, he takes her in his arms, kissing her with the same sense of urgency she's been experiencing all afternoon. The chemistry between them is powerful, a fire she hopes never flickers out. They tear off their clothes and have sex on the living room floor. Afterward, they move to the sofa and cuddle under a blanket.

Jake spoons her from behind. "I love you, Syd. I never stopped." While he's made dozens of comments about them spending their lives together, this is the first time he's told her he loves her since they've gotten back together.

"And I love you . . ." Her voice trails off.

"But?" He gives her a little shake. "Do I hear hesitancy in your tone?"

"I'm worried this is happening too fast. Aren't you?"

"Not at all. We should never have broken up in the first place. We wasted ten years. Why waste another day?" He kisses her neck. "Speaking of which. Seeing you every other weekend is hard. When football practice starts, I won't have as much time. Can I come to Palmetto Island next weekend?"

"Sure. I don't think we have any big events booked, but I need to double-check our calendar."

"Cool. Don't make plans for Sunday night. I have a surprise for you."

"Ooh." She turns to face him. "What kind of surprise?"

He chuckles. "You'll have to wait and see."

She fingers an outline around his lips. "Give me a hint."

"Not a chance."

"Then I'm cutting you off for the rest of the night." Rolling off the sofa, she sashays naked across the living room and up the stairs to his bedroom. He chases her, tackling her onto his bed and making love to her again.

Later, when Jake goes to the bathroom to brush his teeth, Sydney is searching his drawers for a T-shirt to sleep in when she discovers a black velvet ring box. Opening the box, her breath hitches at the sight of the large round diamond set in a halo of smaller diamonds.

Is this his surprise? Tingles of excitement dance across her chest as waves of uncertainty overcome her. Stuffing the ring box back in the drawer, she returns to bed and pretends to be asleep when he climbs in beside her. She lays awake for hours contemplating her future. She agrees with Jake. They shouldn't waste any more time when they're meant to be together. But is she ready for marriage? A month ago, she was single, navigating her life's course on her own. Now she's in a serious relationship. A *long-distance* serious relationship. They share history, one more complicated than Jake realizes. And what about her career? She accepted Birdie's head job to allow for an easy exit when the time comes. But she has a good thing going at Birdie's. She's not sure she wants to leave. While there are plenty of wonderful restaurants in the Upcountry, wherever she lands, she'll have to rebuild her reputation all over again.

Overwhelmed by uncertainties, Sydney only manages a few hours of restless sleep. Stirring before Jake, she rinses off in the shower and tiptoes around the townhome as she gathers her things. She needs to escape before he wakes. He'll want to make love, and she needs to think clearly without her feelings for him clouding her judgment.

After stopping for coffee, she drives around Clemson before heading over to Greenville. Both towns are charming. A lot will depend on where she can get the best job. She loves Palmetto Island, but it's a resort town. A small town will offer a more normal life.

She wrestles with her thoughts during the drive home, and she comes to several conclusions. She loves Jake and doesn't want to risk losing him. She'll say yes when he proposes and lobby for a long engagement. She's ready to leave the past behind, to break the tie that's keeping her in the Lowcountry. But she can no longer live with the secret. When Jake comes down on Sunday, she'll tell him the truth about their breakup.

TWENTY

A melia tosses and turns throughout the night. She can't stop thinking about Becca and Happy, worrying about what will happen to both of them as the disease progresses.

Just after dawn, she nudges Jonathan awake and makes love to him. Afterward, they lay naked with the covers tossed aside and the air conditioning blowing cool air on their damp skin. "What did I do to deserve this lovely surprise?" he asks.

"We need to talk."

He lets out a groan. "I figured there was a catch." Rolling out of bed, he retrieves their robes from the bathroom. "I'll make coffee and meet you on the porch."

She watches him leave the room. Jonathan is a wonderful man. She cherishes their relationship. Is she willing to give him up? Because what she's about to propose may very well drive him away.

Amelia gets out of bed, slips on her robe, and goes into the bathroom. She brushes her teeth, splashes cold water on her face, and studies her reflection in the mirror. She has no choice. She won't be able to live with her conscience if she doesn't follow her heart.

Jonathan is waiting on the porch with two cups of coffee on the table in front of him. "I have a feeling this is about Becca and Happy."

"We have to help them, Jon. They have no other family." She sits down in the chair closest to him.

Jonathan blows on his coffee and takes a sip. "I agree. What's happening to them is tragic. We'll give them some money."

Amelia stares out across the water. "Money won't do them any good. Unless Becca doesn't have health insurance. Which I doubt because she's a teacher at a respectable private school."

"Then what do you suggest?"

"I'm going to offer for them to live here until the time comes for Becca to go into a memory care facility."

"And then what? What will you do with Happy?"

"I'll adopt her." When Jonathan starts to object, she raises a hand in protest. "Let me finish before you say anything. Not having children has created a gaping hole in my life. By bringing Becca and me together, God is giving me a chance to fill that hole."

He sets down his coffee and rubs the stubble on his chin. "You can't seriously be considering becoming a parent at your age."

"I don't think of fifty-four as old. Besides, Happy is not a newborn. She's well on her way to being an adolescent."

Jonathan gawks at her, as though unable to believe what she's suggesting. "And what if I don't approve?"

Amelia doesn't respond. Her silence is her answer.

"That's just great, Amelia. You're willing to throw away our relationship for two people you hardly know." Jonathan is a skilled trial attorney, used to controlling his emotions. But the throbbing vein at his temple lets Amelia know how angry he is.

"That's not true. I've come to care about Becca and Happy a

great deal. I've been floundering these past few months, searching for direction in my life. And I've found it. I'm certain, with every fiber of my being, this is the right choice for me."

"But not for me." He sets his mug down hard, and coffee sloshes over the edges. "I've already raised my children. I have no interest in becoming a parent again."

She reaches for his hand. "I beg you to reconsider."

He jerks his hand away. "I beg *you* to reconsider."

"I can't turn my back on them. Becca may refuse my help. She may already have a plan in place for their futures. But I have to at least try." Amelia stands and crosses the porch.

"Where are you going?" he says to her back.

She pauses in the doorway. "To talk to Becca."

"I won't be here when you get back."

Amelia grips the door frame as she considers the sacrifice she's making. "I'm sorry, Jon. I truly am. But this is something I have to do."

Becca makes Happy's favorite blueberry pancakes for breakfast, and they sit down at the table on the porch to eat. Becca pours syrup on her pancakes and passes the bottle to Happy. "Wanna talk about what happened at the party?" Mother and daughter were both too upset when they got home last night to have this conversation.

Happy stares down at her untouched food. "I was watching the movie with Gus when I heard someone screaming. I thought someone was hurt, and I went to see if I could help. I heard you telling the ladies you have a disease. I could tell it was bad from the way they looked at you. I got scared, so I took off running. I ended up on the beach. I knew I wasn't supposed to be there alone, and I didn't know what else to do, so I went to Mia's house and hid in their outdoor shower until she found me." She looks up at Becca with tears in her eyes. "I'm sorry, Mama. Please don't ground me again."

"I understand you were upset, sweetheart. And I'm not going to punish you. In fact, as of this minute, you're no longer grounded."

Happy's face lights up. "Do you really mean it?"

"I really mean it." Becca will do anything to see her daughter smile. She wags a finger at Happy. "But no more going on the beach alone, either at night or during the day."

"I won't. I promise." Happy forks off a bite of pancakes and stuffs it in her mouth. "What kinda disease do you have? Is it cancer?"

"No, honey. My disease is called Alzheimer's. It's usually thought of as an old-person's disease, but younger people like me can get it too. The disease attacks my brain and makes me forget stuff."

When Happy's eyes get big, Becca knows what she's thinking. Her daughter's already seen the signs. "Are you gonna die?" Happy asks, her question soft on her lips.

"Eventually. But hopefully not for a while."

Happy's eyes fill with tears. "Will I have to go live with Daddy in Colorado?"

"No, honey. Your happiness is the most important thing to me. I won't make you live anywhere you're not comfortable."

Happy swipes at her eyes. "But where *will* I live?"

"I'm not sure yet. I'm still working on it."

"Maybe we can stay on Palmetto Island," Happy says, absently dragging the tip of a sausage link through a puddle of syrup.

"Maybe. Would you like that?"

Happy sits up in her chair. "Yes! I love it here. The beach. And all my new friends."

Happy's friends appear on the beach over the sand dunes,

calling and waving for her to join them. "And here they are," Becca says. "As if you summoned them with your mind."

"Very funny. Can I go with them, Mama?"

"In a milk . . ." Becca purses her lips as she wraps her tongue around the word. "A minute."

Happy yells to her friends, "Be there in a sec."

Becca laces her fingers together and rests her hands on the table. "While you're no longer grounded, because of my illness, I'm enforcing some stricter rules around here. I want you to check in with me throughout the day."

"Can I have a cell phone?" Happy presses her palms together with her fingertips touching her chin. "Please!"

"That's probably a good idea. One with limited features so we can stay in touch."

"Yay!" Happy jumps to her feet. "Can we get it today?"

"We'll go shopping this afternoon." Becca shoos Happy away. "Run along now and let me rest."

Happy starts off and turns back around. "Can I tell my friends? About your disease?"

After last night, the whole island probably already knows, anyway. And Happy will need her friends' support for what lies ahead. "That's fine. As long as you promise to come to me with questions and concerns."

"I promise," Happy calls over her shoulder as she runs off.

Becca watches Happy approach her friends. The girls huddle around her while she's presumably telling them about her mama's disease. When she's finished talking, they glance back at Becca, waving at her before heading off down the beach.

Becca has been dreading this conversation, but she feels her burden has been lifted. Having her secret out in the open will make things easier. She's in a race against time. The sooner she can put things in place the better for everyone involved.

After cleaning up from breakfast, Becca stretches out on the daybed swing and closes her eyes. She's dozing off when there's a knock at the door. She doesn't budge. She isn't in the mood for company. Another knock is followed by a pounding, and she worries something has happened to Happy.

She reluctantly drags herself off the swing. Inside, she finds Amelia on the front stoop, holding up a pastry bag from Birdie's Nest Cafe. "I brought donuts."

"That's kind of you, but we've already eaten breakfast," Becca says in a hostile tone. Her secret is out in the open. She no longer has to fake nice to Amelia. This woman is beginning to irritate her, the way she's constantly inserting herself into their lives.

"Save them for later. Donuts are a treat anytime." Amelia brushes past her, taking the bag of donuts into the kitchen.

Becca follows her. "Why are you really here, Amelia?"

"I was worried about you. Last night was traumatic. I wanted to make certain you're all right."

"I'm fine. Thanks for dropping by," Becca says, sweeping her hand at the door.

"You're not getting rid of me that easily." Amelia eyes the round table in the corner. "Can we talk for a minute?"

"I'm sorry. But I have a splitting headache," Becca says, massaging her temples.

"This won't take long. It's important," Amelia says and helps herself to a seat at the table.

Becca lowers herself to the seat opposite her.

"When were you diagnosed?"

Unable to stomach the pity in Amelia's eyes, Becca drops her gaze. "At the beginning of May. The disease is . . ." She searches for the word, but it isn't there. "Getting bad fast."

"What sort of plans have you made?"

Becca doesn't answer. She continues to stare down at the table.

"Talk to me, Becca. You can trust me."

Becca lets out a loud sigh. Amelia is right. She has to trust someone. She can no longer manage alone. Hannah is busy with the wedding. It wouldn't be fair to burden her. "I've met with the administrator at a memory care facility in Charleston. My paperwork has been approved. I'm all set to be admitted when the time comes."

"What about Happy?"

"I'm working on a plan," Becca snaps.

Amelia draws in a deep breath. "I have a proposition for you. I want you and Happy to come live with me at Point Pleasant. When it becomes necessary, I'll arrange for private nurses for you. After you go into the memory care facility, I'd like to adopt Happy. I can provide a good home for her. I promise she will be loved and well taken care of."

Becca looks up. "I don't understand. Why would you do that for us?"

"For many reasons. Raising children is one of life's greatest gifts. And I missed out. I was never able to have a baby of my own, and my husband refused to consider adoption. My therapist suggested I foster a child. I've been considering it. Your situation fell in my lap, as though it was meant to be. I felt a special connection with Happy the first time we met. I didn't understand it then. But I do now."

"I can't afford private nurses," Becca says, her jaw tight.

"But I can. Happy needs to be with her mama for as long as possible."

Becca thought that initially. But now she's not so sure. She doesn't want Happy to witness her deterioration, day after day. "Your offer is incredibly generous. But you don't understand what you're getting into." She pushes back from the table. "I really need to be alone right now."

Becca exits the house and walks to the edge of the dunes where a gentle breeze cools her skin. Amelia has offered a viable backup if Becca's plan doesn't pan out. But she feels obligated to see that plan through before she makes her decision. A single tear slides down her cheek. This discussion has driven home the brutal reality that Becca will one day turn her daughter over to someone else to raise.

Becca, who assumes her visitor has gone home, is surprised when Amelia appears at her side. The woman is persistent. And while it's difficult to admit, Becca admires that about her.

"I wanted to check on you before I go," Amelia says. "I realize I threw you a curveball. I understand you need some time to think about it."

"How does Jonathan feel about all this?" Becca asks, her eyes on the ocean.

"Truthfully, he has mixed emotions."

"Which means he doesn't approve."

"I love Jonathan. I'll be disappointed if things don't work out for us. However, if he doesn't come around, he's not the man I thought he was." Amelia takes hold of Becca's hand. "I can't explain why I feel so strongly about having you and Happy live with me. I'm in a position to help you, and this is just something I need and want to do."

Becca softens a little toward Amelia. "Your kindness means more than you know. But I can't let you risk your relationship with Jonathan."

"What if Jonathan comes around?"

"Then I'll consider your offer." Becca removes her hand from Amelia's grip and wipes the tears with the hem of her cotton shirt. "This is all so overwhelming."

"I'm sure it is. I think you should talk to my therapist."

"Ha. She can't fix what's wrong with my brain."

"Maybe not. But she can help you sort your emotions and make these difficult decisions. I'll schedule the appointment. And don't worry about the cost. I'm picking up the bill."

Tears of gratitude spill from Becca's eyes. "Thank you. Talking to someone might help."

They turn and walk slowly back to the house. "What else can we do to make life easier for you?" Amelia asks. "Shall we find someone to run errands and manage the household?"

Amelia's use of the pronoun *we* annoys Becca. And she's not an invalid yet. "I'm fine for now," Becca lies. More often than not, she finds herself confused and disoriented when she leaves the house.

"We'll take baby steps," Amelia says.

Becca manages a smile. "Baby steps would be great."

She stands on the front porch long after Amelia's convertible has disappeared from sight. She must accept her new reality. This disease is chomping away at her brain, and she can't do this alone.

TWENTY-ONE

Amelia arrives home from Becca's to find an empty space in her closet where Jonathan's clothes hung neatly a few hours ago. "He didn't waste any time," she says out loud. She's unaware that Bebe is cleaning in the master bath until the housekeeper appears in the closet doorway.

"I was here when he left," Bebe says. "It's not often I see a grown man cry."

"Jonathan was crying?"

"He wasn't boohooing, but he was wiping his eyes with that red bandana he carries around. I can tell when a man is upset. And Mister Jonathan was hurting. What'd you do to him?"

"It's a long story."

Bebe plants a hand on her hip. "Then you'd better start talking."

"Fine. But I need coffee. Let's talk in the kitchen," Amelia says as she brushes past Bebe.

Downstairs in the kitchen, Amelia brews a fresh pot of coffee and pours two mugs. Seated at the breakfast room table, she confides in her old friend about Becca's disease and her offer to adopt Happy. Bebe is like a second mother to Amelia. She's been the family's housekeeper since Amelia was a child. She trusts Bebe not to let her make a mistake.

"Oh, Lord. Those poor folks. My heart aches for them. I gather Mister Jonathan doesn't approve of the adoption?"

"He thinks I'm too old to become a parent."

Bebe gets up from the table and begins dusting the plantation shutters. "You have to respect the man's opinion. His children are grown. He understands, better than you, the commitment you're getting yourself into."

"Are you saying this is a bad idea?"

"Not at all, if this is what you really want." Bebe closes the wooden slats and runs her duster over them. "You have so much to give a child—a beautiful heart and a lovely home."

"What would Mama do?"

"Miss Dottie would adopt the child, no questions asked." Bebe turns to face Amelia. "But she wasn't in love with the man of her dreams." She waves the duster at Amelia. "And I've seen you with Mister Jonathan. You're crazy in love with him."

"I am. I don't deny it." Amelia stares down at her coffee. "I'm hoping Jonathan changes his mind once he has a chance to think about it. Once he realizes I'm determined to see this adoption through."

"This decision seems rather hasty. Why not take a few days to think about it and talk to Mister Jonathan again?"

Amelia shakes her head. "You don't understand."

Bebe returns to her chair. "Then explain it to me."

"During all the years of pain I suffered as Nelson's wife, I never once lost my faith. I have always felt a force driving me forward, giving me the strength to persevere. But I never understood the purpose until now. This is the right decision, Bebe. I feel it in my soul. I am meant to raise Happy."

Bebe takes Amelia's hands in hers. "Those kinds of feelings are best not ignored."

"What do I do about Jonathan?"

"Pray he comes around but accept that he might not. You need to be fully prepared to lose him, baby girl. And I don't think you're there yet."

Reclaiming her hands, Amelia stares out the window at the cloudless morning. "Maybe not. I'm convinced this is the best solution for both Becca and Happy. They can live here together for as long as possible. That way, when Becca has to move into the home, the transition will be smoother for Happy."

A worried look crosses Bebe's face. "I didn't realize Miss Becca is gonna live here too."

"At least for a while. With nursing care, of course. I realize it'll create more work for you. But I'll make it worth your while. I think it's important for Becca and Happy to be together as long as possible."

"I'm not worried about the extra work. What you're doing is incredibly selfless. You're a good soul, just like your mama. Miss Dottie would be proud."

Amelia offers her a sad smile. "That means a lot, Bebe. Thank you."

"You know how much you mean to me, baby girl. I'll support you in any way."

"I'm counting on it. I can't do this without you."

Bebe sips her coffee. "You're going to need more than just my help. My niece runs her own private nursing service. Her employees are certified nursing assistants, not RNs. But Toni runs a tight ship. You'd be in excellent hands with her."

"That's wonderful. Please text me her contact info. Becca is going to need someone sooner rather than later, if only for a few hours a day to help run errands and such."

"Let Toni assess the situation. If all you need is someone to run errands, I'm sure you can find someone cheaper."

"That's true." A chill travels up Amelia's spine, and she shivers. Her life is about to change drastically. Is she ready for it? She stands abruptly. "I'm going for a walk on the beach."

Amelia grabs her running shoes from her bedroom and hits the beach at a fast pace. The midday sun is hot, and perspiration soon breaks out on her forehead and runs down her back. But the physical exertion releases nervous energy and clears her head. The reality of what she's proposing hits hard. But she's not afraid. She feels a sense of calm like she's never experienced. She looks to the sky. Her mama is watching over her. Miss Dottie will guide her. As long as she keeps her faith in herself and in God, the situation will play out as it's meant to.

Ethan leaves at seven in order to make it back to Charleston in time for work at eight. Hannah walks him to the car, clinging to him longer than usual when he hugs her goodbye. Neither of them slept much after the dramatic events of the previous night and the sad revelation of Becca's disease.

Ethan holds her at arm's length. "Are you gonna be okay here alone?"

"I don't have much choice. I have a ton of work to do. But I'm grateful for the distraction."

He kisses her one last time. "I'll try to clear my calendar, so I can come back Thursday night."

A soft smile spreads across her lips. "I would love that."

After driving Gus to day care, she returns to the cottage and settles in at her desk in her second-floor makeshift office. But despite her demanding workload, she can't concentrate. She stares out at the ocean waves breaking on the shore. She's never lost a friend before, never known anyone to die from Alzheimer's. A quick Google search tells her more than she wants to know about the effects of the disease. And what about poor Happy? What will become of that sweet child? Her father wants nothing to do with her. And Becca has no other family. Will she be placed in a foster home?

Lunchtime rolls around, and Hannah's stomach growls. How can she think about food when her friend is in crisis? She considers calling Becca to check on her. But she decides to wait. Becca is a private person. She'll likely need the day to herself.

Her phone vibrates the desk with a call from Ethan. "How's your day going?"

"Terrible. I've gotten nothing done. I've been sitting her staring out the window for hours."

"Me too," Ethan says, and she envisions him standing at the window of his second-floor office in downtown Charleston.

Hannah leans back in her chair, picking at a loose thread on her raggedy Widespread Panic T-shirt. "I can't stop thinking about Becca and Happy. We should do something. I'm planning to take them a casserole later. But that's lame. Taking food to the family is what you do when someone dies. And Becca isn't dead yet."

"Let's adopt Happy," Ethan blurts.

Hannah brings her chair upright. "Do you mean it, Ethan? I've been thinking the same thing."

"Not only will she be an awesome big sister to Gus, she'll be a big help when we have more children. Besides, she's a great kid. She's smart and easy to be around."

"But what about our living situation? There's not enough room for the four of us in your condo."

"We'll buy a house if we have to."

"But what about your parents' house?" The house Ethan grew up in on Legare Street has been in his family for generations and will one day be his.

"We'll work it out. Housing isn't the main issue, anyway. Do you have any idea what Becca has in store for Happy?"

Unexpected tears fill Hannah's eyes. "Last night wasn't the time to ask. I'll talk to her this afternoon, when I take the casserole over."

"Do that," Ethan says. "Feel her out, see what she's thinking, before we give it too much thought."

"All right," Hannah says. "I'll call you later. In the meantime, try to get some work done."

When she hangs up, Hannah makes an attempt at developing a new concept for a website renovation, but she's too distracted and soon abandons her work. Pushing back from her desk, she hurries down the stairs. As she putters about the small kitchen, putting together a chicken tetrazzini casserole and salad, she contemplates the difficulties she and Ethan would face as Happy's parents. The child will require much love and nurturing during the years ahead. Eventually, Becca will be committed to a memory care facility. Happy's visits with Becca will be emotional, especially when Becca fails to recognize Happy. How will all this impact Gus and the other children Hannah and Ethan hope to have?

Hannah is blessed to have a remarkable man in her life. Ethan will be at her side through thick and thin. Hannah and Ethan have enough love in their hearts for a dozen children, regardless of whether they're biological or adopted. They are in a position to help a friend in need. They will make it work.

TWENTY-TWO

Becca wakes from a long nap to find Happy standing over her, studying her. "What is it, Happy? Is something wrong?"

Happy sits down gingerly on the edge of the bed, as though she's afraid of breaking Becca. "Celeste's grandma has Alzheimer's. Last time Celeste went to see her, she didn't recognize Celeste. Is that gonna happen to you? Are you gonna forget me?"

Becca struggles to sit up. "There are a lot of unpleasant aspects of the disease. But I see no point in discussing them yet."

Happy hangs her head, her golden hair like a curtain framing her face. "So, you *will* forget me. We won't be together always and forever."

Becca pulls Happy to her. "You will live forever in my heart, honey. As I will always live in yours. This disease will make me say things and do things that are out of character for me. When this happens, I want you to think back to your memories of the real me. Does that make sense?"

Happy scrunches up her face. "I guess so. Can we go buy my phone now?"

"You bet." When Becca gets to her feet, a wave of dizziness overcomes her, and she stumbles into the nightstand.

Happy grabs hold of her arm and helps her back over to the bed. "Mama, are you okay?"

"I'm fine, sweetheart. I just got a little dizzy." She stands again, more slowly this time. "Now, grab my purse and let's go buy you a phone."

"Yay!" Happy says and runs out of the room ahead of her.

The phone store is located next to the Harris Teeter. Becca has seen it dozens of times, and she drives there with relative ease. But when they enter the store, her mind goes blank and panic renders her paralyzed. Happy tugs on her arm, but Becca is frozen in place.

"What's wrong, Mama?" Happy asks, her eyebrows pinched.

Becca's tongue is heavy, and she can't answer.

A nice-looking young man with caramel skin and amber eyes approaches them. "Afternoon, ladies. My name is Emmett. Can I interest you in a new phone today?"

Happy says, "Yes, please. I'd like to get a phone like my friend has." She tells him the make and model.

"Excellent choice for a starter phone. And we have plenty in stock."

When he heads off across the store, Happy takes hold of Becca's arm and walks her slowly to the display.

After Emmet spends a few minutes demonstrating the different features, he asks Happy, "Are you sure this is the one you want?"

Happy bobs her head. "How much is it?"

"I'll need to pull up your account." Emmett looks over at Becca. "Do you know your account number?"

Becca's lips part, but no words come out of her mouth.

"Can you pull it up by my mom's phone number?" Happy asks.

Emmett gives Becca a quizzical stare. "Sure. Let's go over to the counter."

Once again, Happy takes Becca by the hand, and they follow Emmett to the counter. Becca sits on a stool while Happy conducts the transaction with Emmett. When it's time to pay, Happy removes Becca's wallet from her purse and slides the credit card in the reader. When the reader prompts her to sign her name, Becca drags her finger across the screen in a squiggly line.

Emmett hands Happy the box containing her phone. With a glance in Becca's direction, he asks her, "Is your mom okay?"

Tears well in Happy's eyes. "She has a brain disease. She forgets things sometimes."

"Oh. I'm sorry. That's rotten luck. Are you okay to drive home?" he asks Becca in a loud voice, as though she were hearing impaired.

Becca removes her phone from her purse, accesses the maps app, and clicks on the address for the beach house. She flashes the screen at him.

Emmett gives Becca a skeptical nod. He comes from behind the counter to speak to Happy. "I have a daughter about your age. You know to call 9-1-1 in an emergency. Your phone will come in handy for GPS tracking if you need it. Be sure to learn how to use that feature properly."

Becca's cheeks burn. He's talking about her like she's not in the room. Like she's an elderly lady or a child who can't take care of herself. Because that's what she is. *Happy is now the parent and Becca the child.*

"Yes, sir," Happy says. "Thank you."

Becca follows Happy to the car. They don't talk on the way home, but Becca feels her daughter's eyes on her, watching and waiting for her to falter.

They've no sooner gotten home when Hannah knocks on the front door. She hasn't bothered to knock in weeks, and usually just barges in. Now that everyone knows about Becca's disease, they are treating her with kid gloves. She was afraid of this. She was hoping to avoid it as long as possible. Her life is spiraling out of control, and she's powerless to stop it.

Becca motions Hannah and Gus in. "We brought you dinner," Hannah says raising the casserole dish in her hands. "I hope you like chicken tetrazzini."

"We love chicken tetrazzini," Happy says.

Becca takes the dish from her. "This is kind of you, Hannah. Unnecessary but greatly appreciated."

Gus yanks on Happy's arm. "Do you wanna go swimming with me in the ocean?"

"Sure!" Happy casts an uncertain glance at Becca. "Is that okay?"

"Of course. Go put on your bathing suit."

"Be back in a sec," Happy says, darting into her room and closing the door.

Hannah says, "I can go down to the beach with them if you'd rather stay up here and rest."

After what happened in the phone store, Becca doesn't want to be alone. "That's okay. I'll come with you."

When Happy returns in her bathing suit, Becca and Hannah grab two beach chairs and follow them through the sand dunes. They set up their chairs on the edge of the surf while the kids splash in the waves.

"How're the wedding plans coming?" Becca asks, eager to talk about something other than herself for a change.

"Good. I think. I keep feeling like I'm forgetting something important. Everything is ordered, all systems are a go."

They sit for a while in silence. Becca is unaware she's crying until Hannah places a hand on her arm.

"I'm so sorry, Becca. I can't imagine what you're going through. Do you want to talk about it?"

Becca blots her eyes with Happy's beach towel. "I took Happy to buy a cell phone earlier today. When we got inside the phone store, I froze. I couldn't speak. I forgot how to talk. That's what it's gonna be like. I'll eventually forget how to swallow." She brings a trembling hand to her lips. "Everything is happening so much faster than I expected."

Hannah strokes her arm. "You must be terrified. Have you made any plans?"

Becca explains about the memory care facility.

"What about Happy? Ethan and I would love for her to live with us."

Becca is grateful Hannah doesn't say *adopt*. The word is so final, the formal termination of her parental rights to her child. "I'll add your names to the list." Her sarcastic tone brings on a pang of guilt. "I'm sorry, Hannah. This is difficult for me."

"I'm sure it is," Hannah says. "Who else has offered to take in Happy?"

"Amelia. She was here first thing this morning. She could never have children of her own, and she feels a special connection with Happy."

If Hannah is disappointed, she doesn't show it. "Amelia can provide a good life. Any child would be lucky to grow up at Point Pleasant."

"While that may be true, Jonathan isn't on board with Amelia's decision. And I won't ruin their relationship."

"This all came about so fast. I'm sure he'll change his mind once he's had a chance to think about it." Hannah angles her body toward Becca. "If it makes a difference, Ethan and I are talking about buying a house."

"I'm certain you and Ethan would provide a loving home regardless of where you live. It's just that . . ."

"That what, Becca? What are you not saying? Is there someone else on the list?"

Becca nods. "Happy's biological mother."

TWENTY-THREE

Sydney is going over the evening menu on Wednesday afternoon when Anna, the clerk at the coffee bar, enters the office. "You have a visitor in the cafe."

"A visitor? But I'm not expecting anyone. Did they give you a name?"

Anna shrugs. "She didn't say."

"Okay. Tell her I'll be right there."

Sydney leaves the menu for Birdie's approval and exits the office. Passing through the double doors, she stops in her tracks at the sight of the woman on the banquette. She's staring down at her lap, and even though her face isn't visible, Sydney would know her anywhere.

She moves slowly around the counter and stands beside the table. "Becca? What're you doing here? Is . . ." She stops herself. Sydney knows so much from watching the child over the years. The golden shade of her hair. The red tricycle she raced around the cul-de-sac. The pink backpack she carries to school every day. Yet she doesn't know the little girl's name.

Becca stands to face her. "Happy is fine."

Sydney shakes her head, unsure if she heard her correctly. "You named her Happy?"

"I named her Harper, which is my maiden name. She was such a happy baby, we soon adopted the nickname." Becca gestures at the door. "Can we go outside? I need to talk to you in private."

Sydney follows her outside to the park. The skies are overcast, and a gentle breeze rustles the Palmetto tree fronds. The women stand side by side, staring into the water fountain. After several minutes of awkward silence, Becca turns to face her. "There's no easy way to say this. I have early onset Alzheimer's."

Sydney gasps and her hand flies to her mouth. "I'm so sorry, Becca. I don't know what to say."

"There's nothing you can say. I got dealt a bad hand. It happens." Becca, appearing as though she might faint, staggers over to a park bench.

Sydney rushes to her aid. "Can I get you something? Some water? Sweet tea, maybe?"

"I'm fine." Becca pats the bench beside her. "Please, have a seat."

Sydney sits down. "Does Happy know about your disease?"

"Yes." Becca wipes the perspiration from her face with a linen handkerchief. "She found out by accident, sooner than I wanted to tell her. Although it's probably for the best."

"Your husband must be devastated."

She stuffs the handkerchief in her bag. "My husband left me last year for another woman. He's no longer a part of our lives."

"But he's her father. He legally adopted her, which makes him responsible for her."

"As if that means anything in this day and time. Craig moved to Colorado with his new family. The judge ordered him to give me child support. I haven't seen a dime. Doubt I ever will."

"That sucks." Sydney had spent long hours with her attorney

174

interviewing potential candidates to adopt her child. She picked the wrong couple. "Do you have family who can help you?"

Becca shakes her head. "That's why I'm here."

Sydney narrows her eyebrows. "I'm not sure what you mean."

Becca fiddles with her purse strap. "I thought that . . . maybe . . . since you're older, and she's older, you'd be in a better position to be her mother."

"Let me get this straight. You're suggesting I take her back?" Sydney asks, her heart pounding against her rib cage.

"Why not? She's your biological daughter, after all."

Sydney jumps to her feet. "Is this some kinda cruel joke? Do you have any idea how hard it was for me to give my baby up?"

Gripping the bench's armrest, Becca slowly stands. "I know exactly how hard it was for you to give her up. I saw you at the hospital the day Happy was born. You were distraught. The doctor had to give you a sedative. I gave you a piece of my heart that day, a small portion of the debt of gratitude I owed you for trusting your child in my care."

Sydney turns her back on Becca, once again facing the fountain. "How did you even find me?"

Becca steps closer, her voice near Sydney's ear. "I never lost you. I've kept tabs on you. And I'm not the only one."

Sydney's blood runs cold. "What do you mean?"

"I've seen you parked on the street outside my house."

She spins around. "So what if I checked you out. Sounds like I had plenty of reason to worry."

Becca's chin trembles. "I've been a good mother to Happy."

The air rushes out of Sydney's lungs. "I'm sorry, Becca. I didn't mean that. Of course, you've been a good mother. This is all sudden. You've caught me off guard. I'm not really in a position to care for a child. My career demands I work long hours."

"I understand. Do you have a . . . a person . . . a boyfriend?"

"That's none of your business." Sydney storms off across the boardwalk.

Becca calls after her. "Wait! Sydney! Please, don't go."

Sydney stops when she reaches the railing.

When Becca catches up with her, she's slightly out of breath. "This is hard to explain. All these years, I've wondered if you'd approve of the job I was doing as her parent. I understand now that she was never really mine. She's been on loan to me, and now that I'm facing this health crisis—"

"The adoption becomes void, and the child goes back to its original owner."

"Not necessarily. It is my responsibility to make arrangements for her. If you don't take her back, at least give me your permission to find someone else to care for her."

"So, you're asking me to give my child up all over again."

Becca ignores her comment. "Will you at least meet her? She's a great kid. I've already had two women approach me about adopting her. Nice families with plenty to offer."

Sydney's gut clenches, and she worries she might throw up. Could she make this work? She's often dreamed of one day being reunited with her daughter. But later, when her daughter's a grown woman and can understand why Sydney had to give her up. Maybe God intended it to be this way. She and Jake are back together. Their careers and living circumstances complicate the situation. But this may be her only chance.

She turns to Becca. The sadness in the woman's eyes makes Sydney soften toward her. "I need some time to think."

"Of course, you do." Becca presses a folded slip of paper in her hand. "Here's my cell number and the address for the cottage where I'm staying. I don't know how much time I have, Sydney. But I don't think it's a lot."

"I understand. I'll call you in a few days."

Sydney waits until Becca disappears around the corner of cafe before leaving the railing. She wanders aimlessly around the boardwalk. She's too wrecked to return to work. She thumbs off a text to Birdie. *So sorry. I'm having a personal crisis. I can't come back to work today.*

When she looks up, she finds herself standing at the entrance to Shaggy's. The porch is teaming with the lunch crowd, but she finds an empty seat at the bar. She orders a vodka on the rocks from Lewis, the bartender, but when he brings her drink, she only takes a sip. As tempted as she is to drown her sorrows, getting drunk won't solve her problems. Her phone vibrates the bar with a text from Birdie. *Take all the time you need. I'm here if you want to talk.*

Birdie isn't the one she needs to talk to. She needs to reset. To go back to the beginning. To start all over again, this time telling Jake the truth.

Dropping a ten-dollar bill on the bar, she leaves the porch. Her car keys are in her purse in the office at work. Going behind the cafe to the back entrance, she slips into the coatroom and peeks around the doorjamb into the kitchen. Birdie is nowhere in sight, and the rest of the staff is too busy to notice when she ducks into the office and retrieves her purse.

Hurrying to her apartment building, she gets in her car and drives out of town before she can change her mind. She has a lot to think about during her drive to Clemson. As much as she's pined for her child all these years, and now has a chance to get her back, she's not sure it's the right choice for either Happy or herself. Or Jake. Fortunately, she doesn't have to make this decision alone a second time. Jake will undoubtedly be angry at her for keeping the truth from him. But once he calms down, even if he wants nothing more to do with her, he'll take his responsibility to the child seriously. Of that much, she's certain.

TWENTY-FOUR

Hannah is waiting on Becca's porch when she returns from her meeting with Sydney. "How'd it go?" Hannah says, standing to greet her.

"As expected. Sydney is confused and concerned and angry at Craig for abandoning Happy. I don't blame her. She chose us over a lot of other couples to adopt her child, and Craig—I mean *we* . . . are letting her down."

"You can't help your disease, Becca."

Becca stares at the porch floor. "No, I guess not."

There's a knock at the door, and Hannah says, "Do you want me to get it?"

"Maybe if we ignore it, whoever it is will go away."

Hannah laughs, thinking she's joking.

"I'm serious, Hannah. I'm not in the mood for company."

The front door bangs open, and Amelia bustles in, calling out, "Yoo-hoo." She spots them on the porch. "There you are."

"Shoot me dead now," Becca mumbles.

"Shh!" Hannah hisses. "She can hear you."

Amelia emerges from the house onto the porch. "Hey there,

Hannah. I didn't realize you were here. I just stopped by to check on Becca."

Hannah senses Becca's hostility. Whatever problem Becca has with Amelia, she needs to get over it. She's going to need Amelia in the months ahead. "I could use some fresh air," Hannah says. "Why don't we go for a walk on the beach?"

Becca glances at the heavy clouds. "Looks like rain."

"A walk sounds nice," Amelia says in a chipper voice. "According to the forecast, the rain is supposed to hold off until later in the day."

"Come on. We won't melt if we get a little wet." Hannah waves them on, leading them across the lawn and through the sand dunes.

The beach is deserted, the threat of bad weather having driven vacationers inside. They kick off their shoes and head south. "Where are your kiddos today?" Amelia asks.

"Gus is at day care and Happy is at a friend's house," Hannah answers.

"Happy has certainly made a lot of friends on the island," Amelia says.

Becca stops walking. "This feels like an ambush. If you're going to try to convince me to let you adopt Happy, I'm going home."

Amelia appears wounded. "That was not my intention, Becca. I was just making conversation. I didn't mean to upset you."

"I'm sensing some tension here. And I think we need to clear the air." Hannah turns toward Becca. "You're going through a lot right now. And it's hard for us to watch you suffer. We're trying to help, in the only way we know how. They say it takes a village to raise a child. Let us be your village, Becca."

Tears stream down Becca's cheeks. "You have no idea how hard it is to let go of control of my child."

"You're right. We don't." Amelia reaches out, as though to brush a loose strand of hair off Becca's cheek. But then she thinks better of it and retracts her hand. "We only want what's best for Happy. And for you. Tell us what you want. What you need. And we'll make it happen."

Becca lets out a sob and drops to her knees on the sand. "I need my brain back! I need to think straight! Can you make that happen, Amelia?"

Amelia kneels down beside her. "Oh, honey. If only I could. But I can be your sounding board. I can help you organize your affairs. I can make life easier for you, so you can focus on Happy."

Becca screams, "You just wanna take my child away from me."

"That's not at all true." Amelia pulls Becca into her arms, holding tight when Becca fights against her. "Only you know what's best for you and your child. I'll support you in whatever you decide regarding your futures. Since you don't have any family, I thought you could use a friend."

When Becca begins weeping uncontrollably, Hannah plops down on the beach to comfort her, rubbing her back while Amelia rocks her gently. When her crying finally subsides, Becca wipes her eyes and blows her nose with the tissue Amelia gives her.

"I'm so sorry," Becca says, sniffling. "I have so many decisions to make, and I'm struggling to focus. I need every friend I can get right now."

"We can accomplish more if we work together as a team," Hannah says.

Becca smiles at her. "A village."

Hannah stretches her legs out in front of her. "I'm calling our first official meeting of the town council to order. The primary item on our agenda is to find the best solution for Happy. To do that, we must put all our cards on the table." She turns her head toward Amelia on her right. "You should know that Ethan and I have also offered for Happy to live with us." She looks at Becca on her left. "And you should tell Amelia about Sydney."

Fidgeting with her hands, Becca says in a slow and low voice, "I adopted Happy as a baby. Sydney is her biological mother."

Amelia's brow shoots up. "Sydney? As in Birdie's chef, Sydney?"

Becca nods. "I went to see her earlier today. Sydney's older now, and Happy's no longer a baby. I thought she might want her back. Needless to say, Sydney was shocked. She's taking some time to think about the situation."

"Is Sydney married?" Amelia asks.

Becca shakes her head. "When I asked her if she was seeing someone, she told me it was none of my britches . . . my business."

A flash of memory comes back to Hannah. "About a month ago, on the day of my painting party, Sydney canceled at the last minute when an old friend came to town. A few days later, she admitted the old friend was actually her old boyfriend. I wonder if he could be Happy's biological father."

Becca shakes her head. "When we were going through the adoption process, Sydney told me she didn't know who the baby's father was. I guess it's possible she was lying. What else did she say about him?"

"Let me think." Her conversation with Sydney at the cafe replays in her mind. "They still have chemistry, but they have some logistical challenges to work out."

Becca looks heavenward. "How wonderful would it be for Happy to be reunited with both her biological parents?"

Hannah watches for Amelia's reaction. The grimace, while slight, tells Hannah just how much adopting Happy means to Amelia.

"Does Happy know she's adopted?" Amelia asks.

"No." Becca rubs at the back of her neck. "Against my wishes, my ex-husband made the decision not to tell her. Craig was embarrassed by my infertility. He didn't want anyone to know."

Amelia gets to her feet and gives Becca and Hannah a hand up. When they start walking again, Becca says, "This situation will take some time to sort out. I've turned in my resignation at school. Happy loves it here, and she's made so many new friends. Since I won't be going back to work in the fall, I was thinking I'd sell my house in Mount Pleasant and rent the cottage on a month-to-month basis. The rate is considerably less during the off-season."

"That's a brilliant idea," Amelia says. "Happy can go to school here, and the two of you can ease into the next stage of your lives. I have nothing but free time on my hands. I can help organize the sale of your house and the move." She slows her pace. "I don't mean to be so pushy. That's just my nature."

Becca smiles, the first Hannah has seen from her in days. "I'd appreciate your help. It would be a load off my back."

Hannah grins. "See how much we can accomplish when we work together."

Becca loops her arms through Amelia's and Hannah's as they continue down the beach. "You two didn't know me before. By nature, I'm easygoing, But I'm angry a lot of the time now. I lash out at everyone without meaning to. Some of it is the disease itself. Although the fear and uncertainty of what I'm experiencing is also to blame. There will come a time when I have no clue what I'm doing."

"We will be here for you when that happens," Amelia says.

Becca's voice is tight. "While I may not always act like it, I'm grateful for your friendship and your concern for Happy's and my well-being."

Hannah rests her head on Becca's shoulder. "You're in good hands. Your village will take care of you."

TWENTY-FIVE

Jake has yet to get home from work when Sydney arrives in Clemson late afternoon. Sitting on the front stoop of his near-campus townhouse, she watches the summer students stroll past with eyes glued to phones and shoulders stooped under the weight of their backpacks. She waits nearly an hour before Jake's truck appears from down the road. He whips into the parking lot and screeches to a halt in the space beside her car.

When he notices her, his face registers first surprise and then bewilderment. His tall frame climbs out of the front seat. "What're you doing here? Never mind. I'm glad to see you, whatever the reason." Taking her in his arms, he unlocks the door and walks her backward inside the townhouse. Pressing his lips against hers, he paws at her clothes.

Sydney pushes him away. "We need to talk."

"I figured that. Whatever it is can wait." He kisses her again with more urgency.

"Stop, Jake!" She shoves him harder. "This can't wait another minute."

He fumbles with his pants as he rearranges his privates. "What're you talking about?"

"I need to tell you the truth about our breakup."

"That happened years ago. We're back together now. Whatever it was doesn't matter anymore."

Sydney shakes her head. "You're wrong. It mattered then. And it matters even more now."

He gives her the once-over, noticing her attire for the first time. "Why are you wearing your uniform? Did you bring a change of clothes? Are you planning to stay?"

"I'm not sure you'll want me to after you hear what I have to say."

"You're scaring me, Sydney. Let's sit down," he says, motioning her to the sofa.

She looks at the sofa and back at him. She suddenly finds it difficult to breathe. "Actually, can we take a walk?"

"Whatever," he says in an irritated tone.

Jake strides ahead of her out of the apartment and down a block to a small park overlooking a playground. He stands beside a bench waiting for her to sit first. Children's laughter fills the air. Of all places for him to bring her.

Plopping down beside her, he says, "What's this about, Sydney?"

"I . . ." She'd rehearsed her speech many times in the car, but when she opens her mouth to speak, her mind goes blank. Is this what it's like for Becca? She pauses a minute to collect her thoughts. "The day after my father was awarded the position in Japan, I found out I was pregnant."

Jake's body goes still. "Pregnant? Was it my child?"

"Of course, it was your baby. I was always faithful to you, Jake."

"But—" he starts, as she raises a hand to silence him.

"Please! This isn't easy. Let me finish." She lowers her hand. "My mom found the pregnancy test and told my dad without talking to me first. He was furious. He blamed me for sabotaging his big career opportunity. He wanted me to have an abortion, but I refused. I made a deal with them. I agreed to give the baby up for adoption if they let me live with my sister in Atlanta until the baby came."

Jake stands and begins pacing back and forth in front of her. "Why didn't you tell me? If it was my baby, I had a right to know about it."

"Because you're an honorable man, and I knew you would've insisted on doing the honorable thing in marrying me. And I couldn't let you give up your football career, your dreams of going to the NFL."

He stops pacing and glares at her. "Yet you gave up my child, my own flesh and blood, without even talking to me first. We could've made it work."

Sydney stands to face him. "How? Neither of us had jobs or college educations. We had our futures ahead of us. We weren't ready to be parents."

"So says you. I would have appreciated the chance to decide that for myself." He rakes his fingers through his brown waves. "Why are you telling me now?"

"I can't live with this secret between us anymore. I was planning to tell you this weekend, but then Becca, the adoptive mother, came to see me earlier today. She's been diagnosed with early onset Alzheimer's disease. Her husband left her for another woman, and she has no other family."

A flash of anger electrifies his blue-green eyes. "So, she expects us to take the kid back?"

"It's not like that, Jake. Becca thought that, since I'm older, my circumstances may have changed, and I might want my child back. *Our* child back."

Jake takes her by the arms. "Are you lying to me, Sydney? Is this really *my* child? Because the Sydney I loved would have told me about the pregnancy. My parents would've helped us."

She tears her eyes away from his. "I thought so too."

"What does that mean?" When she doesn't answer, he gives her a shake. "What does that mean, Sydney? Are you saying my parents knew about the pregnancy?"

She nods. "At least your mom does. I don't know if she ever told your dad. I went to see her after I took the test. Before my parents found out. Your mom and I had grown so close. I just knew she'd help us. But she turned on me. She called me a slut and accused me of ruining your life. And she was right, Jake. Fathering a newborn while attending college and playing football would have eventually taken its toll on you. I made the right choice for both of us."

"Ha. You made the selfish choice. The only person you were thinking of was you."

Anger pulses through her, and she pounds her fists against his chest. "Selfish? Do you have any idea how hard it was to let go of my baby after carrying her in my body for nine months?"

He locks his arms around her so she can't move. "Okay. Calm down. I need to know the truth, Sydney. Did this Becca woman reach out to you today? Or did she contact you back in May? Is that why you connected with me on social media? Is that why you wanted us to get back together?"

Sydney wrenches free and takes a step back. Sweeping a hand down her body, she says, "Look at me! I'm still wearing my uniform. Becca came to see me at the cafe. She told me about her disease. I told her I needed time to think. She left, and I got in my car and drove straight here."

"I'm not sure what or who to believe. Everything about my life for the past ten years has been a lie." Jake turns his back on her and walks away, leaving her standing alone in the park.

Sydney waits until he's out of sight before moving to the chain-link fence. Tears blur her vision as she watches a young mother pushing her little girl in a swing on the playground.

She rubs her upper arms where Jake squeezed her. He's not a

violent person, and he's never been physically rough with her. He's angry and upset, understandably so.

Unburdening herself of the secret she's been keeping for a decade provides an enormous sense of relief. Now, she must pick up the pieces of her life. If Jake wants nothing more to do with her, she'll find a way to move on. At least she'll have closure.

The little girl in the swing tosses her head back and smiles lovingly at her mommy. The way Sydney has seen Happy smile at Becca dozens of times. The way Sydney yearns for Happy to smile at her. She's missed out on nine years of Happy's life. Is it even possible for Sydney to pick up where Becca leaves off?

She trudges back to Jake's townhouse. He's standing inside his storm door. He watches her, but he doesn't wave, and he doesn't come outside. He doesn't stop her from leaving. She gets in her car and drives off.

Sydney imagines Jake on the phone with his mother. Will Patti tell the truth about what happened ten years ago? Or will she lie and blame Sydney for running away without telling Jake about the baby? Sydney was just a kid back then. Their parents were the grown-ups, yet they were all too eager to rid themselves of Sydney when she found herself in trouble. She expected as much from her own parents. They were not the loving type. But Patti, who was like a second mother to her, turned her back when Sydney needed her the most. Now Patti will have to answer to her son.

If only things had been different. Jake would've married her. But what would their lives be like now? Would they still be together? What kind of parents would they be? Would they have survived Jake's college years, the demands of football and the girls constantly throwing themselves at him? Would Sydney have found her way to a career as a chef?

As she exits onto the highway heading south, the enormity of how much her career means to her hits home. She's worked hard to establish herself as one of the South's up-and-coming chefs.

And she refuses to let anyone or anything interfere with that. Besides, she can't pay her bills without her job. And she can't raise a child with no income. Is she seriously considering being a single mother to Happy? Why not? Happy is a nine-year-old little girl. She doesn't need round-the-clock care like an infant. The thought of having her child back both terrifies and exhilarates Sydney.

She turns up the volume on her favorite country music station. For the rest of the long drive, despite the way she left things with Jake, she wears a broad smile on her face as she contemplates a future as Happy's mom.

TWENTY-SIX

Traffic is heavy on Friday afternoon heading from Charleston back to Palmetto Island. When cars on both sides of the road slow to a crawl, Amelia whips off the highway into the Dairy Queen parking lot.

"What're you doing?" Becca asks, bracing herself against the dashboard.

Amelia pulls up to the drive-through menu. "Getting some ice cream. Do you want some?"

"Sure." Becca leans across the console to read the menu. "I'll have a chocolate dipped cone."

"Excellent choice," Amelia says, and orders two chocolate dipped cones from the woman on the loudspeaker.

When they pull around to the check-out window, Becca insists on paying. She's grateful Amelia doesn't argue. The woman has done so much for her. An ice cream treat is the least she can do.

Amelia hands her a cone, and Becca bites off the chocolate swirl on top. The sugary sweetness is a nice reward after the stressful meeting with the Realtor.

When they return to the highway, Amelia says, "Your Realtor is convinced you'll get a good price for your house. You have plenty of equity built up. You should be able to live in the beach cottage as long as you'd like."

"As long as I *can*," Becca says under her breath.

Amelia takes a dainty nibble of her cone. "Selling your house is a big step. Do you think you're ready?"

"I had mixed emotions at first. This is my child's home, the only home I've ever owned. We've shared many happy memories there. But there's also a sadness that has taken up residence in the house since my husband left. More than anything, I feel relieved, as though I'm shedding the ball and chain that has dragged me down this past year. I can finally move on. With whatever life I have left to live."

"The ocean has magical healing powers. You and Happy will thrive at the beach."

In a disgruntled voice, Becca says, "I sure hope so. If I can get all this business taken care of. I need to figure out what to do with my eclectic mixture of junk. I'll keep a few pieces for Happy, for sentimental reasons, and get rid of the rest."

Amelia glances over at her. "We can rent a mini-warehouse in Palmetto Island."

The lines in Becca's forehead deepen. "Why are you doing all this for me, Amelia?"

Amelia pauses, licking at her ice cream. "Every day is a struggle when you're married to an abusive man. I've been so self-absorbed for so long, but I'm finally climbing out of the dark hole I've been living in for decades. I find that focusing on someone else for a change is therapeutic."

Becca studies Amelia while she drives. She sees the pain of the past etched in the tiny lines around Amelia's eyes. "I was wrong about you, Amelia," she says in a soft voice.

Amelia smiles over at her. "No, you weren't. I come on too

strong sometimes. I can't help myself. I'm a fighter. Jonathan says I'm way too intense for my own good."

"I imagine you had to be to survive what you've been through." Becca wonders what kind of mother Amelia would be. She's wiser and stronger because of her life's experiences. And Amelia can offer her daughter financial security. She would drive Happy to be her best self, to achieve great things. Isn't that what all women want for their children? "About your offer to adopt Happy . . ." Becca's voice trails off as she loses her train of thought.

"My offer stands as long as it takes you to make up your mind. I understand this is a difficult decision. Part of me believes Happy would be better off with her biological parents."

This surprises Becca. But she's glad Amelia is putting Happy's best interests ahead of her own. "How so?"

"There's nothing quite like the biological bond between parent and child. Of seeing yourself in the face of another."

"What about the other part?" Becca asks. "What makes you the better candidate to be Happy's mother?"

Amelia thinks about her answer before responding. "The desolation of not being able to have a child is all-consuming. You adopted Happy. You know what I'm talking about?"

Becca thinks back to those miserable years she spent trying to conceive. "All too well."

"If things work out for me to adopt your daughter, I will give her my heart and soul."

Becca's throat swells, but she chokes out, "That means a lot, Amelia."

They ride in silence while they finish their ice cream cones.

Amelia wipes her mouth with her napkin, balling it up and dropping it into the cup holder. "How do you feel about the medical care you're receiving? Are you satisfied with your doctors?"

"Mostly. I have an excellent team at MUSC. But I'm worried about how fast the disease is progressing. And some of my meds have strange side effects. I have an appointment on Tuesday of next week. I hope to get answers to my long list of questions."

"I'll go with you, if you'd like. I can help you get those answers. I can be pushy when I need to be."

Becca laughs out loud, a sound that is foreign to her own ears. "I've noticed. But I would appreciate your company."

"After your appointment, we could grab some lunch and head over to Mount Pleasant. We can tag the items you want to store, and then later in the week, I'll organize movers to transfer them to the storage unit. If we hire a professional service to clean early the following week, you'll be able to put the house on the market in two weeks' time."

Becca knits her eyebrows. "That's a lot of driving back and forth for you."

"I don't mind. Driving my mama's sporty convertible makes me feel closer to her."

Becca looks up at the car's roof. "I never noticed this was a convertible."

"Do you wanna put the top back?" Amelia asks with mischief playing on her lips.

"Yes! I'd love it."

Amelia presses a button and the convertible top folds back. The traffic clears as they head for the open roads of the Lowcountry's barrier islands. She turns up the volume on the classic rock station, and they sing at the tops of their lungs, the wind whipping their hair about their faces. Becca closes her eyes, relishing a few moments of contentedness that are becoming fewer and farther between.

Happy, with Mia on her heels, comes running out of the cottage when they pull into the driveway. Happy dances around the convertible. "Can I ride in the car with the top down, Mama? Please!"

Becca gives her child a half hug. "No, honey. Amelia and I had a long day. We need to let her get home to her supper."

Amelia calls out, "We'll do it another time, Happy. Soon! I promise."

The threesome waves to Amelia as she drives off. Unexpected tears of gratitude sting Becca's eyes. After feeling alone for so long, Becca has found someone to lean on in Amelia.

Happy loops her arm through Becca's. "I missed you today, Mama. What's for dinner?"

Becca smiles at her. "You missed me so much, you can't wait for me to cook your dinner." She locks eyes with Mia over the top of Happy's head. "Would you like to stay for dinner?"

The babysitter gives her a quizzical look. Despite all the time she spends with Happy, Becca has never invited her for a meal. "Thanks, Miss Becca. But I need to get going. I have plans with friends later."

"I understand." They move toward Mia's car. "Before you go, are you free to keep Happy on Tuesday? I need to go back to Charleston for the day."

Happy crosses her fingers and squeezes her eyes shut, waiting for Mia's response.

Mia tousles Happy's salt-crusted hair. "Yes, ma'am. I'm available all day."

"Yes!" Happy says, giving Mia a high five.

Mother and daughter wait for Mia's car to disappear before entering the house together arm in arm. Happy drags Becca into the kitchen. "Can we have grilled cheeses for dinner?"

"That's easy enough. And then maybe we'll go for a bike ride on the beach."

"Yes! Let's!" Happy reaches for the loaf of bread. "Why are you in such a good mood, Mama?"

Becca cuts a slab of butter and places it in a pan on the stove. "I have something to tell you. I think it's good news. I hope you will as well."

Happy slaps two slices of cheese between four pieces of bread. "What is it?"

"Let's make dinner first."

"No! Tell me now! Are we getting a puppy?"

"Definitely not. The last thing I need is something else to care for." She spoons healthy portions of fresh fruit onto two paper plates. "How would you feel about moving to Palmetto Island permanently?"

Happy freezes, cutting her enormous eyes at Becca. "Are you serious? I would love that. But what about our house? And where would we live?"

Becca flips the sandwiches in the pan. "We'd sell the house in Mount Pleasant, and we'd continue to live here, at the cottage, for the foreseeable future."

"Will I get to go to school with my new friends?"

"That's the plan."

"Yay!" Happy twirls around the kitchen. "This is so awesome! Thank you, Mama."

"You're welcome. This is a good move for us. We're gonna be very happy here. We'll get a real Christmas tree this year. And put it over by the window."

Happy's demeanor becomes serious as she gathers napkins and forks from the drawers. "Have you decided who I'm gonna live with when you die?"

Becca removes the toasty sandwiches from the pan, placing them on the plates alongside the fruit. "I'm still working out the details. But a number of people have offered."

"Is Amelia one of them?"

Becca debates how much to tell Happy. Is her daughter old enough to be part of the process? "She was the first. But there are others. Once I figure everything out, you and I will have a nice long talk." She turns to her daughter, taking Happy in her arms. "I hope you and I will be together for a long time. The road ahead of us won't always be easy, but you have a lot of friends here who care about you, and who will support you through the hard times. Not just your girlfriends, but Amelia and Hannah and Birdie as well."

Happy relaxes against Becca. "I know, Mama. But it won't be the same."

Becca tastes salt when she kisses her daughter's hair. "Always remember that you and I will be together forever in our hearts."

Amelia, after dropping off Becca, arrives home to find Jonathan coming up from the dock.

"Amelia," he calls as he approaches from across the lawn. "I hope you don't mind me being here. I had some things I needed to take care of on the boat."

She eyes the back door, anxious to avoid a confrontation. "Of course not, Jon. Keep the boat here as long as you'd like."

He gives her an awkward peck on the cheek. "I'll call first next time."

She steps away from him. "That's not necessary. Feel free to come and go."

He removes his sunglasses to see her better. "You look tired. Where have you been?" He catches himself. "Sorry, I don't mean to pry."

"It's fine," she says. "I don't have any secrets. I went to Charleston with Becca to take care of some business."

"I assume this means you're going through with the adoption."

"It's not that simple. Becca is considering several factors, one of them being Happy's biological parents."

His jaw slackens. "You mean, Happy was adopted?"

"Yes, but don't tell anyone, because Happy doesn't know yet."

Jonathan kicks at the gravel in the driveway. "We had something special, Amelia. I can't believe you're throwing it all away because of a . . ."

A surge of anger jolts Amelia. "Because of a what, Jon? A lovely little girl with a beautiful spirit who is about to lose her mama and needs a home?" She jabs her pointer finger at the ground. "God dropped this child in my path. In my heart, I believe I'm meant to help this family." Her tone changes from angry to sorrowful. "Our relationship wasn't so special, not if you're unwilling to support me in the most monumental endeavor of my life."

She strides off toward the house, letting herself in and leaning against the door until she hears Jon's car start up and the crunch of gravel in the driveway. She pours herself a glass of Sancerre and takes it out to the rockers on the porch. It's Friday night, and she's all alone. No dinner plans, and no one to keep her company. She closes her eyes, letting the evening sun warm her face as she contemplates future Friday nights. If Becca and Happy come to live with her, life will be hectic and one day will bleed into another. After Becca transitions into the memory care unit, assuming Happy remains at Point Pleasant, Amelia will spend her Friday nights chauffeuring Happy to various activities—dances and sporting events.

Soon enough, Happy will go off to college and Amelia will be an empty nester. Amelia rests a hand on the arm of the empty rocker beside her. And she'll once again be all alone in this big house. In ten years' time, Amelia will be sixty-four. God willing, she'll have plenty of life left ahead of her. But she'll have no one to spend it with. Unless she finds a special someone along the way. She thought Jonathan was that special someone, the love of her life, her reward for surviving years of an abusive marriage. But he isn't the man she thought he was. Just as Nelson failed to live up to her expectations. No man will ever truly make her happy.

The person responsible for her happiness is herself. For the first time in her adult life, she is free to make her own choices, to follow her heart. She made a commitment to Becca. And she will not renege on that obligation. Regardless of how the situation plays out.

TWENTY-SEVEN

When Birdie and Stan offer to keep Gus overnight on Saturday, Hannah jumps at the opportunity to have some much-needed time alone with Ethan. They enjoy a leisurely dinner at Birdie's Nest Cafe, sharing salads and appetizer specials and a bottle of sparkling rosé. They're finishing a slice of blueberry and peach cobbler when Hannah notices Sydney moving from table to table, greeting guests. Her posture is stooped, as though her problems are weighing heavily on her. Hannah suspects those problems have something to do with Happy.

Hannah waves her over. "Hey there, stranger! You outdid yourself with tonight's specials. Particularly the tuna tartare." She lowers her tone and whispers conspiratorially, "I hear the boss has taken the night off. Can you join us for a glass of wine?"

Sydney hesitates a beat before signaling a server to bring her a glass of Pinot Grigio. When she sits down opposite them at the table, Hannah says, "I hear you got a promotion."

"A promotion?" Ethan says. "Congratulations! What exactly does that entail?"

"We're reorganizing to incorporate the catering business Birdie is launching."

"I believe I heard something about that." He nods. "Go on."

"We've begun the process of looking for a new dinner chef and event planner. I'll be in charge of them once they're hired." Sydney turns to Hannah. "By the way, I made a few changes to your menu. I'll email you the final version tomorrow."

"I'll be on the lookout for it," Hannah says. "Which reminds me, I've been meaning to talk to you about the wine selections."

Ethan pushes back from the table. "Excuse me, ladies. I see an old friend on the boardwalk. I'm going to speak with him while y'all talk wedding."

Sydney and Hannah watch him leave the dining area and greet his friend with a handshake and man hug. "He's such a nice guy," Sydney says. "Did you ever have any doubts about him?"

"When we first met. But my life was more complicated back then." Hannah shifts her gaze from Ethan to Sydney. "How's it going with your budding romance?"

"Complicated," Sydney says with a smile. "Let's just say, the past came back to haunt us."

"Does this past have anything to do with Happy?" When Sydney's face registers surprise, Hannah explains, "Becca is renting the cottage next to mine. We've become friends, and she confided in me about her situation."

Sydney presses her lips into a thin line. "Who else did she tell?"

"Only Amelia. Because we're concerned about Becca. As you might imagine, she's going through a lot right now."

The server brings Sydney's wine, and she smiles her thanks.

"If it's any consolation, Happy is a well-adjusted, much-loved little girl," Hannah says.

Sydney sips her wine. "I often park across the street from their house in Mount Pleasant, hoping to catch glimpses of her. She's growing up so fast."

"Children do that." Hannah studies her more closely. "She looks a lot like you. She has your pert nose and full lips. Except your eyes are gray and hers are an interesting shade of blue-green. Ice eyes, I would call them."

A faraway look crosses Sydney's face. "She has Jake's eyes."

Hannah presses her. "So, Happy is the past that came back to haunt you?"

"Things were going great," Sydney says while staring down at her wine. "Until he found out I got pregnant and gave his baby up for adoption without telling him."

"I'm sorry. I know how that goes. Gus was three years old before his biological father found out about him."

Sydney's head jerks up. "I didn't know that. Why didn't you tell him?"

"Because he cheated on me, and by the time I discovered I was pregnant, we'd broken up. I didn't want him in our lives." Hannah shrugs. "I was young."

"How did he react when he found out?"

"He was furious at first. But then he wanted us to get back together, to be a family. I tried, but we were all wrong for each other. Ethan entered my life around this time."

"Is that what you meant by *complicated*?"

"Exactly." Hannah thinks back to that confusing time. If Ethan hadn't come along, she might have married Ryan for the wrong reason, so her son could be with his biological father.

"I wanted to tell Jake from the beginning," Sydney says. "But my parents didn't support my decision to keep the baby, and his mom turned against me. Jake had just been offered a football scholarship to Auburn. A wife and baby would've interfered with his future."

"Would you do things differently if you had to do it all over again?"

Sydney takes another sip of wine and slides her glass away. "Honestly, I don't know. I admire you for choosing the difficult path. I took the easy way out by finding someone else to raise her."

"Come on, Sydney. You and I both know the easiest way out is not putting your child up for adoption. You were much younger than me when you got pregnant. I probably would've done the same thing in your shoes."

"In a way, I've been given a chance for a redo. Getting my daughter back is a dream come true for me. But I'm not sure how a nine-year-old fits into my hectic schedule."

"You've built a life for yourself. No one will judge you if you decide not to take her."

"I'll judge me. I won't be able to live with myself."

"Then what's stopping you from taking her back?"

"Fear of failure," Sydney says without hesitation, as though she's given it considerable thought. "I'm not strong like you."

Hannah's chin drops to her chest. "Seriously? You're stronger than you think. You rule the kitchen with an iron fist."

"That's different. I'm not sure I have it in me to be a single parent."

"Give Jake some time to adjust. He'll come around. Even if he doesn't, you won't be alone. You'll have plenty of support. Ethan and I will be around most weekends. Amelia adores Happy. And you can always lean on Birdie. She loves children. She's been my rock these past few years. I never would've survived without her." Hannah thinks about the road ahead for Happy. "An older child will be easier in some ways and more difficult in others. She'll be dealing with the loss of her mother and will need a lot of patience."

"Right. Patience I'm not sure I have." Sydney balls up little pieces of her cocktail napkin. "How will I ever measure up to Becca? She's the quintessential mom."

"Don't view it as a competition. Be yourself. In time, you'll form your own relationship with Happy. You need to meet her. You'll be more comfortable with the idea after you've spent some time with her. I have an idea." Hannah slaps the table near Sydney's arm. "Come for dinner tomorrow night. We'll throw some burgers on the grill. I'll invite Happy and Becca."

Sydney groans. "That would be too awkward."

"Why? Happy doesn't know who you are. But, if you're worried about it, I'll invite Mom and Stan to break the ice."

She sucks in a breath as she rises to her feet. "You're right, Hannah. The time has come for me to meet my daughter. What can I bring?"

"Not a thing. Tomorrow is your day off. Let someone else cook for a change."

"I'll bring dessert."

"Only if you have cobbler leftover from tonight. It was delicious."

"Done." Sydney smiles down at her. "You have a good heart, Hannah. Thank you for doing this."

Hannah's eyes remain on Sydney as she continues on to the other tables. Ever the professional, she forces a smile on her face as she mingles with the patrons. She's worked hard and accomplished a lot for someone so young. She shouldn't have to choose between her career and parenting. Hannah wouldn't want to be in her shoes. Whatever she decides, the road ahead won't be easy.

TWENTY-EIGHT

Sydney stays in bed past noon on Sunday. She rarely sleeps in and never gets up later than ten. But a day without Jake isn't a day worth living. Her heart will always belong to him. She can't decide how Happy fits into her life until she settles things with him. And the only way to do that is to go see him again, to beg him to give her another chance.

After a quick shower, she dresses in a sundress with a skirt that dances provocatively around her slender thighs. Stuffing some clothes in an overnight bag, she brews a coffee for the road and throws open the door. Jake is standing in the hallway with his fist raised, poised to knock.

"Sydney!" He eyes the duffel bag slung over her shoulder. "Are you going somewhere?"

"To Clemson, believe it or not. What're you doing here?"

"I came to apologize. I would've been here sooner, but my mom flew in to see me. She didn't leave until last night."

She grips the handle of her duffel. "What did Patti have to say?"

"She feels terrible about the way she treated you. She's carried this burden around all these years."

"Yeah? Well, she's not the only one who's been carrying a burden." Spinning around, Sydney tosses her bag on the sofa and moves over to the window. "What other words of wisdom did your mom impart?"

"She thinks we belong together. And I agree with her." Sydney senses his presence behind her, feels his breath on her neck. And when he speaks, his voice is near her ear. "What do you think, Sydney?"

She turns to face him, placing a hand on his cheek. "I think I don't wanna live without you."

He kisses the inside of her wrist. "We have a lot to talk about. Wanna grab some sandwiches and go to the beach?"

"I'd like that." She drops her hand from his face. "Let me put on my bathing suit."

He nods. "I'll change out here."

She goes into her room and closes the door. As much as she yearns for his touch, she's grateful he doesn't try to seduce her. She needs a clear head to make decisions about her future.

He calls out to her through the closed door. "Will you wear the blue polka dot bikini? The one you wore on the Fourth of July?"

She hollers back. "Sure! Since it's the only bathing suit I own."

She changes into her bikini, slips on a cover-up, and throws a few beach essentials into a tote. When she emerges from her bedroom, he's dressed and waiting by the door. They walk together to the parking lot.

"Let's take my car," Sydney says. "The beach chairs are already in the back."

"That works. Let me grab my cooler." He removes a soft Yeti cooler from the bed of his truck and stores it in the back with the chairs.

When he folds his tall frame into the passenger seat beside her, she asks, "What's in the cooler?"

He shrugs. "The usual. Some water, a couple of soft drinks, a few beers."

The Sandwich Shack is crowded, and they stand in a long line to place their order. Important issues hang in the air between them, and they say little while they wait. When they reach the beach, they set up their chairs near the surf. Jake digs into his sandwich, but Sydney merely nibbles at hers. When Jake polishes off the last bite of his foot-long sub, he goes after her leftover panini. He gathers up the paper and stuffs the trash back in the bag. Opening a bottled water, he gulps down the whole thing at once. Watching a man of his size eat is something to behold. Sydney wonders what it will be like to keep his appetite satiated.

"So," he says, screwing the cap back on the empty bottle. "Why don't we start from the beginning. I wanna hear what it was like for you, being pregnant and giving up the baby."

Sydney stares out at the ocean as she relives that painful time in her life. "Giving her up was the hardest thing I've ever done. But I had no choice. I had no means of supporting her. Our parents had turned their backs on me. My sister was ready to get me out of her house. You've gotta believe me, Jake. I did what I thought best for our baby."

Jake takes her hand and brings it to his lips. "I believe you, Sydney. And I don't blame you. I was hell-bent on playing football. I can't say for sure I would've given up my scholarship. I admire you for the sacrifices you made. So many girls would've terminated the pregnancy. What happened in the past is over. We need to figure out how to move on."

She eases her hand away from his. "We can't move on until we decide what to do about Happy."

"We need to decide what to do about us first." Jake's gaze lifts to the sky at the sound of an approaching low-flying plane. Shielding his eyes from the sun, he points. "Look! That plane is towing a banner. I can't see what it says. Can you?"

Looking up, she reads out loud as the plane passes in front of

ASHLEY FARLEY

them. "Will. You marry me. Sydney? Wait." She blinks to clear her eyes. "What is this? Did you do this?"

Groups of people gather nearby, staring up at the plane. There's a hum of murmurs as eyes dart about. The question on everyone's lips: *Who is Sydney?*

Jake jumps up, pulls her to her feet, and drops to his knees in front of her. He produces a familiar black velvet box. She's been too distracted these past few days to think about the ring she found in his drawer.

"Having you back in my life is a dream come true for me. I will do everything in my power to make you happy. Will you marry me, Sydney?"

She doesn't hesitate in answering yes. She has no doubts about being his wife and sharing his life.

He gets to his feet. Removing the engagement ring from the box, he places it on her finger. "It's a perfect fit."

She stares down at it as the sun beams rays of color off the diamonds. "It's stunning."

When she stands on her tiptoes to kiss him, the crowd breaks out in cheers. She buries her face in his chest. "This is embarrassing."

"Let's really give them something to talk about." He scoops Sydney up and carries her into the ocean. When he's waist deep, he sets her down and presses his lips to hers in a display of affection that results in more cheers from the onlookers.

"I can't believe we're engaged," she says, admiring her ring.

"Not for long. I aim to make you my wife as soon as possible."

She tears her eyes away from her ring. "How soon?"

"We can decide on the date later. I'm going to haul you off to an all-inclusive wedding destination in Jamaica or some such tropical paradise."

The idea warms her body. She's all for eloping. It's the *as soon*

206

as possible part she has a problem with. But she won't spoil the moment.

He bites her lower lip. "I have a bottle of champagne in the cooler. My plan was to crack it out here. But, considering our audience, I'd rather take it back to your apartment and celebrate in private."

"Let's do it," she says and body surfs out of the water with Jake right behind her.

They gather their belongings, and Sydney speeds back to her apartment, where they spend the afternoon drinking champagne and making love. They finally come up for air around four thirty.

Jake wraps his arms and legs around her. "I love you, Sydney. I want us to be together—now. I'm willing to move to Greenville if necessary. Will you start looking for jobs right away?"

Sydney pulls the covers over them. "You need to be patient, Jake. Finding the right job could take some time. After that, we'll have our whole lives together."

Moving onto his side, he props himself on one elbow. "True."

"There's something more important we need to decide, Jake."

He twirls a lock of her hair around his finger. "There's no decision. We're going to reclaim our child," he says, examining the ends of her hair.

Sydney jerks the lock of hair away from him. "It's not that simple. She's not an infant. She's a nine-year-old girl whose mother is dying. We can't just tear her away from her life, her friends, and the people she cares about."

"I thought this was what you wanted," he says, rolling onto his back.

"I want what's best for all of us." She sits up with her knees tucked beneath her chin. "The natural progression is for people to finish their educations, establish their careers, find their life's partners. And when they're ready, they have children. Taking Happy out of the equation, I wouldn't be ready to have children for at least a few more years. You and I have worked hard to get where we are. We shouldn't have to give up our ambitions. And we shouldn't feel guilty about wanting our share of success."

"I'm not sure I'm following what you're saying."

Sydney lets out a breath and collapses against the pillows. Staring up at the ceiling, she says, "Me either, honestly. I'm still sorting my feelings on the issue. This may sound selfish, but I believe our happiness is as important as Happy's. If we give up our dreams, we could end up resenting her. Let's not get ahead of ourselves. Hannah has invited all of us to dinner tonight. Let's at least meet Happy first."

Jake's eyes sparkle. "Can I come?"

"I think you should. I'll text Hannah. I'm sure she won't mind. But we have to be careful. Happy doesn't know she's adopted."

His face falls. "Oh. I see. This *is* complicated."

"Very. But we'll take it one step at a time. Let's first determine how we might fit into this child's life, and how she might fit into ours."

Sydney understands the risk. She lost her baby once. She's not sure her heart can survive another direct hit. But she has Jake by her side this time around to cushion the blow.

Sydney waits until they are on the way to the cookout—with Jake driving his truck and her sitting beside him with a warm cobbler on her lap—to tell him more. "You should know, other people have offered to adopt Happy."

Jake glances over at her. "What other people?"

"Hannah and Ethan, for starters. Although I can't really see that happening with them living in Charleston. The situation with Amelia is more serious. She's older—in her midfifties—and could never have children of her own. She could provide a stable home. Plus, she's super wealthy."

"So, we have some competition," Jake says, his facial muscles tight. He's always been competitive. But Sydney reads something more in his determined expression. Although he hasn't yet met her, his child is important to him.

"I don't view this as a contest," she says. "Although, I admit, I feel like I'm going to a job interview. What if Happy doesn't like us?"

Jake reaches for her hand, fingering her engagement ring. "What's not to love? I'm charming and good-looking, and you're beautiful and talented."

Sydney cuts her eyes at him. "Be serious, Jake."

"Okay." He drops her hand and returns his to the steering wheel. "The truth is, I doubt Happy pays us any attention, since she doesn't know who we are."

"Unless . . ." Sydney bites on a fingernail. "Do you think she might sense the connection?"

Jake shakes his head. "How can she when she doesn't know she was adopted?"

But when Hannah introduces them a few minutes later, Happy tilts her head one way and another as she studies Jake's eyes. They are the same unique shade of blue-green as hers. Ice eyes, as Hannah called them.

The buzzing of her phone breaks Happy's fixation, and she lowers her gaze to read the text.

When Becca comes over from next door, Happy says, "Mom, my friends are down on the beach. Can I go hang out with them?"

Becca looks from her daughter to the empty beach and back. "I don't see them. How do you know they're on the beach?"

Happy waves her phone at Becca. "They texted me. They're hidden behind the sand dunes. But they're out in front of our house."

"I thought we agreed your phone was only to be used in an emergency."

Happy stomps her foot. "Mo-om. They texted me. I didn't text them."

"All right, fine. But don't go far. I'll text you when dinner is ready."

"I thought the phone was only for emergencies," Happy says in a sassy voice.

"Go!" Becca says, shooing her daughter on.

All eyes are on the child as she disappears into the sand dunes.

"She's a beach girl at heart," Hannah says.

Becca nudges Hannah. "Takes one to know one."

Sydney swallows down the lump in her throat. "She's amazing." Her daughter, her own flesh and blood.

"She has good genes," Becca says in a soft voice.

Sydney looks at Becca in surprise. "What a lovely thing to say."

When Becca turns to Jake, her breath hitches. "Your eyes! You're Happy's biological father." Her gaze shifts back to Sydney. "So, you lied to me. You knew who the father is."

"I'm . . . um . . . we . . ."

Jake comes to her rescue. "We'd broken up at the time. I didn't know she was pregnant."

"But you're together now?" Becca says.

Sydney is aware of Hannah hovering nearby, waiting for the answer. "We haven't seen each other since high school. We reconnected a few weeks ago. I know it seems fast, but we got engaged this afternoon." She flashes her ring.

Jake pulls Sydney in for a half hug. "I'm not letting her get away again," he says, and everyone laughs.

Hannah moves in to inspect the ring. "Congratulations! I'm so excited for you. I knew you two would work things out."

Ethan appears with a tray of drinks. "What're we celebrating?"

"Jake and Sydney got engaged this afternoon." Hannah passes

out the drinks and holds hers up for a toast. "To Jake and Sydney."

Sydney clinks glasses and takes a sip. "This is delicious. What is it?"

Ethan beams. "Cucumber vodka mixed with soda, muddled cucumber, and a squeeze of lime."

Sydney licks her lips. "Hannah, we may have the signature drink for your wedding."

Hannah smiles. "I approve. But tonight is about you. Tell us, how did Jake propose?"

Everyone listens spellbound as Sydney recounts the story of the personalized sky banner.

"Isn't that romantic?" Hannah says with a love-struck expression.

Ethan appears wounded. "Hey, don't I get some credit? I gave you a beach cottage when I asked you to marry me."

"Yes, you did." Hannah plants a kiss on his cheek. "And I love my cottage."

"When's the big day?" Ethan asks.

"Soon!" Jake says.

Sydney casts him a warning look. "We've only been engaged a few hours. We have much to decide."

Ethan takes Hannah by the hand. "Come with me to the kitchen. Let's give these three a chance to talk."

After they're gone, Jake says, "Let's sit down," and guides Becca and Sydney over to the rockers on the porch.

A few minutes of awkward silence pass before Becca blurts, "I assume your engagement means you've decided about taking Happy back?"

Sydney shakes her head. "Not necessarily. This is all very sudden, and we have a lot to sort out."

"There's no hurry. I'm selling my house in Mount Pleasant, and I've extended my lease on the cottage next door. Happy and I will live there until . . ." Becca's voice trails off. She doesn't need to finish her sentence. Everyone understands what *until* means.

Jake clears his throat. "I understand Happy doesn't know she's adopted."

Becca nods. "My ex-husband was opposed to telling her, and I went along with him. I always considered Happy *my* child, regardless of her DNA. I figured I'd tell her one day, when the time was right. I think maybe that time has come."

"Will you tell her about us?" Sydney asks.

"With your approval. Under the circles . . ." Becca scrunches her face as she struggles to get the word out. "Circumstances, we should all be on the same page. I don't trust my failing mind, and I don't want there to be any secrets. The more I think about it, the more I think it's best to let the situation play itself out. My daughter's happiness is the most important thing to me. She's growing more mature by the day. We should consider her input when deciding her future."

"I totally agree," Sydney says. Some of the tension she's been carrying around for days fades away. She's not alone in this decision. Others are involved. Most importantly, Happy will be involved. She won't be forced to live with Sydney and Jake against her will.

TWENTY-NINE

An exhausted Becca is content to let Happy read the last chapter of *To Kill a Mockingbird*. When she finishes reading, Becca closes the book and turns out the light. Soft moonlight fills the room, and the overhead fan blows cool air on their bodies.

"Admit it," Becca says. "You enjoyed the novel."

"Better than I thought I would," Happy says. "Can we go back to Harry Potter now?"

"I guess. But first tell me what you learned from Scout?"

Happy giggles. "That I don't have to wear dresses if I don't want to. And it's okay to beat up boys. Except I would never beat up Gus. He's a cool kid. I wish he was my little brother."

Happy has always wished for a sibling. Becca could never give her one. But now, if she goes to live with Sydney and Jake, she might one day get that little brother or sister. "Be serious for a minute, sweetheart. Did you learn anything important from Scout?"

Happy pauses a beat before answering. "That it's okay for me to be different." She rolls onto her side. "Why am I different from you, Mama?"

Becca's heart races. "What'd you mean?"

"Your hair is brown. Mine is blonde. Your eyes are hazel. Mine are light. Hannah calls them ice eyes. I've never seen anyone with eyes like mine until tonight. Until I met Jake."

Fear renders Becca speechless, but Happy doesn't seem to notice.\

She talks on. "And Sydney holds her fork the same as me, between my second and third fingers like you're always telling me not to. Am I related to Sydney and Jake?"

Becca inhales a deep breath. She's not ready for this conversation. But she can't pass up the opportunity. "Yes, honey. Do you know what it means to be adopted?"

"A girl at my old school was adopted. Her real parents gave her away when she was born."

Rolling onto her side, Becca props herself on one elbow. "There's way more to it than that. Sometimes women aren't able to care for their babies. Sometimes they're too young. And sometimes they're financially unstable. On the other hand, there are lots of women who desperately want to have a baby and can't."

"Why not?"

Becca fingers a strand of blonde hair out of Happy's face. "Because the parts of their bodies that make babies don't work the way they're supposed to. This happens more than you would think. And it happened to me. My body couldn't make a baby, and Sydney's body made one when she was too young to care for it. She gave her baby to me to raise in a process that is called adapt . . ." Of all the times for her words to fail her. She tries again. "Adoption."

A single tear rolls down Happy's cheek. "So, you're not my mama."

"I am totally your mama. You were one day old when you came to live with us. We went to court and the judge legally made you my child."

"Our first night here, we went to Shaggy's for dinner, and you stopped in the park afterward, while we ate our ice cream cones. You said you weren't looking at the woman in the white coat, the one I thought was a cook. But I know now that it was Sydney you were watching. Is that why we came to Palmetto Island this summer? Are you planning to give me back to her?"

Wrapping an arm around her daughter, Becca holds her daughter close. "This may be hard for you to understand, but I feel obligated to let Sydney know what's going on. Sydney's life has changed since she gave birth to you. She has a career, and she can take care of you. But only if that's what you want."

With a quivering lower lip, Happy says, "I want to live with Amelia."

"And that's a fine option, as well. But you've only just met Sydney and Jake. You should at least get to know them before you decide. We're not in a hurry. I'm not going anywhere anytime soon."

"You don't know that for sure." Happy tries to push away, but Becca holds her tight.

"None of us knows for sure what tomorrow will bring." Becca kisses the tip of Happy's pert nose. "You have another thing in common with Scout."

"What?"

"You're too smart for your own good."

"No, I'm not," she says in a huffy tone. "I'm not like Scout. I wish things could go back to the way they were. Before Daddy left."

"Is that what you really want? I thought you loved Palmetto Island. What about all the new friends you've made down here?"

Happy doesn't answer. After a long minute, in a soft voice, she says, "I don't wanna talk anymore, Mama. Please leave."

Sliding out of bed, she kisses her daughter's forehead and tucks the covers tight around her small body. "Call me if you need me."

An hour later, as Becca lies awake in her own bed worrying

about her daughter's future, she hears Happy sobbing in the next room. She longs to go to her, to comfort her and tell her everything's going to be fine. But everything won't be fine. And pandering to her will do more harm than good. Her daughter must take ownership of her life. That's asking a lot of a nine-year-old child. But she has faith in Happy. Learning to cope with life's challenges early on will make her stronger in the long run.

As the days and weeks roll on, Becca senses Happy pulling away from her. As difficult as it is for Becca to experience, her daughter is doing exactly what she hoped. Happy is embracing her new reality. And Becca is proud of her. Happy is growing stronger. And maturing. She no longer complains about doing her chores and takes on more responsibility without being asked.

Overnight, Happy has become the most popular girl on the island, receiving invitations from all ages. Long days spent on the beach with her friends often extend into the evenings with cook-outs and movie nights at one of their homes. On weekends, Sydney and Jake take her on water-related excursions during the day—sailing and wave runner rides and tubing—and out to dinner at night. While Happy says little about her time with them, she always returns home in a good mood. But her daughter craves Amelia's company the most. Happy jumps at every opportunity to run errands with her, and they often go for bike rides or walks on the beach together in the late afternoons. As much as it pains her to watch another woman taking her place in her daughter's life, Becca is grateful Happy has found someone she looks up to and can trust.

Amelia insinuates herself into every aspect of their lives. But Becca no longer resents of the intrusion. She lets her guard down and embraces Amelia's support. And she finds Amelia's presence comforting. Amelia intuitively knows when Becca needs companionship and when she prefers to be left alone.

Once she accepts Amelia into her life, Becca discovers that she admires her a great deal. Amelia makes friends with everyone she meets by flashing her winning smile and turning up her southern charm. She has a way of getting people to do her bidding without them realizing they've been manipulated. In preparation for Becca's appointment at MUSC, Amelia researches medications for Alzheimer's patients. Certain there are better choices for Becca, Amelia convinces her team of doctors to experiment with her prescriptions. Almost immediately, Becca feels more like herself.

Amelia orchestrates the moving of furniture from Becca's house in Mount Pleasant to the mini-warehouse they rented on Palmetto Island. They bring two carloads of Becca's and Happy's clothes and other personal belongings to the cottage, items that make her feel more at home like her fake fur throw blankets, goose down pillows, and small library of cherished novels.

Becca's Realtor puts her Mount Pleasant home on the market on Wednesday of the third week of July. The Realtor calls Becca on Friday afternoon with the news that she's received four strong offers.

Becca, who has just woken up from her nap, emerges from her bedroom in search of Amelia. She finds Amelia and Happy together in the daybed swing, deep in conversation with their heads close together.

They don't hear Becca approach, and they both appear startled when she looms over them. "What're you two talking about?" Becca asks.

"Oh, you know . . . just the birds and the bees," Amelia says in an offhanded manner.

Happy scrambles out of the swing. "I was waiting for you to get up from your nap. Is it okay if I ride my bike to Celeste's house now?"

Becca smiles at her daughter. "As long as you text me when you get there."

"I will!" Happy says and skips off toward the beach.

Amelia throws her legs over the side of the swing and gets to her feet. "Did you have a nice nap?"

"I did. Thanks." Becca shields her eyes from the sun as she watches her daughter disappear down the beach on her bike. "What were y'all really talking about just now?"

Amelia smiles. "I wasn't kidding. We were talking about the birds and the bees. Happy caught me off guard. She was confused about a number of things, primarily how a woman has a baby when she's not married. She didn't mention any names, but I got the impression she was referring to Sydney. We had a long talk about love and respect. I hope I didn't overstep any boundaries."

Becca can't help but feel jealous of Amelia. Teaching her daughter about the birds and the bees is her job. But she's able to hide her feelings. "Not at all. You can't control when these teachable moments occur. And you have to take advantage of the opportunity while children are in the mood to listen. I'm glad she feels comfortable talking to you about such important matters."

Amelia's brow knits. "I hope I said the right thing."

"In my experience, if it comes from the heart, it's the right thing."

Amelia considers this a minute. "That's good advice. I'll have to remember that."

"On another note, I just got a call from the Realtor. She has four offers on the house. She's emailing them over to me. Will you help me sort them?"

"Of course. How exciting. Where's your laptop? I'll go grab it."

"I'm not sure. Check the kitchen." Becca sits down at the picnic table to wait. Amelia is gone for some time, and Becca is getting worried about her when she finally returns. "What took you so long?"

"I had trouble finding your laptop. It was in the refrigerator."

A week ago, this would've embarrassed Becca, but today she bursts into laughter. Amelia joins in, and the two women laugh until tears stream down their faces.

When they finally collect themselves, Becca says, "I don't know what I'd do without you, Amelia. How can I ever repay you for all you've done for me?"

"You're sharing your daughter with me. That is repayment enough."

"What about . . . um . . ." Becca scrunches up her face. "Your boyfriend? What's his name?"

"Jonathan."

"Yes. Sorry. Have you heard anything from Jonathan?"

Amelia stares down at her hands. "I see him when he comes to work on his boat. He waves, but he never stops to chat. I consider myself a good judge of character. But I was really wrong about him."

"Not necessarily, Amelia. Jonathan knows what's involved in raising children. His children are grown. He's looking forward to retirement. And I don't blame him. You should talk to him again before you move forward with the adoption. He can make you understand what you're getting yourself into."

"He'll give me a lecture about sacrifices and commitment. And I don't need that. I adore Happy, and that's enough for me. Helping you has given my life the kind of purpose I've been yearning for. The three of us—you, Happy, and me—are becoming a family. No way am I turning my back on you now."

"Just talk to him," Becca says in a pleading tone. She hates that she's come between Amelia and Jonathan. He's a good man. Happy needs a father as much as Amelia needs the man she loves by her side.

Amelia pats her hand. "If it'll ease your mind. But it won't change the way I feel about the situation."

THIRTY

After interviewing candidates with varying degrees of experience, Birdie takes a risk by hiring two young women fresh out of cooking school in Atlanta. Louise and Jana are talented and ambitious, and Sydney has no doubt that they'll work well together. Due to their lack of experience, Birdie asks Sydney to stay on through the holiday season to train them. Birdie has been good to her. She can hardly say no. Sydney video interviews with a handful of restaurants in Greenville. One intrigues her more than the others. And the timing is ideal, as the current head chef won't retire until the end of the year.

Watching Jake fall head over heels in love with their daughter tugs at Sydney's heartstrings. She cautions Jake not to get his hopes up. She remains unconvinced that taking Happy back is the best solution for any of them. Her gut instincts tell her Happy is better off living on Palmetto Island. Like Hannah said, *She's a beach girl at heart.* Despite her mother's illness, the child is thriving in her new environment. Happy is already losing so much. How could they ask her to leave the place that makes her happy?

When it comes to her own feelings, Sydney is proceeding

with caution. She loves her child. She's always loved her. But she gave Happy up once. She's protecting her heart in case she must give her up again.

"We'll have other children that we'll love just as much as we love Happy," she reminds Jake on the phone late one night.

"I don't get it, Syd. Why are you giving up on Happy?"

"Because I want what's best for her. That's all I've ever wanted. I've loved her from afar for nine years, Jake. She's grown up right before my eyes. I've watched someone else mother her. Pushing her in a stroller. Helping her in and out of her car seat. Teaching her how to ride a bicycle. There were days my heart ached so much I thought it would shatter into tiny pieces. But never once did I regret my decision. Because Becca was in a better position to take care of her, and she was doing a fine job of being her mother."

"Well, now she's not in a better position to take care of her. Becca has a debilitating disease, which puts our child's safety at risk. Anything could happen. Becca could forget to pick her up from the movies one night. Or drive her into an unsafe part of town and get her killed."

"Puh-lease. You're being melodramatic. Happy isn't in danger. She's surrounded by people who love her. Besides, there aren't any unsafe areas on the island."

"We have the opportunity to get her back, Syd. And I, for one, am going to fight for her."

"Becca isn't dead yet, Jake. God willing, she isn't going anywhere anytime soon. Meanwhile, I'm interviewing for jobs in Greenville, and you're on the coaching staff for one of the top football teams in the NCAA. We have some serious logistical challenges. Amelia has offered to take care of Becca as long as possible. This sounds selfish as hell, but I'm not willing to turn my life upside down to take care of a woman with Alzheimer's disease. Are you?"

"Maybe," he says, but his defeated tone suggests otherwise.

"We're both tired. Let's talk more about this tomorrow." Sydney ends the call, but she can't sleep from thinking about their conversation. At what lengths is Jake willing to go to in order to get his daughter back?

She doesn't have to wait long to find out. Two nights later, on Thursday evening during the third week of July, she's going over the night's specials with her waitstaff when Jake shows up out of the blue.

She drags him into the coatroom, away from the noise of the kitchen. "What're you doing here? Why didn't you tell me you were coming?"

"I wanted to surprise you. I'm interviewing for head football coach at Palmetto High tomorrow morning."

Sydney shakes her head. "I think you're making a mistake. But whatever."

"This is something I've gotta do, Sydney."

"Wait, a second. Football season starts next month. Why is this position just becoming available?"

"Sadly, Coach Ridman, who has been there for thirty years, was just diagnosed with pancreatic cancer. He's taking early retirement."

"Oh. I'm sorry to hear that."

"I hope you don't mind me crashing with you," Jake says.

"Ha ha. No. Let me get my keys." She goes to the office and returns with her keys. "I'll see you when I get off."

But he's sound asleep when she arrives home, and she decides not to wake him. He needs to rest up for his interview. If he takes this job, they can stay on the island, and Happy will come to live with them.

Sydney tries not to get her hopes up. And she's not surprised when Jake returns from his interview wearing a dejected expression.

"I can't do it, Syd. High school football isn't for me." He

plops down on her sofa. "I wanted it to work out, so you could keep your job, and Happy could grow up at the beach."

She sits down beside him. "In order to be successful, we need to be passionate about our work. I refuse to settle for second best. And you shouldn't either. Let's figure out our lives, and if Happy comes to live with us down the road, we'll help her adjust."

He rakes his fingers through his thick hair. "Maybe I should find a more stable career. I could go back to school. Maybe law school."

She elbows him in the side. "Are you joking? Football is your life. You've only been coaching a few years. Give it a little longer."

"In order for me to move up the ladder, I'll have to jump from team to team. That means moving from city to city."

"I expected as much. We'll be fine as long as we're together."

He pulls her to him. "Speaking of which . . . The team has a bye the third week in September. What say we elope? I've been researching wedding destinations. We could go to Aruba or St. Lucia or the Cayman Islands."

"Any of those sound heavenly to me. Are we inviting our families?"

He walks his fingers up her arm. "I was hoping to keep it small. As in two, you and me."

"I love it." She pulls him down for a kiss. "Now that you're here, can you stay the weekend?"

He kisses her back, his lips soft and moist against hers. "As long as you promise to make it worth my while."

"You'll have to entertain yourself while I'm at work the next two nights."

"I'll catch up with Ethan and Hannah."

She cuts her eyes at him. "Mm-hmm. I know you. You're hoping to run into Happy."

He flashes her a guilty grin. "Maybe."

"Hannah's invited some friends over for drinks to meet Ethan's parents on Sunday night. I'm sure you'll see Happy then."

"Yes!" Jake punches the air. "Maybe we can take her to lunch or for ice cream sometime over the weekend."

"Maybe." Sydney glances at the clock on the stove. "I have awhile before I have to be at work. We can either spend it in bed or we can book our wedding."

He stretches out on the sofa, pulling her on top of him. "How about a quickie, and then we book our wedding?"

Her phone vibrates in her pocket with an incoming call. "Sorry. This might be work." She digs the phone out of her pocket. "I don't recognize the number. It's the same area code as yours."

"That's probably my friend, Barry Boone. I forgot to tell you. I gave him your number. He's calling you about a job. You should talk to him. He has an interesting proposition."

She pushes herself up as she accepts the call. "Sydney Olson."

"Sydney, my name is Barry Boone. Jake gave me your number. I hope you don't mind me calling you."

"Not at all." Feeling Jake's eyes on her, Sydney steps out to the balcony for privacy.

"I understand you're moving to the area, and I have a business proposition for you. I own a fast casual salad restaurant in Greenville called Bowls. We serve only the freshest ingredients. We've done so well here I'm opening another location in Clemson. I'm looking for someone with your background to help me develop a franchise program. If you're interested, I'd like to set up a time for a video conference next week."

She pauses a beat as she considers her response. "I'll be honest. This isn't exactly what I had in mind, but I'm intrigued enough to have a conversation."

"Wonderful. How does Wednesday morning at eleven sound?"

"I can make that work." They discuss the logistics of the video conference before hanging up.

She remains at the railing, staring out across the marsh.

While she'll miss this view, she's willing to sacrifice living on the water in order to be with Jake. But there are some things she refuses to give up. She just lectured Jake about not settling for second best. Yet here she is considering a job with normal hours that would allow her to be at home with Happy in the evenings. There's no harm in learning more about it. Who knows? The job might provide a unique set of challenges that interest her. She'll keep an open mind and trust in God that everything will work out as it's meant to be.

THIRTY-ONE

Hannah and Ethan are busy in the kitchen—she's slicing avocados for the guacamole, and he's mixing a pitcher of margaritas—when his parents arrive twenty minutes early for the party.

Clara presses her cheek to Hannah's. "I hope you don't mind us coming early. We have something important we want to talk to you about before the other guests arrive."

Hannah surveys the trays of heavy hors d'oeuvres spread out on the counter. She was already running behind. Now the food won't be ready when the party starts.

Clara wanders into the living room. "The cottage is charming. Can we have a tour first?"

Hugh gives Hannah a hug. "I'm sorry," he whispers in her ear. "I wanted to call, to tell you we were on the way, but she insisted we surprise you."

Hannah softens. She adores her future father-in-law. He's a true southern gentleman. "It's fine. Really."

"Want me to show them around?" Ethan asks as he fills glasses with the margarita mixture.

"No. I'll do it. You finish that."

The tour of the small cottage takes less than five minutes. When they return to the living room, Ethan hands his parents a margarita. "What did you want to talk to us about?"

Clara sets her drink on the coffee table and folds her hands in her lap. "We've decided to give you the house on Legare Street. We've been traveling so much and spending more time on Sullivan's Island, we figured it was time to downsize."

"Wow," Ethan says. "I knew I'd get the house one day. But I wasn't expecting it so soon."

Clara angles her body toward her son. "If you approve, we'd like to move into your condo. That way we have a place to rest our heads when we're in town for parties and other events."

"That makes sense." Ethan looks around his mother at Hannah. "What do you think?"

"I think it's incredibly generous. Your home is lovely. Gus will be a lucky little boy to have such a wonderful yard to play in. But what about all your furniture?" she says about their collection of priceless antiques that are not Hannah's taste.

"We'll take what we can use to the condo and sell whatever you don't want." Clara pats Hannah's arm. "Decorate the house to your liking, dear. We expect you to make changes. You won't hurt our feelings."

"The idea of decorating a house like that intimidates me," Hannah says.

"Hire an interior designer," Clara says. "I can give you the names of several to interview. They are expert at executing your vision."

"They're also expert at spending your money," Hugh says with a snicker.

"Don't worry, honey," Ethan says. "We'll figure it out."

The front door bangs open and the other party guests file in. Sydney and Jake followed by Max, Davis, Birdie, and Stan. Amelia brings up the rear. After Ethan introduces his parents, the crowd erupts into chatter.

Jake makes his way over to Hannah. "Is Happy here?"

Hannah smiles. "She's out on the swing with Gus."

"Awesome," Jake says and makes a beeline to the backyard.

On the other side of her, Amelia leans in close. "Where's Becca?"

"She stayed home. She's not feeling well."

Amelia narrows her eyes. "Maybe I should go over and check on her."

"I think she's probably fine. She was going to heat up some of Sydney's homemade tomato bisque and go to bed early."

"All right. I'll wait a bit."

Hannah claps loudly to get her guests' attention. "Please, everyone, make yourselves at home. I'll have some food out momentarily."

She returns to making guacamole in the kitchen. "What can I do to help?" Ethan asks when he joins her a few minutes later.

"Get the shrimp and bowl of pimento cheese out of the fridge." She points her knife at a tray of pita chips. "The pimento cheese goes on that tray."

He opens the refrigerator, removes the items, and comes to stand beside her at the counter. "Are you happy about the house?"

She smiles over at him. "Are you kidding? I'm thrilled. Did you know about this?"

"I told my parents we were considering adopting Happy and might be looking to buy a house. I guess they figured the timing was right now to give me the house." Ethan's face falls. "Looks like we're out of the running to be Happy's parents. Jake is crazy about that kid."

"Sydney too. Although she's more concerned about doing what's best for Happy. I honestly think Becca and Happy would be better off with Amelia. At least, for the time being."

"You're probably right."

Hannah and Ethan make several trips, transferring the trays of food from the kitchen to the porch table, which she has covered in a pink gingham cloth and adorned with an arrangement of pink hydrangeas from her yard.

In their absence, the group has separated. The women are gathered on the porch and the men are standing in a circle on the lawn. With the exception of Jake, who is still in the swing with the kids.

Hannah senses tension when she joins the group of women. Leaning into Sydney, she says, "What's going on?"

"Your future mother-in-law and I were just discussing the rehearsal dinner. She has in mind to change venues." Sydney wears a smile on her face, but her tone carries a hint of annoyance. "Clara, have you told Hannah your idea yet?"

"Not yet." Clara gives Sydney a hard smile before turning her attention to Hannah. "Wait until you see our rental house. The place is fabulous. We have enough bedrooms to comfortably sleep twenty. And the grounds are spectacular. I was suggesting to our wonderful event planner that having the rehearsal dinner in the garden would be glorious."

Sydney says, "And I was explaining to Clara that we'd never find rentals at this late date."

Hannah checks her weather app. She's tracking it closely, now that the wedding date is within the ten-day forecast. "Even if we could, the extended forecast is calling for strong storms on Saturday night."

"We may have to serve dinner inside the cafe as it is," Birdie says.

"That's dreadful," Clara says. "I wasn't aware of the potential for foul weather."

"The good news is, Sunday looks beautiful for the wedding," Hannah says.

"And cooler," Max adds. "This week is supposed to be miserably hot."

"In that case, we'll leave well enough alone." Clara places three steamed shrimp on a clear plastic plate and adds a dollop of cocktail sauce. "Hannah dear, Hugh and I have been looking forward to meeting your father. Will he be joining us tonight?"

Hannah's been dreading this conversation. She opens her mouth to explain about her estrangement from her father when Cary emerges from the living room. "Did someone mention my name?"

Hannah's eyes meet Birdie's. "What's he doing here?" Hannah mouths and Birdie shrugs.

Clara sets down her plate and extends her hand. "At long last. I'm Clara Hayes. Thrilled to finally meet you."

"Charmed." Cary kisses the back of Clara's hand in a gesture that makes Hannah want to puke. "I'm Cary Fuller, father of the bride."

Hannah glares at him. "Dad, I need a word with you in private."

He objects. "But—"

"Now." Grabbing his upper arm, she marches him across the porch.

Birdie is on their heels. When the three of them are alone in the living room, she says, "Cary, what on earth are you doing here?"

He looks back and forth between Birdie and Hannah, his gaze finally landing on Hannah. "I didn't know you were having a party. Thanks for the invitation, by the way. I stopped by to tell you the good news."

Hannah's stomach sours. "What good news?"

"I'm going to be in town for the wedding after all."

"What happened to your Mediterranean cruise?" Birdie asks.

"Violet and I broke up. I'll be able to walk Hannah down the aisle after all."

"Sorry, but that job's taken," Hannah says. "Mom is walking me down the aisle. You're not invited to the wedding. Like you weren't invited tonight. Now, please leave."

"Hannah, don't be like this," Cary says in a pleading tone.

Hannah's so angry, she worries her head might explode. "Like what, Dad? I forgave you once for walking out on us, for letting me believe you were dead. But you chose to go on a cruise with your girlfriend over coming to my wedding. I will never forgive you for that." Her arm shoots out with a finger pointed at the door. "Leave. And don't come back."

"But . . ." He steps toward her, and she jumps back.

Her face set in stone, Hannah snarls, "Get out of my house. I have company and you are not welcome here."

Her father hangs his head. "I'm sorry, Hannah."

"Too late for apologies." Hannah strides across the room and swings open the paned door. "Out." She holds the door open until he leaves, and then closes and locks it behind him.

Her body trembling with anger, Hannah leans against the door taking deep unsteady breaths.

"I'm so sorry, honey." When Birdie moves to touch her, Hannah smacks her hand away.

"Mom, please. I need a minute alone to collect myself."

"I understand," Birdie says and reluctantly leaves Hannah standing by the door.

Turning her back to the living room, Hannah watches her father's car pull away from the cottage. Things will never be the same between them again. But he brought it on himself.

After a few minutes, when Hannah feels more like herself, she rejoins the party. The women have moved from the porch to the yard and are now mingling with the men. She pulls Clara and Hugh aside. "I should have explained about my father a long time ago. The two of you are such loving and supportive parents, and he's . . . well, he's a jerk. Dad and I were close when I was growing up. But he was a different person back then. On New Year's Day of my senior year in college, he cleaned out my parents' bank accounts and ran off to Maui with another woman."

Clara gasps, and Hugh says, "How awful for you and your mother."

Hannah nods. "Dad came back to Palmetto Island three years later, and I forgave him, hoping we could salvage our relationship. But things between us were never the same. The final straw was when he decided to go on a Mediterranean cruise with his current girlfriend instead of coming to my wedding. Apparently, he broke up with that girlfriend and wants to walk me down the aisle."

"What did you tell him?" Clara asks.

"That Mom is giving me away, and I kicked him out of the house."

"Good for you," Hugh says.

Hannah stares down at the ground. "I'm sorry to dump all this on you. I thought you should know since we're going to be family."

Hugh puts an arm around her shoulders. "You deserve better, my dear. You're a wonderful girl, and you'll make a fine wife for my son. If you'll let me, I'd like to be your surrogate father. Ethan will tell you I'm full of fatherly advice."

Hannah smiles at him. "That means a lot. Thank you."

The moment is interrupted when Becca bursts out of the cottage next door screaming, "Help! Fire!"

Everyone springs into action at once. Happy, Jake, and Amelia hurry across the yard to Becca. Gus runs to Hannah's side, wrapping his arms around her legs. Ethan darts into the house for their fire extinguisher, and Birdie calls the fire department.

Seconds later, Ethan exits the house with the fire extinguisher. "Don't go in there, son," Hugh calls after him. "Wait for the fire department."

"Don't worry," Ethan yells back. "I'll be careful."

The crowd moves to the edge of the lawn to watch the scene

unfold. Jake and Ethan enter Becca's cottage, and they're still inside when the fire trucks arrive with sirens blaring.

The guests murmur amongst themselves, speculating as to the source of the fire. Huddling together, Sydney chews on a fingernail and Hannah placates a scared Gus. In the yard next door, a hysterical Happy clings to Becca, who is also crying, while Amelia tries to calm them both down. Relief washes over Hannah when Ethan and Jake emerge from the cottage. Jake, wearing an angry scowl, strides ahead of Ethan toward them.

"I'm done with this situation," Jake says to Sydney. "We're taking Happy home with us tonight."

"Good luck prying her off of Becca," Sydney says.

"What happened?" Hannah asks Ethan.

"Becca was heating something on the stove and fell asleep," Ethan says. "Whatever was in the pot burned and smoke set off the fire alarm. There were no flames and no damage. Just a lot of smoke."

"This is all my fault," Hannah says. "Amelia wanted to go check on Becca earlier. I told her she was fine."

Ethan pulls her close. "This is not your fault. You had no way of knowing."

"It could've been a lot worse," Jake says. "Happy could've been in the house. There could've been a real fire."

"I know you're worried," Hannah says, her fingers grazing Jake's arm. "But they're in excellent hands with Amelia. She knows how to handle the situation. And Becca trusts Amelia."

Jake snaps at Hannah, "Becca is not the one I'm worried about."

Sydney looks apologetically at Hannah. "I agree with Hannah. We need to let Amelia handle it." She puts an arm around Jake's waist. "Let's go home. You have to leave at the crack of dawn to get back to Clemson for work."

Jake mumbles a grumpy *thank you for the party* as they turn their backs on Happy and walk toward the house.

"Jake's got it bad for that little girl," Ethan says, his eyes on Happy. "He was furious when we were inside that house."

"I can well imagine how confused he must be having just found out about her and now all this," Hannah says, gesturing at Happy and Becca.

Hannah's heart breaks at the sight of the weeping mother and daughter. This incident will change everything. She knew something like this was bound to happen, but she hoped Becca and Happy would have more time together in the cottage. They can't wait any longer. The decision regarding Happy's future will have to be made immediately. While she believes Happy and Becca are better off living with Amelia, she has a sinking feeling Jake won't readily agree to the arrangement.

THIRTY-TWO

Amelia is grateful when the firefighters restrict entry to the cottage for twenty-four hours. Becca and Happy are in no condition to be left alone tonight. Becca is a zombie, barely able to string two words together, and Happy is inconsolable. She takes them home with her to Point Pleasant where she finds suitable clothing for them to sleep in and tucks them into bed in her guest room.

Amelia sleeps little that night as the reality of what she's getting herself into hits home. She yearns to call Jonathan, desperately needing to hear him say everything will be okay. But everything won't be okay. Not for this woman and her little girl.

Breakfast the next morning is a dismal affair despite the smorgasbord of food Bebe prepares. Becca is distraught, confused about why she's at Point Pleasant and claiming to remember nothing about the fire. And Happy can't stop crying long enough to eat her pancakes. When Amelia can't take it anymore, she excuses herself from the table and goes to her study to call Martie.

After explaining the situation, Amelia asks, "Is it possible for a nine-year-old to have a nervous breakdown?"

"She's dealing with a lot," Martie says. "And she's too young to understand how to process her emotions. I have some free time before my first appointment. Do you want me to try talking to her?"

"I think it might help."

"I'll be there shortly," Martie says.

When Martie arrives twenty minutes later, Amelia and Happy have moved to the porch rockers and Bebe has taken Becca upstairs to Amelia's closet to find something suitable to wear.

Amelia turns her rocker over to the therapist, and Martie introduces herself to Happy. "My job is to help people sort through their feelings when they have problems they can't handle. I work with a lot of kids your age, Happy. I believe I can help you if you'll let me."

Happy stares blankly at Martie without responding. While the child is no longer crying, Amelia can tell new tears are not far away.

"Would you like to go for a walk on the beach?" Martie suggests, and Happy nods.

The two have no sooner disappeared over the sand dunes when Sydney comes around the side of the house. "I rang the doorbell, but no one answered. Where's Happy? I need to see her."

"She's not here at the moment."

"Where is she? This has gone too far, Amelia. Jake is really upset. He's threatening to sue for custody."

Amelia stares her down. "Everyone's upset, Sydney. Happy is an emotional basket case. She's down on the beach, talking to my therapist as we speak. I don't see how taking her away from her mother is going to help."

Sydney's demeanor softens as her gaze shifts to the ocean. "Poor kid. She must be so confused. I don't want to make things worse for her, but after what happened last night, Jake and I are concerned for her safety."

"As are we all," Amelia says. "Last night could've been a lot worse. Becca and Happy will move in here with me as we originally planned. I'll bring in caregivers on a limited basis to start with and adjust the schedule as needed."

"As *you* originally planned," Sydney says. "Jake and I have not agreed to that. He had to leave town, but he's coming back on Friday. We want to talk to Happy then, before anything definite is decided."

Irritation crawls across Amelia's skin. "Of course. You're within your rights as Happy's biological parents. Call when he's back in town and we'll set up a time. As you know, I'm hosting Hannah's wedding here on Sunday. The weekend will be busy. Now." She sweeps her arm in the direction Sydney came. "If you don't mind seeing yourself off."

Sydney spins around and storms off.

Amelia drops to the chair. Would it be so bad for Happy to live with Jake and Sydney? For Becca to go to the memory care facility? Amelia will rekindle her relationship with Jonathan, and they'll live happily ever after. Except Amelia won't be happy. Not without that little girl in her life. Damn Jonathan for making her choose.

Amelia remains on the porch, racking her brain for a better solution to the situation. Thirty minutes later, she spots the top of Happy's golden head as she makes her way up from the beach. When she comes into view, Happy is wearing a smile, and the kick in her step has returned.

"I'm gonna check on Mama," Happy says to Amelia on her way inside.

"Okay, sweetheart."

Martie sits down beside her. "That went well. She's a great kid. She's very mature for her age. She just needs reassurance that someone is looking out for her best interests. She adores you, Amelia. Are you sure this is what you want?"

"I was just asking myself the same question. But the answer is unequivocally yes." Amelia tells Martie about her visit from Sydney. "I will fight tooth and nail to keep Happy and Becca together as long as possible. Afterward, when Becca is committed to the memory care facility, I will parent Happy to the best of my ability."

"And what about Jonathan?"

"Jonathan showed his true colors when he refused to support me in this decision. I miss him like crazy. But I'll survive. My life is about to be very busy."

Amelia's phone rings, and Jonathan's picture appears on the screen. "Speak of the devil."

Martie gets to her feet. "I need to go, anyway."

"Thanks again, Martie." Amelia waits until she's disappeared around the side of the house before accepting Jonathan's call.

"I heard about the fire," Jonathan says. "I gather Becca and Happy are living with you now."

"They are," Amelia says in a curt tone.

"Is this really what you want, Amelia?"

She grinds her teeth. "No, Jon. This is not what I want. I want Becca to have a miraculous recovery and everyone's lives to go back to the way they were. But that's not going to happen."

Jonathan sighs. "You don't understand what you're getting yourself into. Can we meet somewhere? And talk this thing through?"

"There's nothing you can say that I haven't already considered. I'm scared out of my mind, Jon. But I know in my heart I'm doing the right thing. These people need me. I will not turn my back on them the way you turned your back on me."

On Monday afternoon, Amelia drives Becca and Happy to the cottage to retrieve enough clothes to get them through the weekend. Becca agrees to wait until after the wedding to decide about her permanent living situation. But as the week progresses, Amelia becomes increasingly aware of Becca's deteriorating condition. She does an excellent job of covering for herself, but her mind is slipping, and small things are happening that will soon become major issues.

Becca doesn't object when Bebe's niece, Toni, sends the first round of caregivers. Becca is content to spend her days on the porch, looking out over the ocean. She likes for the caregivers to read selections to her from Amelia's collection of classics. Amelia often wonders what's running through her mind, but when she tries to strike up a conversation, Becca has little to say.

Happy stays close to Amelia. She enjoys helping prepare for the wedding. For the reception send-off, they tie pink rose petals in mesh sachets and paint cute sayings on plastic bubble bottles. They spend an entire morning replacing the annuals in Amelia's containers with fresh plants ordered from a nearby nursery.

When Happy confesses she doesn't have a dress for the wedding, Amelia takes her to the children's shop on Ocean Avenue and buys her a simple sleeveless frock with a full skirt in a cheerful shade of yellow-green.

The threesome is settling into their routine nicely, the fire all but forgotten, when, on Thursday evening, Becca receives a call from the owner of the beach cottage. They have just sat down at the table with plates of Bebe's steaming crabby mac and cheese in front of them. Amelia knows something is wrong when the color drains from Becca's face.

"But I've paid you in advance for the rest of the summer," Becca says.

She listens a minute more and hands the phone to Amelia. "He's kicking us out."

Amelia takes the phone from her and goes into the kitchen.

"I'm Amelia Archer, a friend of Becca's. Is there a problem?"

"I own the beach house she's renting. I've just learned about the fire. My source tells me she has Alzheimer's. She should not be living alone. Definitely not in *my* house."

Amelia paces the floor while she talks. "First of all, there was no fire. Soup burned in a pan. There were no flames, just a lot of smoke and a ruined pan. I don't know the law regarding these situations, but I'd be willing to bet evicting someone because of a health issue is grounds for a discriminatory lawsuit."

"And you may very well be right." He breathes heavily into the phone. "Look, lady, I don't want any trouble. My wife is terminally ill with cancer. I'm renting out the cottage to pay her medical bills. I can't afford for something to happen to my property."

"I see." Amelia leans against the counter. "And I'm sorry for your troubles. Becca and her daughter have been staying with me this week, anyway. Can we have until next week to move out?"

"I'm sorry, but no. Sunday is the end of the month, and I have a new tenant who wants to move in on Monday."

"All right, then. We'll figure something out." She's about to hang up when she remembers to ask, "Do you mind telling me how you learned about the fire?"

"Some guy claiming to be the kid's biological father called me. I've forgotten his name. Sounds like that woman has a mess on her hands. I hope you can help her sort it out."

"I'm trying," Amelia says, and ends the call. She stares at the phone. Why would Jake rat Becca out to the property owner? He's up to something.

When Amelia returns to the breakfast room, Becca and Happy look up from their plates. She hands Becca her phone. "He wants you out by Sunday. Poor man's wife has cancer. He can't afford for anything to happen to the cottage."

Relief crosses both mother's and daughter's faces. After what happened, neither wants to return to the cottage.

Amelia reclaims her vacated seat. "Bebe will help us. We'll have you moved out in no time."

"Yes!" Happy's bottom rises several inches off the banquet. "Does this mean we get to live here forever?"

Becca looks expectantly at Amelia, as though she, too, is a child waiting for the answer.

"I can't promise that yet, sweetheart. We still have some things to work through. But I do think it's time for you to have your own room."

Happy's face falls. "Are you sure you'll be okay alone?" she asks Becca.

"I won't be alone. You'll be right down the hall."

"Can I sleep in your old room, Miss Amelia?"

Several times this week, Amelia has found Happy wondering around her childhood bedroom, examining her old horse show ribbons and tennis team trophies. "Sure thing. After the wedding, you and I will sort through my things together. I'll pack up whatever you don't want and put it in the attic."

Becca's phone rings again. This time Sydney is the caller. She pushes the phone across the table to Amelia. "I don't want to talk to her."

Amelia accepts the call. "Hey, Sydney. This is Amelia. Becca's eating dinner. Can I help you with something?"

"Jake and I want to spend some time with Happy. Is she free tomorrow around three?" Sydney says in a businesslike tone.

Amelia's stomach knots. Jake and Sydney are going to try and take Happy away. "Let me check." She presses the phone against her chest while she speaks to Happy. "Jake and Sydney want to spend some time with you tomorrow afternoon. Does that work for you?"

A broad grin spreads across Happy's face. "Sure!"

Amelia locks eyes with Becca. "Is that okay with you?"

Becca gives her a solemn nod. Both women understand that everything is about to get a lot more complicated.

THIRTY-THREE

"You're going about this the wrong way," Sydney says to Jake on the way to Point Pleasant to pick up Happy. "Having Becca evicted was underhanded. I never knew this side of you."

"I had to do something. Happy isn't safe living alone with Becca in that cottage. Why doesn't anyone else understand the gravity of the situation?"

"Amelia understands. Becca and Happy have been staying with her all week."

"There you go again, pushing Happy off on Amelia. Do you even want her back?"

"Of course, I want her back. But only on Happy's terms. She wants to stay on Palmetto Island. How is that supposed to work when I live in a one-bedroom apartment and I work most nights?"

Jake grips both hands on the steering wheel. "Just let me talk to her. I can convince her to move to the Upcountry with us."

"I hope you know what you're doing," she says under her breath.

They arrive at Point Pleasant to find Amelia unloading

clothes from Becca's van. "Becca got evicted from the beach cottage." Amelia cuts her eyes at Jake. "But you already know that, don't you?"

"Amelia—" Sydney starts, but Amelia raises her hand to cut her off.

"Don't say anything, Sydney. This is a difficult situation. It's best if we don't discuss it."

Happy comes running up from the dock. Behind her, Jonathan waves to them from the stern of his sailboat.

"Are you and Jonathan back together?" Sydney asks.

Amelia shakes her head. "He's keeping his boat here for the time being."

Jake crouches down and Happy jumps onto his back. He takes off with her across the lawn, kicking and bucking like a wild horse.

"I'm sorry, but I have to say this, Amelia. Jake and I are Happy's birth parents. We have rights. You're a single middle-aged woman. What do you have to offer?"

Amelia spreads her arms wide. "Look around you, Sydney. I can give her a stable home. She can continue to live with her mother as long as it's feasible."

"Her adoptive mother," Sydney murmurs.

"You're the one who gave her up for adoption."

"For all the right reasons. Not that it's any of your business." Sydney digs her thumb into her chest. "Becca approached me about taking Happy back. This is what she wants."

"That was before I offered to adopt her." Amelia removes the last load of hanging clothes from the minivan and slams the sliding door. "Now, if you'll excuse me, I need to check on Becca." She enters the house without looking back.

"Let's go, Jake," Sydney calls out.

"Coming," he says, and gallops back across the yard to the car.

As he's pulling out of the driveway, he turns up the volume

on the radio so Happy can't hear them talking. "I take it that didn't go well."

Sydney folds her arms over her chest. "Nope. We're at war."

Jake attempts to lighten the mood in the car by singing loud and off-key to the country music station. Happy thinks it's hilarious and belly laughs most of the way to town.

It's a sultry afternoon, and Scoops is teaming with customers, many of whom are still wearing their bathing suits and cover-ups from the beach. "What do you want, Syd?" Jake asks as they wait in line.

"I don't care for anything." She's too angry to eat, and she rolls her eyes when he orders triple scoop chocolate cones for himself and Happy.

They take their ice cream to an umbrellaed table on the sidewalk out front. Jake purposefully eats messy, and half his cone ends up on his face. Happy removes a wad of napkins from the dispenser and hands them to him. "You're incorrigible."

Jake stuffs the last of his cone in his mouth and licks the tips of his fingers. "I am? What exactly does that mean?" he asks in a teasing tone.

Happy shrugs. "I'm not sure. My mom calls me that sometimes," she says, her lips pressed thin.

Jake wipes his mouth and balls up the napkins. "Been a tough week, huh, kiddo?"

"Sort of. I've had fun helping Miss Amelia get ready for the wedding. But my mom . . . it's like she's off in space all the time now."

Jake's expression is now serious. "You understand Sydney and I are your biological parents, right?"

Happy squirms. "Yes."

"Do you know what that means?" Sydney asks.

Happy bites on her lip. "It means Jake was your boyfriend and a baby happened."

Sydney can't help but smile. "That pretty much sums it up.

You may have Jake's eyes, but you remind me of myself when I was your age."

Happy's face lights up. "Really?"

"I enjoyed the outdoors as much as you. And I loved my friends. I watch you when you're with your friends. And I feel like I'm your age all over again."

"Did you know Sydney and I are getting married?" Jake asks.

Happy bobs her head. "Mom told me."

"Did you know Jake coaches football for Clemson?" Sydney says.

Happy's ice eyes get big. "Really? That's so cool. My friends are Clemson fans. Wait until I tell them."

"Jake can't move to Palmetto Island because of his job," Sydney explains. "So, once we're married, I'll be going to live with him in either Clemson or Greenville, depending on where I find a job."

Jake scoots his chair closer to Happy. "We'd love it if you'd come live with us. I know how much you love the island. But you'd love the Upcountry, too, if you'd give it a chance. There's hiking and whitewater rafting and fly-fishing."

Happy scrunches up her nose. "Fishing. Yuck."

Jake laughs. "Okay, well, there are plenty of other outdoor activities to choose from. We'll be a family. We'll buy a house, and one day soon, you'll have a baby brother or sister."

Sydney reaches for Happy's hand. "Maybe not *that* soon. I have a lot of making up for lost time to do with you first."

"What about Mama? Can she come too?"

An annoyed expression crosses Jake's face. "Becca will be living in a place where doctors and nurses know how to take care of her."

"That place is near Charleston," Sydney says. "We'll bring you down here often to see her."

"But what about my new friends? And where will I go to school?"

Jake bumps his elbow against Happy's. "You'll make new friends in your new school in Greenville or Clemson."

Happy's eyes glisten with unshed tears. This was the wrong thing to say.

"You can invite your beach friends to come up for football games," Sydney says.

"I can get you box seats, and you can meet some of the players," Jake adds.

"That'd be cool, I guess." Happy looks down at her unfinished ice cream, which is now melting down the cone and onto her hand. "I can't eat anymore."

Sydney smiles at her. "That's fine, sweetheart. Jake is the only person I know who can eat three scoops of ice cream. Throw it away and go wash your hands."

When Happy leaves the table, Jake turns to Sydney. "You were right. If we try to force her into living with us, she could end up resenting us. I have no clue how to handle the situation. She's our child. We have rights."

"Give her some time, Jake. We still have a lot to figure out in our own lives."

"Speaking of which. How did your virtual interview go with Barry?"

Sydney looks away, watching for Happy. "The salary is excellent. The hours would enable me to be home at night. I would have an opportunity to invest in the corporation. Fast casual fresh is the way of the future. I'd accept the job in a heartbeat if I thought we had a chance of getting Happy."

"But it doesn't excite you. I can see it in your eyes."

"I love being a chef. I can return to it later." In her case, she understands later could very well mean never. By the time Happy reaches high school, Sydney and Jake will hopefully have more children. And by the time she's an empty nester, the culinary world will have left her behind.

"Happy's been gone a long time. I should go check on her." Sydney is pushing back from the table when Happy returns.

"Sorry. My friends are inside. I was just talking to them for a minute." Happy stands beside the table, but she doesn't sit down. "Can we go now? I promised Miss Amelia I'd help her unpack our clothes."

"Of course," Sydney says, rising from the table. She walks to the parking deck with a heavy heart. She's lost Happy to Amelia. Then again, Happy was never meant to be her child. Her one remaining hope is that Happy will agree to be a part of their lives in some form or fashion.

THIRTY-FOUR

After a line of thunderstorms tears through the area on Saturday night, Hannah's wedding day dawns with cooler temperatures and a cloudless periwinkle sky. Hannah, wearing a white satin robe with her mahogany hair piled on top of her head, stands at Amelia's bedroom window watching the scene unfold on the sprawling green acres below. Her florist winds garlands of citrus-colored flowers and greenery around a white lattice arbor and workers from the party rental company arrange rows of folding white chairs into two sections. Under the tent, servers adorn banquet tables with creamy linens while the four-piece bluegrass band tunes its instruments on the stage in front of the dance floor.

Giggles erupt from the en suite bathroom where her two bridesmaids—long-time best friend, Liza, and new business partner, Chris—are having their hair professionally styled.

The bedroom door swings open, and Birdie enters the room. When she sees Hannah, she stops short, and tears fill her eyes. "You look lovely, sweetheart."

"So do you, Mama," Hannah says of Birdie's taupe-colored, lace-covered gown. "Where's Gus?"

"Downstairs in Amelia's study with Ethan and his grooms-men. I tried to pry him away, but he refuses to leave Ethan's side."

"Ethan better not let him get dirty," Hannah says.

"Don't worry. Gus is taking his job as ring bearer seriously."

Gus is dressed similar to the groomsmen, who are wearing khaki pants, white button-down shirts, coral-colored bow ties, and blue blazers. Only Gus's khaki pants are short, with gray suspenders in place of the blazer.

"It's almost time," Birdie says.

"Can you believe it?" Hannah places a hand over her heart. "In less than an hour, I'm going to be Mrs. Ethan Hayes."

Birdie smiles at her. "And the two of you are going to have a fairytale life together. Now." She claps her hands. "Let's get you into that scrumptious dress."

She summons the bridesmaids from the bathroom to help Hannah into her dress. The hair stylist is securing her veil atop her head when Max arrives with a tray of mimosas. Hannah thanks her bridesmaids for being part of her big day and several rounds of toasts are made.

Liza sets down her mimosa. "I have something borrowed and blue for you." She ties a thin satin blue ribbon around Hannah's wrist. "Remember this?"

Hannah nods. "From our childhood. We always insisted on wearing matching ribbons." She kisses the air beside her cheek. "Thank you for being my best friend."

Ethan's mother bustles into the room in a designer lace gown that must have cost thousands. She declines Max's offer of a mimosa and pulls Hannah to the side. "You are absolutely breathtaking. Ethan's teeth will fall out when he sees you."

Hannah blushes. "You're too kind, Clara."

"I'm being serious. Before you walk down the aisle, I wanted to tell you how overjoyed I am to welcome you and Gus into the family. I wish you and Ethan a lifetime of happiness."

"That means so much, Clara. And thank you again for last night. The rehearsal dinner was lovely."

Clara laughs. "Despite the raging storms. However, I admit the weather made it more festive." She leans in close to Hannah's ear. "You're the perfect wife for my son. He's my world. Please take care of him."

Hannah's throat swells, and she fights back tears. "He's my world, too, Clara. I promise, I won't let you down."

Clara draws away. "I'd better get back downstairs."

"Can't you stay for one mimosa?"

"I'm afraid not. My job is to keep those rascal groomsmen from getting too rowdy."

"Please keep an eye on my Gus."

"Don't you worry. He's such a sweet boy. I'm flattered he already thinks of me as his grandmother." A wicked glint appears in Clara's eyes. "Although, when he asked if he could call me grandma, I told him I prefer Nanna."

Hannah laughs out loud. "I don't blame you. Nanna it is," she says, hugging Clara once more.

Clara is leaving the room when Bebe appears in the doorway. "Miss Hannah, I hate to disturb you, but your daddy is here to see you."

A chill travels through Hannah. "Tell him to go away. He's not invited."

Cary appears behind Bebe. "Please, Hannah. I only need a minute."

When Hannah looks to her mom for help, Birdie says, "He's your father, Hannah. You can talk to him for a minute."

The other women bustle about, gathering their things before clearing the room.

When Birdie moves toward the door, Hannah says in a pleading tone, "Please, don't go, Mom."

"I'll wait right outside in the hall if you need me."

"Traitor," Hannah says under her breath.

Cary enters the room. He looks handsome in a gray suit and blue-and-white striped tie. Is that a tear in his eye? She can't remember ever seeing him cry. He smiles down at her, and memories from early mornings spent on the water together come rushing back. A lump develops in her throat. "Please, don't cause a scene. I can't afford to mess up my makeup."

"I won't upset you. I promise." Cary moves toward her. "You're stunning, Hannah. Ethan is a lucky man."

She softens a little toward him. "Thank you for saying that."

"I couldn't let the day pass without telling you the truth. Violet broke up with me after I told her I couldn't go on the cruise. I don't know why I agreed to go in the first place. A momentary lapse of judgment, I guess. I would never have missed your wedding."

"Why didn't you tell me this the other night?"

"You didn't give me a chance."

Hannah thinks back to Sunday. Perhaps she kicked him out prematurely. "I've just been so angry at you, Dad. Since you came back to town. Every time I think I'm getting over it, you do something else to make me mad. I don't want to feel this way, but—"

"I deserve it. My head has been screwed on wrong these past few years. I realize that now, and I'm going to see a therapist. I have a long way to go, but if it's the last thing I do, I'm going to make you proud of me again."

The thought brings a smile to Hannah's face. "I'm glad you're getting help, Dad."

"I'm sorry I've caused you so much pain, Hannah. I love you more than you'll ever know. I'd really like to see you get married. I'll sit in the back row. I won't cause any trouble, I promise."

"I would ask you to give me away, but—"

Cary shakes his head. "Your mom deserves that honor. She's

been your rock these past few years." He squeezes her arm. "Will you save me a dance?"

"I would love that," she says, standing on her tiptoes to kiss his cheek.

"The next time I see you, you'll be a married woman, no longer my little girl."

"A part of me will always be your little girl." Hannah means this with all her heart. She'll give him another chance. And another, and another after that. As many as it takes. Because he's her father. Her family. And family members forgive one another. Hannah would rather live with an imperfect father than no father at all.

As Hannah requested, Becca and Happy sit together in the row reserved for the bride's family. The weather and setting are picture-perfect for an outdoor summer wedding. When the music transitions to "Trumpet Voluntary," the guests stand and Hannah, carrying a bouquet of bright flowers, descends the aisle on her mother's arm.

Becca relishes the moment. She probably won't remember much about it tomorrow. Even if Becca is still alive when Happy gets married, she'll be too far gone to attend the wedding. She assumes Jake will walk her down the aisle. Or maybe Jonathan if he ever comes to his senses. Two months ago, Becca was a stranger to this close-knit group of island locals. She now considers them friends. More importantly, she trusts them to take care of her daughter. These loving people are now Happy's family. Her village.

When Hannah reaches Ethan, the music stops, and the congregation sits down. Becca closes her eyes and tilts her face skyward, letting the sun warm her face. She imagines herself on Jonathan's sailboat with the wind whipping her hair and the water rushing toward her. Her destiny is in someone else's hands. She can now relax, and when the time comes, she'll sail away.

Sydney, dressed as a guest in an emerald sheath and single strand of pearls, is too busy monitoring the food tables and stocked bar to enjoy herself. Two hours into the reception, however, once the guests have had a sufficient amount to eat and drink, she accepts Jake's offer to dance.

The song is a slow one. He holds her tight, and she rests her head on his chest.

"You outdid yourself, Syd. Everyone is raving."

"Thanks. I'm pleased with the way everything turned out. Although, with perfect weather like this, anything that goes wrong is forgiven." Sydney notices Happy watching them from the edge of the tent. "I saw you and Happy out here awhile ago. She's a good little dancer."

"Naturally, she inherited my athletic ability."

She smacks his chest. "She appears to be in a good mood tonight."

"She's having fun. And she looks so pretty in her green dress." Even though Sydney can't see Jake's face, she hears the tenderness in his voice.

She closes her eyes and imagines their wedding in Aruba in September. After they're married, everything will fall into place as it's meant to be. When the time comes, they'll have more children—a little boy who loves football and a little girl who brings joy to the lives she touches.

When the song ends, Happy walks out onto the dance floor and takes Sydney and Jake by the hand. "Come with me." She drags them over to the porch, instructs them to wait for her there, and disappears into the crowd.

"Wonder what she's up to," Sydney says.

Jake chuckles. "Who knows? That kid is full of surprises."

A minute later, Happy returns to the porch with Amelia in tow.

"Where's your mom?" Amelia asks Happy.

"She went upstairs with the nurse to rest. I need to tell y'all something." Happy motions the three of them to the rockers. Standing in front of them, she says, "I've made a decision. I want to live at Point Pleasant with Amelia. So I can be with Mom as long as possible." She turns to Sydney and Jake. "That doesn't mean I don't want the two of you in my life. A girl can have more than two parents, right?"

They all laugh. "I don't see why not," Jake says.

"I can come visit on the weekends and go to football games. Maybe you can come down here some too?"

A broad smile spreads across Sydney's face. "We absolutely can. Maybe we'll buy a small cottage like Hannah and Ethan."

"That would be cool." Happy turns to Amelia. "Is it okay with you if I live here?"

Amelia gets up and pulls the child to her. "More than okay. We'll figure out the legal logistics. I'll either become your legal guardian or your foster parent, whichever makes sense." She looks over at Jake and Amelia. "I promise to take good care of her in your absence. Co-parenting is the perfect solution. We'll make all the major decisions regarding her education and care together."

Jake and Sydney also stand, each placing a hand on Happy's bare shoulders. "We will be here for you whenever you need us," Jake says, and Sydney adds, "And lots of times when you don't."

Gus comes running over to the porch. "Happy! Come quick. It's time for bubbles. Mama and Ethan are leaving."

It's not lost on Sydney when Happy looks to Amelia for permission. "Can I go?"

"Of course, sweetheart. Blow extra bubbles for me." Amelia gives her another squeeze before turning her loose.

Sydney leans into Jake. "Are you okay?"

He offers her a sad smile. "I will be. This solution feels right to me. We'll have more children one day, and Happy will make one hell of a big sister."

"That she will."

Amelia remains on the porch when the guests migrate to the driveway to blow bubbles and throw rose petals at Hannah and Ethan as they make their grand exit in Ethan's Porsche. She's lost in thought, reflecting on the events of the afternoon, and she doesn't hear Jonathan approach from behind until he's standing near her.

"Hello, Amelia."

She flinches, her hand flying to her racing heart. "You startled me. How long have you been standing there?"

"I just walked up. You were kind to open your home for the wedding." He steps close enough for her to smell his woodsy cologne. "Your generosity knows no bounds."

Her eyes remain on the dispersing crowd. "I've had a nice day, Jon. Please don't spoil it for me."

"I don't intend to. I heard your conversation with Happy."

"So, you were spying on me."

"Not intentionally. I was coming up from the dock. I thought I'd take a peek at the bride and groom. As I got near the porch, I heard Happy talking. I didn't want to interrupt, so I remained around the back corner of the house until she left." Taking her by the arm, Jonathan turns her toward him. "Happy's been helping me on the boat this week. She's an amazing kid, a true delight to be around. I admit I've grown quite fond of her. She's going to need all the love and support she can get in the months ahead. I very much want to be a part of her life."

"If you're asking whether you can keep your boat here, I'm fine with it."

He lets out a breath. "I'm not talking about my boat. I've missed you, Amelia. I'm embarrassed by my behavior. The prospect of being a parent again freaked me out. I was focusing on the tough parts of parenting, constantly worrying about their grades and their friends and their health. But Happy helped me remember all the miraculous things about being a parent. The joy of teaching your child something new. And watching them learn to navigate the world on their own."

"Happy and Becca are a package deal, Jon."

"I realize that."

"It will be a long road with an endless stream of caregivers," Amelia warns. "Watching her deteriorate won't be easy."

"All the more reason for me to be here. Not just for Happy, but for you. You can't do this alone, Amelia."

Amelia's breath hitches as she turns away from him toward the ocean. "I'm scared, Jon."

He places a hand on the small of her back. "I'm scared too, Amelia. That's part of the reason I've stayed away. I also needed time to think, and after giving it careful consideration, I'm convinced this is the right thing. Becca and Happy need us. And we're able to help them. You have the biggest heart of anyone I know, and you share your love so freely. You're going to make a wonderful role model for that little girl."

She relaxes against him. "I've felt so alone without you. I'm not sure I can take it if you leave again."

"I'm not going anywhere. Ever. I promise."

The conviction in his tone tells Amelia he means it. And she trusts him, because he always shoots straight with her. Their personalities, while different, complement each other. Amelia jumps into things headfirst while Jonathan warms up to a situation on his own terms. Together, they'll make a formidable force for what lies ahead. Who knows where this path will lead them, but Amelia is ever so grateful not to travel it alone.

Happy and Gus dart across the yard with Birdie and Max following at a leisurely pace. Happy calls out, "Come with us, Miss Amelia. We're going for a walk on the beach before it gets dark."

She casts an uncertain glance at Jonathan. "Go! Have fun with your friends."

"Will you wait for me to get back?"

The gold flecks in his hazel eyes sparkle. "If that's what you want."

Standing on her tiptoes, she gives him a feathery kiss on the lips. "That's what I want." Kicking off her shoes, she hurries to catch up with her friends, who are waiting for her at the edge of the yard.

Birdie looks at Amelia over the top of her sunglass frames as she approaches them. "Are my eyes deceiving me, or did I just see you kiss Jonathan?"

Amelia beams. "We're working things out."

Birdie hugs her. "Oh, honey. That's wonderful! Happy shared the news that she'll be staying with you on the island. You're going to need his support in coping with Becca's illness and raising a spirited nine-year-old."

Amelia is only half joking when she says, "I'm may limit his parenting authority for fear Happy turns out like his daughters."

Amelia's phone vibrates in her dress pocket, and she reads the text from Anna. Speaking of the devil diva. "This is Jonathan's daughter, Anna. She's an event planner. She saw the pictures of Hannah's wedding on Instagram and wants me to call her tomorrow to talk about the flowers."

Birdie elbows Amelia. "See! I told you they'd come around."

A warmth floods Amelia's body, and she places a hand over her heart. "I feel like all the stars are aligning for me. If only they'd find a cure for Alzheimer's."

Happy, who is already on the beach with Gus, yells at them. "Come on! What're y'all waiting for?"

The three old friends walk single file through the sand dunes. When they reach the beach, they loop their arms and trail behind Happy and Gus who are running zigzags with their arms outstretched through the edge of the surf, oblivious to the water splashing their wedding clothes.

"We should've made them change first," Birdie says.

"Let them be kids," Max says. "Why spoil a perfect day?"

Amelia says, "Today was perfect, wasn't it? Things have been so hectic, I never asked Hannah where they're going on their honeymoon."

"They're driving down to the resort at Palmetto Bluff," Birdie says. "They're only staying a few days. Hannah's been neglecting her business, and they're both eager to get Gus settled in their new home before school starts."

"How does it feel to have a married daughter?" Amelia asks.

Birdie lets out a contented sigh. "I feel at peace. I'm not losing my daughter. I'm gaining a wonderful son-in-law. Ethan worships Hannah. I can stop worrying so much about her, because I know he's looking out for her and Gus."

"It's a comforting feeling," Max says. "Knowing someone else, in addition to yourself, has your child's best interests at heart."

"Mm-hmm," Birdie says. "Now I can focus on moving in with Stan."

Amelia stops walking and turns to her friend. "So you pulled the trigger? Good for you!"

A wide grin spreads across Birdie's face. "And I couldn't be happier about it. I have an excellent management team in place. I can work as much or as little as I want."

Max says, "It wasn't that long ago, during the reopening cele-bration for the hotel, when the three of us were at odds with our men. Look at us now. Jonathan and Amelia are back together.

Birdie's moving in with Stan. And Davis and I are buying a house together."

"What?" Birdie and Amelia say in unison.

Birdie appears wounded. "Why didn't you tell me? When did this happen?"

"You've been busy with the wedding. Davis and I have been talking about it for weeks. I'm following your lead, Birdie. I'm hiring a hotel manager. I want more time with Davis. Like you, I'll still be very much involved in the business without so much of the day-to-day stress."

Birdie turns to Amelia. "I'm sorry, honey. We're going on about our semi-retirements and you're just beginning your parenting journey. You can count on us to support you. Whatever you need, don't hesitate to ask."

Amelia squeezes Birdie's arm. "That means so much, Birdie. And I will definitely be looking to you for guidance. I'm getting a late start, but all my dreams are finally coming true. Like you, Birdie, I feel at peace, although for different reasons. I'm blessed to be able to live out my days at Point Pleasant. And fortunate to be raising an amazing child like Happy. I've found a wonderful partner in Jonathan, and I'm finally putting my troubled past behind me." She pulls her friends in for half hugs. "Most importantly, the two of you are back in my life. You are my village. Whatever happens with our men, we will always have one another."

"Friendships like ours are rare," Max says, and with unshed tears glistening in her eyes, Birdie adds, "We must nurture them until our dying days."

———

Thank you for reading *Sail Away*! If you enjoyed the series, please consider reading my Hope Springs series. Join the unforgettable

ASHLEY FARLEY

cast of characters at the historic inn for romance, family drama, and adventure.

You might also like some of my stand alone novels. Be sure to visit my website where you'll find a host of information regarding my inspiration for writing as well as book trailers, reviews, and Pinterest boards from my 20+ other books.

And . . . to find out about my new and upcoming books, be sure to sign up for my newsletter:.

ALSO BY ASHLEY FARLEY

Palmetto Island

Muddy Bottom

Change of Tides

Lowcountry on My Mind

Sail Away

Hope Springs Series

Dream Big, Stella!

Show Me the Way

Mistletoe and Wedding Bells

Stand Alone

Tangled in Ivy

Lies that Bind

Life on Loan

Only One Life

Home for Wounded Hearts

Nell and Lady

Sweet Tea Tuesdays

Saving Ben

Sweeney Sisters Series

Saturdays at Sweeney's

Tangle of Strings

Boots and Bedlam

Lowcountry Stranger

Her Sister's Shoes

Magnolia Series

Beyond the Garden

Magnolia Nights

Scottie's Adventures

Breaking the Story

Merry Mary

ACKNOWLEDGMENTS

I'm grateful to many people for helping make this novel possible. Foremost, to my editor, Patricia Peters, for her patience and advice and for making my work stronger without changing my voice. A great big heartfelt thank-you to my trusted beta readers —Alison Fauls, Anne Wolters, Laura Glenn, Jan Klein, Lisa Hudson, Lori Walton, Kathy Sinclair, and Jenelle Rodenbaugh. A special thank you to my behind-the-scenes, go-to girl, Kate Rock, for all the many things you do to manage my social media so effectively.

I am blessed to have many supportive people in my life who offer the encouragement I need to continue the pursuit of my writing career. I owe an enormous debt of gratitude to my advanced review team, the lovely ladies of Georgia's Porch, for their enthusiasm for and commitment to my work. To Leslie Rising at Levy's for being my local bookshop. Love and thanks to my family—my mother, Joanne; my husband, Ted; and my amazing kiddos, Cameron and Ned.

Most of all, I'm grateful to my wonderful readers for their love of women's fiction. I love hearing from you. Feel free to shoot me an email at ashleyhfarley@gmail.com or stop by my website at ashleyfarley.com for more information about my characters and upcoming releases. Don't forget to sign up for my newsletter. Your subscription will grant you exclusive content, sneak previews, and special giveaways.

ABOUT THE AUTHOR

Ashley Farley writes books about women for women. Her characters are mothers, daughters, sisters, and wives facing real-life issues. Her bestselling Sweeney Sisters series has touched the lives of many.

Ashley is a wife and mother of two young adult children. While she's lived in Richmond, Virginia for the past 25 years, a piece of her heart remains in the salty marshes of the South Carolina Lowcountry, where she still calls home. Through the eyes of her characters, she captures the moss-draped trees, delectable cuisine, and kindhearted folk with lazy drawls that make the area so unique.

Ashley loves to hear from her readers. Visit Ashley's Website @ashleyfarley.com

Get free exclusive content by signing up for her newsletter @ ashleyfarley.com/newsletter-signup/

facebook.com/ashleywfarley

twitter.com/AshleyWFarley

instagram.com/ashleyfarleyauthor

CPSIA information can be obtained
at www.ICGtesting.com
Printed in the USA
LVHW051354270721
693813LV00005B/136